Follow That Mouse

Follow That Mouse

by Henry Melton

Wire Rim Books
Hutto, Texas

WRB

Follow That Mouse © 2010 by Henry Melton
All Rights Reserved

Printing History
First Edition: September 2010
ISBN 978-0-9802253-7-2

Website of Henry Melton
www.HenryMelton.com

Cover art © Brad W. Foster 2010 - www.JabberwockyGraphix.com

Printed in the United States of America

Wire Rim Books
www.wirerimbooks.com

Acknowledgements

True friends who have told me what was wrong.
Alan McConnell, Colleen LaSoya, Jim Dunn, Linda Ellott, Mary Ann
Melton and Mary Solomon

Special thanks for the inspiration of Stanley Marsh III and his artwork
that has escaped well beyond the confines of gallerys.

For my hometown, and yours.

Salt Lake
City

Provo

Utah

Green River

Ranch Exit

Table of Contents

Ranch Exit

Ranch Exit, Utah is beautiful in its own way. Dot Comal kept her head down to avoid the dust. *But I don't think I can call it a 'town'. Would I get points counted off if I did? Poetic license and all that.*

Ned Kelso shifted gears on his motorcycle. Holding onto him tightly, she looked over his shoulder. They were riding Ned's shortcut. Decades before she'd moved here, there had been a railroad through the valley that served a long abandoned coal mine. The metal rails were gone, reclaimed for the steel. The crossties were gone as well, shipped east, she was told. Sold to homeowners to decorate their gardens.

All that was left was the road grade itself. Dot knew how much effort it took to level her own garden. She couldn't imagine what it'd taken to build that massive path. To her it was like Ranch Exit's own Great Wall. Engineers had cut through the hills and filled dips, making the grade straight and level for twenty or thirty miles.

Abandoned, it was Ned's playground now. Too narrow for anything but his motorcycle, it passed through the Kelso ranch and just past the entrance to the Comal property. The north end stopped at a pile of rubble miles to the west, the collapsed entrance to the coal mine. South, it had been cut off long ago when they built the interstate highway.

The "Kelso Express" just happened to be the quickest route home from school. She'd walked it several times, but never on purpose. Two and a half hours each way was a clear waste of time, and she'd rather work on her school project.

The road grade was twenty feet above the valley when he pointed off to the west.

"Bill's got satellite!" he yelled. "They even get Internet."

Dot's interest perked up. She hadn't had an Internet connection in two years. *I wonder if my account has expired?* Telephone connections out here were noisy and the best modem speeds were much too slow to load web pages without half the images timing out. Plus, everywhere was long distance. Dad had let their regular voice phone connection lapse to save money.

A lone signpost whipped by on the side of the narrow railroad right of way. Dark pink and circular, the sign said, "Cadillac Crossing" in bold white letters.

After about five miles, Ned leaned forward and picked up speed.

She poked him in the ribs. "Ned! Don't you dare jump the bridge! I'm warning you!"

Where the creeks crossed the road grade, old wooden bridges once supported the locomotives and the endless cars of coal. The one near Dot's house had partially collapsed. Last summer, Ned built a ramp of stones so he could jump the gap. He talked about doing it, but the pile had never been stable enough to actually try. The rocks shifted underfoot. She had talked him out of it.

For an instant she wasn't sure he heard her, then the motor started popping as he let off the gas.

Ned yelled, "Hang on!"

She gripped him tighter. Something was wrong.

The motorcycle slowed. Ned cut sharply to the right. Her stomach dropped out from beneath her and for an instant she saw someone on the road grade up ahead.

Ned leaned, keeping the tires on the ground as they slashed through the sagebrush down the steep-sided shoulder. Dot could feel the branches slapping at her leg. If she hadn't worn her usual thick jeans today, her leg would be bloody.

They hit ground level with a bounce and Ned circled around.

"Are you okay?" he asked. "I didn't see him coming. He just appeared, like out of a heat haze."

Dot coughed from the dust, then yelled, "I'm okay. I knew I would be riding with you today, so I dressed for the occasion." She tapped the side of her motorcycle helmet. Half of her scars and scrapes had Ned's name on them.

"Who was it?" she asked.

"I'm not sure. I was busy." He revved the engine and put the bike in low gear. Dot grabbed tight. As he powered up the steep slope, it was the only thing keeping her from sliding off.

Back on the top, Ned killed the engine and leaned the bike on its kickstand.

"Where did he go?"

Dot hopped off and beat the dust from her clothes. Jeans and a flannel plaid shirt were her usual, at least until the weather got too hot. She was a dirt poor rancher's kid and it did no good to pretend otherwise with city fashions they couldn't afford.

The railroad grade stretched in a straight flat line in both directions as far as they could see. There was heat haze, as Ned mentioned, but no sign of anyone.

Dot looked off both sides of the grade, but no one could be seen in the low scrub vegetation. "I saw him too, but he's gone now."

Ned had his eyes scrunched up, peering into the distance. "I think it was Old Man Wanekia."

"Who?"

Ned gestured, "You know! That old Paiute shaman that you see walking down the road all the time." He looked back down the grade. "That would explain it."

Dot sighed. Ned could be opaque at times.

"Explain what?"

"Why we can't see him. He vanished. Indian magic." He nodded, confidently.

"Ned?"

"Yes, Dot?"

"Get back on your bike and drive."

...

Pokey saw her coming. With deep horsey thoughts, he debated whether Dot would have a treat for him. Slowly, he started up the trail from his barn to the fence line. The deep rut was only as wide as his hooves, twisting through the sloping terrain. Pokey checked the vegetation, but any grass in his pasture had long since been pulled up by the roots.

Dot arrived. Ned let her off by the road and then roared off towards his home, another two miles down the road. He was her closest neighbor.

"Hey, Pokey," she called. The lazy horse sped up to a slow walk. She waited at the fence until he arrived.

She opened her palm, and a pair of sugar-cubes scavenged from the school's lunch tray appeared. Pokey's nostrils widened and he strained his neck in her direction.

The sugar vanished. And then he nuzzled at her pockets, nipping at the white paper sticking out.

The mail she'd picked up at the general store had gone into her wide pocket unexamined when they made a brief stop after leaving school. With no home delivery to the individual ranches in the valley, most of the older kids picked up their family mail after school. The three white envelopes were probably just bills. Since the subscription to Reader's Digest lapsed a few months earlier, there'd never been anything to interest her. Occasionally, one of the major stores would send them a flier by mistake and she liked to browse the brightly colored photos. Since the nearest department store was a hundred and fifty miles away, they were off everyone's mailing list.

"Stop that," she pushed the horse away. If he thought it might taste good, he would willingly eat the mail. She stuffed the envelopes deeper into her pocket.

She used to ride Pokey, but he slowed down as she got taller. All he did now was eat and relax in his barn.

Dot frowned as she stroked his nose. Dad had made it clear that her horse was her responsibility.

"Well, let's check your feed." She climbed over the fence at the post where she could use the wires as a ladder, and led the way to the barn.

There were fresh marks on the door to the feed storage room. Pokey chewed on the door when the mood struck him. She was sure it wasn't hunger. The hay-bales Dad had given her last month were only half gone.

She opened the barrel where they kept the grain, and reached in.

A brown field mouse was sitting still, in the mouth of the yellow plastic grain scoop, staring at her.

"Ahhck!" Her hand jerked away. Not that she was scared of mice, but she wasn't expecting it. She waited for it to vanish in that brown blur of mouse-panic that she'd witnessed dozens of times here in the barn. Mice were always there, even when she didn't notice them. No self-respecting mouse could possibly pass up the grain she spilled, or fail to take advantage of the myriad hiding places among the old farm equipment and jumbled piles of excess lumber.

But this mouse didn't escape. It stared at her. She could even see its whiskers move, still chewing.

"Scoot. Get out of here," she urged, but it didn't move until she quickly tapped her finger against the scoop. It moved with mouse-quickness to the shelf on the wall a few inches from the grain barrel, but even then it stopped, in plain sight, and stared at her.

Mice don't act like that, she told herself. She'd seen enough of them to know. *I wonder if it's sick.* That was a scary thought.

She grabbed up the scoop and filled it with a *shoosh* into the barrel and took it out to Pokey, who was stamping his hooves and snorting at his feed trough. When she took the empty scoop back, she didn't see the mouse anywhere.

...

Dot was elbows deep in compost, preparing another bed for their garden, when the old pickup pulled in. It used to be white, before the rust.

Dressed in bright blue, like a marching-band drummer, complete with a shiny matching cap topped with yellow feathers, Ruben Comal waved to his daughter and went into the house. She washed off her hands and followed him in.

Dot looked Dad up and down as he poured himself some tea from the refrigerator. "Okay. What did Mr. Mort think of today?"

Ruben smiled at his daughter. "We built a crop circle."

"Like the UFO things?"

"Right. We paid Jed Fellerman for his hay crop, then went in there and tramped down about three acre's worth. Mort had a diagram we had to follow. Towards the end of the day, he flew over in his eagle and called us on the radio with some fine-tuning."

Dot picked up the shiny blue cap and stared at the yellow feathers. "And what does this have to do with crop circles?"

Her father just shook his head and sighed. "Mort's idea of a worker's uniform, I guess. He had one for me and one for Aaron. How he got my sizes I'll never know. There's special washing instructions too."

She groaned. She did the laundry, and Dad bought Pokey's hay.

"Don't look like that." He shook his head at her. "Having a crazy man richer than Midas living in Ranch Exit keeps me from begging in the street."

"Dad! You told me never to call Mr. Mort crazy. 'If they've got money, they're eccentric.' That's what you said."

He kept his smile restrained. "Okay. But whichever he is, he helps keep the bills under control.

"By the way, did we get any mail?"

Dot looked over to her room. "Oh, yes. I'll get 'em." She went through the door and called out, "Some of them may have teeth marks. Pokey was...."

Her father took another sip of tea, waiting for her.

"Dot?"

There was no answer. "Dot? Are you still there?"

After a few seconds, he got up from the table and went to her door.

Dot was holding one of the letters, the white envelope opened at her feet. He took one look at her face. "What's wrong?"

She held out the letter, her voice shaking, she explained. "It's from Aunt Elizabeth.

"She wants me to come visit her."

...

Watson Wanekia stroked the bearskin band around the top of his walking stick and stared at the road sign shaped like a heart and trimmed in green, an ugly contrast with the glowing sunrise.

'HONORARY FOREST' it proclaimed in bold black letters. The sign towered over a short cluster of sagebrush.

He shook his gray head at Crazy Coat's latest magic spell. The nearest tree was down by the road, beside the lone store and post office that gave Ranch Exit its claim to existence. If George Filmore didn't water it regularly, even that one would be gone—no matter what incantation the rich man put up.

Watson shook his head and put his old bones in motion. Still, Crazy Coat was getting closer. He'd watched the blue men make a power circle in the hay field. If the pattern had been a little tighter, he might have conjured a spell that could bring rain. As it was, it would upset the coyotes until it grew out.

Maybe ... the mouse? He shook that thought away. No, more likely the Man-Under-the-Mountain was affecting them.

...

Ned Kelso whipped into their driveway and spun his rear wheel on the gravel as he pulled to a stop in front of her. He loved the morning run to school. The air was cool and sometimes dew kept the dust down.

He killed the engine, and with one look at her face, asked, "All right. What did I do this time?"

Dot pulled her helmet on and snapped the chinstrap.

"Nothing. You didn't do anything."

"Well, something's wrong. What is it?"

She straddled the bike behind him. "My aunt invited me to spend the summer with them in Seattle."

"Wow! I don't see anything wrong with that. Unless you're afraid of the rain?"

"No. Now get going, or we'll be late for school."

He kicked-started the engine and spun gravel.

Dot held on tight as he sped on up the side of the railroad grade—the Kelso Express.

Ned doesn't understand. I'm not sure I understand.

It had been a scary time, when her mother died. What made it worse was Aunt Elizabeth. She had blamed the cancer on Dad, somehow, and tried to take Dot away from him. They hadn't gotten as far as going to court, but there had been lawyers. Dot remembered the lawyers.

It was ugly. An ugly time.

But that was years ago. Aunt Elizabeth sent her cards at Christmas and her birthday. But Dad made no attempt to contact that side of the family, and until now, she'd made no attempt to do anything more either.

I understand why Dad never wanted anything to do with them after that. But why did he tell me to think about their offer? As if I would want to leave!

The motorcycle's engine began popping as Ned let off the gas. Dot leaned to the side to see what was up.

The color of dry sage, a coyote stood on the center of the pathway. It looked up, seeing them bearing down on it. It hesitated, starting to the left, and then changing its mind and running off to the right.

But even then, it changed its mind again, and as they puttered past its position, the animal was heading back up to the trail.

Ned yelled back, "I feel that way too. I've got a speech to give first period."

...

Smith School was probably the smallest school in Utah—certainly the smallest that served a non-Indian population. The one-room building was ancient, built by Mormon missionaries to serve the Indians.

"The reason," explained Ned, "that I can't be sure it is the smallest is that I couldn't find Ranch Exit on the state's school-districts website.

"And my dad said I couldn't spend more than fifteen minutes on-line. The pages loaded so slow that I ran out of time."

The Gibson twins giggled, and Bill Cartulio smirked from his elevated status with unlimited satellite bandwidth.

"Girls! Stop that!" Ms. Carson, who had the twenty-four students for the first three hours of the day, was already worn out by the antics of the little ones. She was fully convinced that teaching in a one-room school, with everyone from first-graders to graduating seniors sharing the same space was a lost art, and deservedly so. Her resume for a job at a modern urban school was already circulating.

"Ned, continue."

He grinned, "So my proposal is to create a website for Smith School. We can take pictures of the place and make our claim to being the smallest. Then if no one complains, we win the title by default."

Dot shook her head. Being the smallest, most under-funded school around wasn't her idea of something to brag about.

Just let Aunt Elizabeth hear about it. She felt her face flush at the thought. She loved Ranch Exit, but it would just make them look worse.

Ned finished his proposal, and Ms. Carson had the show of hands. It passed.

Larry Samuelson was next with a proposal to talk Mr. Mort into getting a McDonalds for Ranch Exit. All the students voted for that one, even Dot, but Ms. Carson vetoed the idea as impractical.

Only the older students had proposal speeches. Dot kept a calm confident face as Ms. Carson scanned the classroom for the next speaker. This teacher liked to call on the nervous ones first.

Dot had a presentation—a flowerbed for the school, but it wasn't something she was happy with. Tuesdays were proposal days, so with a little delay, she could have another week to prepare something better.

"Latoya?"

Ranch Exit's only senior clutched her nicely bound presentation papers and walked up to the lectern. She was wearing the dressy rust-colored suit her mother had bought her last month. Dot had only seen her in it once, a couple of Sundays ago. She looked very professional.

"I propose that businesses in the Smith School district establish an annual scholarship fund for the valedictorian of the year's graduating class."

There were groans, and she stammered through the next few sentences. It was a well-prepared presentation, with statistics showing what other school districts were doing, but everyone knew it was just another of the endless proposals to ask Mr. Mort for more handouts.

Dot watched the clock, and mentally urged Latoya to keep talking. She glanced at Mr. Filmore who had joined the class for his two-hour stint.

She wondered what he thought of this idea. Other than Mr. Mort and a few ranchers with no money, his store was the only business around here. He didn't even get paid to teach, as far as she knew. Greg Filmore and Nora Baker, a photographer, and sometimes Luke Samuelson took turns helping the part-time paid teacher they hired to keep the school running. Her dad had said that the instant this arrangement fell through, the Ranch Exit students would have to commute seventy miles to the nearest school.

"Hey!" yelled Quad Brewster, interrupting Latoya's summation. "There's a pack of coyotes in the yard!"

Half the class dashed to the window. Dot was with them. Coyotes weren't rare, but they avoided humans and human places.

These four were frolicking among the cars as if the parking lot were their home den.

Mr. Filmore went to the door and opened it, where the predators could see him.

"Go away!" he called. "Scat!"

The darkest one turned its head, and regarded the human.

"Get out of here. Go home!"

One of them yelped, and they scattered, heading in all directions.

Ms. Carter said, "That's the strangest thing I've ever seen."

George Filmore laughed. "You haven't been in Ranch Exit very long, have you?"

Mouse Chase

Ned paused as they approached the interstate off-ramp. They were going the wrong way on a one-way road, but since there was no traffic, he had no worries.

"What's that?" He pointed towards a freshly painted double line across the pavement.

Dot took a glance at narrow yellow stripes and grinned. "Take a look at the sign."

Ned slowed to a stop and took a look backwards at the warning sign. "LIZARD CROSSING".

"I should have guessed. You knew about this one?"

"Dad did the painting. Mort wanted it across the interstate, but that's against the rules. Painting the off-ramp might be too, but no one will notice it."

Ned admired the little crossing, only as wide as his hand. "Do you think too much money rots the brain? Oh, look! There's a lizard. Do you think he wants to cross?"

Ned eased his motorcycle past the lines, but the lizard stayed put, resting on a rock in the sun.

"I guess not." He hit the gas and moved off onto the shoulder of the interstate, heading for the off-ramp sign.

'RANCH EXIT' graced the large green sign, and below it in blue, 'NO SERVICES'.

Dot took off her helmet while Ned dug into his saddlebag. She frowned at the huge text. She was offended.

"Why do they say that? Filmore's store has food, and a public telephone. Isn't that 'services'?"

Ned pulled out the digital camera he had borrowed from Mrs. Baker.

"But he doesn't have gas. I asked him once. Unless he spends a fortune on a gas station that would pull in interstate traffic, it just wouldn't pay. As it is, Mr. Cartulio sells me my gas, like he does to the other ranchers, and he doesn't want interstate traffic pulling into his ranch at all hours of the night.

"So no gas, no 'services'."

Dot shook her head. It was just one more thing that kept her town from getting any respect.

Ned looked through the viewfinder of the camera and frowned. "Do you know how to work this thing?"

She took one look and slid back the lens cover. The camera lit up.

"Ah." He stepped back and framed the road sign. "I'm gonna make this the home page."

"Ranch Exit, no services?"

"Well, yes, and a menu to the other pages."

"Good luck." She shook her head. At least it wasn't her project.

"At least let me take a picture of you in front of the sign." She held out her hand for the camera.

He looked puzzled and then did as she asked, riding his bike in front of the sign.

"Dot? Do you have time to stop by Bill's house? I want to check out the free web account he promised to set up for me."

"If it doesn't take too long. Pokey expects to be fed this time of day."

"It won't. Hop on."

They sped down the off-ramp, relishing this short stretch of smooth pavement. Nothing in Ranch Exit was paved.

As the engine noise died away in the distance, the lizard perked its head up, and then dashed across the road, its tail whipping back and forth across the yellow lines.

...

The old railroad grade didn't reach all the way to the interstate. The spur route had been abandoned before the highway came through and the elevated path had been cut back a hundred yards, leaving room for the exit ramp and, more recently, the side-road to the Mort Ranch.

The main road through the valley curved and branched off to the various homesteads. The Kelso Express was much more direct.

Ned drove up the side of the road grade and gained speed. Dot held on and scanned the passing valley. The elevated road consistently had the best view of the surrounding landscape. She could identify all of the distant ranch houses.

Yesterday, the person walking the path had surprised them. Today Dot had her eyes open. She was rewarded.

She hit Ned on the side. He jerked and she pointed.

Several hundred yards off in the sage, Old Man Wanekia was running. At first glance, she thought it was a younger man—he looked like he was an experienced runner. But as Ned slowed down, she could see that he was limping, using his stick. He was an old man, running too fast for an old man's legs.

Ned peeled off the side of the elevated grade. They approached slowly, catching up to the runner.

Wearing a wide felt hat against the sun, the shaman had stopped. Dot was shocked when his words were loud enough to hear. Most of it was some Indian language, but a few of the curse-words were plain English.

He shook his stick at the sky, pausing only to cough and catch his breath.

"Are you okay Mr. Wanekia?" Dot asked as they pulled up and stopped.

He mumbled some more words they didn't understand. Then added, "I'll curse that hawk out of the sky! I didn't come all this way for my health."

"A hawk, Mr. Wanekia?" Ned asked.

The wrinkled face looked them over. "Kelso. Did you know you're stretching the valley with that thing? Back and forth, back and forth. Hmmp." He plainly was not pleased to see them.

"And the girl with the sick horse—tell your father to be careful. It's not safe sticking your fingers into a wizards' duel."

Dot's mouth was open. Pokey wasn't sick! And what did the rest of that mean?

Ned asked again, "You were chasing a hawk?"

The shaman looked off at the sky again. "No, I was chasing a mouse. Now go away." He rapped the front tire of the bike with his stick, and then limped away.

Dot fished the camera out of Ned's saddlebag and snapped a shot of him.

"Why did you do that?" Ned asked quietly.

Dot was angry. She would know if Pokey was sick and she was offended that someone thought he was.

"For your website. You need pictures of some of the weird characters that live around here."

...

Pokey seemed happy enough. Dot checked his eyes and his teeth. He made the apple she had bought at school vanish in a couple of authoritative crunches.

"You're fine, Pokey, aren't you?"

Ned had let her off about a quarter mile from her house when the motorcycle's engine started sputtering.

"Oh no! Old Man Wanekia cursed my bike!" Ned frowned, twisting the carburetor settings.

"Don't be silly, Ned. You know this happens all the time. It's an old machine."

Ned shook his head. "You saw what he did."

The engine caught, and he headed down the grade, getting a hundred yards before he had to stop and fuss with it again.

Ned worried her. He was taking all this Indian magic stuff far too seriously.

It's this isolation. We never get out of Ranch Exit except for market trips. How many people do I know? No more than dozens. How many people does Ned know? And how many of them take magic seriously?

She walked Pokey over to his barn. When she opened the grain barrel, the mouse was waiting for her.

...

This isn't the same mouse Mr. Wanekia was chasing. It couldn't be. That had been too far away.

Tiny black eyes watched her. She reached for the scoop and banged it against the side of the barrel.

In a brown blur of motion, the mouse moved to a crossbeam in the wall, and then vanished behind a pile of old junk.

She was relieved. That was what a mouse was supposed to do.

But maybe Pokey needs more exercise. She glanced at her saddle and riding gear. The leathers hadn't been oiled in more than a year.

Maybe just bareback.

Pokey accepted the bridle with deep distrust. Dot was disgusted at the effort it took her to climb on his back—she needed a large boulder as a stepladder. She was getting bigger and heavier. The motorcycle helmet was hardly 'horsy' but she didn't want to go back for the other one.

"Get." She rocked on his back. "Get a move on." She shook the reins.

Slowly, and regretfully, he took a step, and then another. Dot could walk much faster, but the whole point was getting Pokey some exercise. She urged him on faster.

She almost had him up to a slow walk by they time they reached the road. And then he stopped.

"Pokey, don't do this to me. We've gone this way many times before. Now move." She shook the reins.

Pokey snorted, and shook his head.

"What's the matter now? Have you...?"

As Dot leaned forward, she saw the motion on the ground. A brown streak zipped across the pathway, almost touching Pokey's hoof. The horse stomped his forefeet, unnerved by the mouse.

But the creature kept going, tiny feet propelling him up into the middle of the road. Then it paused at the far edge.

It's waiting for us. She couldn't see its tiny eyes from their distance, but it had turned to face them.

"Git. Keep moving." Pokey stepped forward. Satisfied, the mouse scurried on another fifteen feet and waited for them to catch up.

Dot wasn't a big believer in magic, but something strange was going on. She put her skepticism on hold and urged Pokey to follow.

The mouse was unimaginative, but persistent. It dashed ahead to an open place among the sage, or on a rock, and waited. Pokey never advanced faster than a walk, but they made time.

The mouse approached the railroad grade and then turned north, towards Ned's ranch. By blazing runs and long waits, the mouse was keeping pace with the best that Pokey was willing to provide.

About a mile from her home, a coyote appeared out of the sage.

The mouse vanished into the rocks. In a flash, the coyote was after him, pawing at the rocks.

"Hey!" yelled Dot. "Leave him alone!"

The coyote snarled at her, lunging towards them. Pokey reared back, flashing its hooves at the beast.

But Dot wasn't ready. She slid off and landed hard on the rocks.

Yellow eyes and sharp teeth confronted her. She could smell its foul breath. A low growl came from deep within its chest.

For a long, unforgettable moment, they stared at each other. Dot was frozen with fear. All her life, coyotes had been part of the landscape, just over the hill, or off in a field, hunting for mice or prairie dogs. They were pretty—a touch of the wild.

Never had she considered them a threat. Not until now.

Pokey shook her out of it. He neighed and pawed, not getting any closer, but responding like any horse did to a threat.

Dot felt her hand curl around a rock. She threw it.

Her aim was wild, but the stone bounced close to its paws, and it turned.

"Go away!" she screamed. She picked up another rock and this one glanced off its flank. It kept running over the hill.

A sharp cold sting on her arm told her she was scraped up. By the time she got to her feet, she knew she was bruised as well.

One quick look to make sure that the coyote was gone, and then she concentrated on calming down the horse. It had been a bad day for Pokey. She patted his flank and spoke soothing words. He almost reverted to his habit of checking her pockets for treats, but he started to shake again.

The mouse was nowhere to be seen. Dot didn't think the coyote had gotten it, but she wasn't sure. She picked up a couple of rocks for her pocket and started walking Pokey back home. Her hip ached with every step, but neither she nor her horse were up to riding.

Had the hawk caught the mouse Mr. Wanekia was chasing? Was that why he was so upset?

Are all the mice in the valley acting strange?

The mice, the coyotes—were there any other animals that were going to act crazy. She looked at Pokey and Pokey looked back.

Is he thinking the same thing about me?

...

The refrigerator magnet held a note from Dad.

"Working late at the Samuelsons. Don't wait supper."

With no phone, the notes they left each other had to do. Dot was a little relieved. She could take care of her own first aid and only tell him about the coyote if she needed to. Every time she came home with an injury, he spent days worrying about his job as her father. It was much more comfortable when they were partners, sharing the chores.

Ruben Comal's ranch was a little too small to make ends meet. He had run cattle. He had grown hay. But when tax time came and he added up the numbers, it was clear the ranch was slowly eating away what little money they had.

For the last three years he had leased his pastureland to neighbors and spent his time doing odd jobs for other ranchers—and even odder jobs for Mr. Mort.

Dot had seen his records, and the notes he wrote to himself that he hadn't shared with her. As long as he could keep food on the table, he was happy in Ranch Exit.

But when she graduated, there would be no money for college. He had sketched out his future then—sell the ranch and move to the city.

Dot's only hope was to get a scholarship, but even that seemed far-fetched. Maybe their life here was doomed, but she wasn't going to cut it any shorter by giving Dad more to worry about.

Duncan's Dwarf

Ned swerved at Dot's driveway, just missing the mouse in the middle of the road. He glanced back. It was still sitting there.

"Stupid mouse. You wanna be roadkill?"

At least the engine was purring like it should. He'd wasted an hour, and missed his chance to check out the website, just because he had to disassemble and clean the carburetor yesterday.

Dot came to the door, dressed as usual, but wearing a yellow scarf. "Early aren't you?" she asked.

"Hey, Dotcom. I thought I would take the road this morning, if you don't mind."

"Giving up the Kelso Express? Afraid of another Indian curse?" She grinned.

"No! It's not that. I just need to look around town for more pictures."

Thankfully, she bought it. "Good idea. Did you ask Mrs. Baker for suggestions when you borrowed her camera? She sells photos for a living, you know."

"Of course." Although he hadn't. The girl could be bossy at times.

She left to collect her books, and Ned waved at Mr. Comal. They were at peace again, now that Dotcom had her helmet and she was all healed up from that spill a couple of months ago. He had been sure the man would kill him when he brought his daughter back from that attempt on the North Mesa, her scalp bleeding and her arm in a sling.

Still, she must like the motorcycle. She was the only one of his friends who rode with him, so he had to put up with her.

...

Wednesday was Dot's day to monitor the little kid's recess time. April and May, the Gibson twins, were her favorites. The three of them had a make-believe tea party with imaginary cups and saucers. Dot sat next to the stone fence where she could keep an eye on the others.

It wasn't a job for the careless. Little Ross Brown had discovered rocks and his aim and power were getting better by the day. She was almost the school nurse for the little ones, and Ross had caused a run on the colorful bandage strips. Luckily, she had discovered that a shout, delivered at just the right moment in his windup, would cause him to fumble the throw. The time she chased him down, she got a pebble on her shin.

Duncan Bly's hole in the ground was getting quite respectable. He had started it three months before, and on days where the weather was warm enough, he would bring out the pail and gardening spade and work hard the whole recess. He claimed there was a dwarf that lived underground, and he needed help. Dot couldn't actually see Duncan, but there was a regular rain of dirt and gravel erupting from the hole. She would have to help him out of the pit and send him to the washroom to clean up five minutes before recess was over. Mr. Filmore had gotten him several feet of yellow "Construction Area—Warning!" tape to surround the hole.

Luckily, the others were engrossed in some run-around-the-playground-chasing-a-soccer-ball game and didn't need her to interfere.

It was then that the eagle flew overhead. Silent, for once.

The giant shadow flickered over the playground and everyone looked up.

Dot caught it just as it revealed the sun.

"Ah, ha!" She saw the true outline of the plane, lined with gold, just before she had to blink from the sun.

Mort's small plane was a marvel of disguise. A giant bald eagle was painted on its underside, and the remainder was so carefully matched to the color of the sky that most of the time, it couldn't be seen.

Frequently, the old billionaire took to the sky and surveyed the town of Ranch Exit and the surrounding lands. At low power, the engine was nearly silent, but when he had to speed up or gain altitude, the little turbine jet sounded a much deeper note than the shriek of the real bird.

Mort had another plane too, but it was a more sedate twin-engine Beechcraft that he used to commute to the civilized world. That was his public plane. No one outside of Ranch Exit ever saw the eagle.

The little jet engine whined louder and the plane shot up at a steep angle and out of sight.

As Dot looked away, she caught sight of Ned running towards his bike. But then, he stopped as the plane left, and he turned back.

Dot glanced at her watch and hurried over to Duncan's pit.

A dirty face smiled up at her.

"I saw him!"

"Who?" Visions of dwarves flickered through her mind.

"The eagle—he was looking right down at me."

She reached down to grab his hand, grateful he wasn't any heavier. "Come on, you need to get cleaned up."

Duncan came up readily, and then dashed off to tell his friends what he had seen.

Ms. Carson hit the school bell with a hammer. Recess was over. Dot counted heads as they retreated back indoors.

Ned walked up and joined her.

"What are you doing out here?" she asked. "You were supposed to be studying."

"But I had to try to get a shot of the eagle! That would make a great webpage."

"I don't know. One time Mrs. Baker took a picture of the eagle, and Mort paid her off to never sell it, and to take no more. I don't think he would like it."

Ned shrugged. "So what. He couldn't stop me."

She let it pass. What did Mr. Mort want? He was secretive about some things, and then pulled outlandish, public pranks like the Apple.

Off to the left, just visible from the interstate, she could still see the sagging remnants of a giant apple. Created by stuffing a huge red plastic bag with hay bales, it had not fared well under the sunlight. The color had faded to a pale pink, and the plastic was splitting. Soon enough it would just be a mound of moldering hay.

Maybe I'm just timid because Dad works for him. She wouldn't do anything to risk her dad's income. *Ned doesn't have that worry.*

...

Bill Cartulio was proud of his satellite dish. They spent a few minutes just flipping through the endless list of television channels before going over to his computer.

"The old man erased my P2P software, but the web browser still works," he shook his head sadly. "I had several gigabytes of stuff—and he erased it all."

Dot asked, "Why did he do that?" Bill said nothing and Ned shook his head from behind Bill's back. She got the message. *Don't ask.*

Ned clicked the web browser. "Did you get me a website?"

"Not yet, but I know where to go."

Within a few minutes, Ned had registered at one of the free website hosting services. They had to put up with advertising banner windows, but Ned was pleased to be able to put up his crude homepage. "Come visit Ranch Exit (no Services)—the smallest place around."

"I'll have to bring the pictures tomorrow. I don't have them downloaded from the camera yet."

"Fine. Maybe by then I'll be able to show you ... something."

Dot pretended she didn't hear that last. Bill had no grudge with her, and if he had something private to share with Ned, then it was obvious she didn't want to be in on it.

No wonder your father wiped out your downloads, pervert!

...

When the sound of the motorcycle died, Dot asked, "Ned, could you stay here while I feed Pokey?"

"Huh? Sure." He dismounted and followed.

"Still the laziest horse in the world, aren't you?"

Dot scolded. "Don't pick on him! He rescued me yesterday."

"What? What do you mean?"

She told the story of the mouse, and the coyote. In this version, Pokey was her valiant defender and chased the predator off.

Ned nodded. "I thought you were riding a little stiff back there. Bruises?"

She didn't deign to answer. They entered the barn.

Dot cautiously checked the grain barrel.

The mouse was waiting.

Ned frowned. "What are you doing here, Roadkill?"

Dot glanced at her friend. "You recognize it?"

"Hard to tell. All mice look alike. But there was a mouse just like it coming down your driveway this morning. I barely missed it."

"He doesn't try to escape unless I startle him." She thumped the barrel. It jumped to the edge and out onto the ground. They watched it dart over to the door, where it waited. Pokey edged back.

Ned asked, "So what do we do now?"

"I feed my horse."

"And then what?"

She looked at Ned. "If you think we ought, we could follow it."

...

Ruben Comal was mildly puzzled when his daughter wasn't there to greet him when he arrived home. The note on the refrigerator didn't help much. Of course, she and Ned were out doing something, but what else was new?

At least she had put supper out to thaw.

The latest paycheck from Mort was putting a trip into town that much closer. Ranch Exit had no bank and George Filmore had stopped taking third-party checks after that ugly incident with Samuelson. A check was only good if someone would cash it.

He stared at the check again. He had no worry that Mort couldn't cover it, but something felt wrong. It was hard to put a name to it.

When Mort came back from his flying around today and pulled out his checkbook, he seemed more distant and distracted than ever. The Midas of Ranch Exit was never a friendly man, but as bosses go, Ruben had no complaints.

And if he has to bury his worries with a few more crazy signs, I'll be happy to do the work and take the pay.

...

"DOUBLECROSSROAD" said the sign in black letters on gray.

"I knew it!" said Ned, when the mouse walked up to a rock and rested in the failing sunlight.

"Knew what?"

They coasted to a stop on the motorcycle, letting the mouse take a rest. It had to wait for Pokey yesterday, but it could never keep up with Ned's bike. Dot was seriously worried about the little thing. How far could a mouse go? Run and hide was its lifestyle, not long distance travel.

"When I first saw this sign, last summer sometime, I wondered what it meant. Sometimes Mort's signs do mean something, you know."

Dot nodded, "And?"

"Well, I got to thinking. This stretch of the old railroad grade is generally straight. You could draw it on a map with a ruler. But look here," he pointed to the side.

"See the side of the elevated grade. As far as you can see, it's even, smooth sided, and covered with sage that's grown up since it was built. But right here, the grade it just a bit narrower, and the rocks are bigger, and there isn't as much sage.

"I think there used to be another spur off this line. It joined the track here, but later they removed it—bulldozed away all signs of it, and then tried to fill in the scar."

Dot nodded wisely. "And who exactly is this 'they'?"

He shrugged. "I dunno. Railroad people I guess."

She laughed, "That I don't buy. Railroad people will come back and remove the rails because the steel is valuable. They will even take the cross-ties and sell them to landscape people, but they don't clean up an old grade just for fun. There's no money in it."

"Oh well. It's just a theory."

"Don't get defensive, Ned. I'm not making fun of you. This time."

"This may not be the place. The mouse looks like he's getting ready to move."

"He'd better get there soon. The sun is going down. Did you bring a flashlight?"

"No, but the bike has a headlight."

"Look! He's leaving the grade."

Ned started the engine. But he hesitated.

"I can't go that way. He's into those big rocks. They'd cut my tires to shreds."

Dot hopped off. "Well we can't lose him! Not after coming this far." She followed the mouse down the slope, losing sight of their little brown leader, and dashing on when it reappeared.

Ned's voice came from close behind. "I hope we're not going too far. I'd hate to climb back up this way in the dark."

She stopped. The mouse was nowhere in sight. Ned landed heavily on her toe. "Ouch!"

"Sorry. Where's the mouse?"

"I'm looking."

The railroad grade was twenty feet above normal ground level here, and the whole side was a pile of fractured boulders three to six feet across. It hadn't occurred to her before, but there was something wrong with the rocks.

"Ned? These are granite."

"So."

"The rocks in our valley are sandstone, shale, sedimentary things like that. Granite isn't. These had to be shipped in from somewhere else."

"That's not unusual for a railroad. They haul that kind of stuff all the time."

"I guess so." In the fading light the mouse was invisible in the rubble.

Ned looked around, "What do we do now? It's gone."

She shook her head. "If the mouse wants to be found, it knows where we are."

"If not, we go home, right? It's getting cool."

"Right." But if they left now, they might never understand the mystery.

In this deep, rural landscape, with no smog, low humidity, and for today, little dust, there was nothing to scatter the light. Sunset happened quickly, and dusk was on a stopwatch.

Rocks that had been baking in the sun dropped quickly in temperature. With not even a cloud overhead to reflect the heat, the air grew nippy.

Ned tapped her arm. "It's time to go. I don't have a coat and when we get moving, it'll be cold."

Dot strained her eyes, but it was hard to see anything now. "Okay."

...

He led the way, climbing boulders. He waited as she followed. If she slipped he didn't want to have to climb back down to get her.

She stopped.

"Come on. Time's a wastin'."

"Ned, did you leave your headlight on?"

"No."

"Then what is that?" She pointed back across the rocks.

At first he saw nothing, but then he saw a diffuse light, not quite as if the facing cliff was glowing, more like moonlight on the rocks, or his bike's headlight shining down on it.

But his motorcycle didn't even have a battery to run the lights—it only worked when the engine was running.

"Let's climb."

They reached the top of the railroad grade with only minimal scrapes. Ned looked back and forth, panicking until he caught the outline of his bike, almost invisible in the dark. They had come up a couple of dozen feet down the way.

He helped Dot up the last boulder, and they stared off into the blackness. The strange light was a patch at the base of North Mesa, no more than twenty feet across, and it was fading as they watched.

Dot said, "I read a book once about plankton or seaweed or something that glowed in the ocean at night. But I've never heard of something like that in the desert."

Ned scraped his shoe on the ground. "It's about gone now. There's nothing we can do tonight. Let's go."

Walking over to his bike, he started the engine. Ned winced as the headlight cut through the darkness.

"Dot. Come here, quickly."

She approached.

"Hold this steady." He dismounted and stepped quietly forward a few paces, and then jumped.

"Gotcha!"

"Ned? What...?"

"The mouse. He was waiting here for us." He held his hands together, cupping it.

"Don't hurt it!"

Ned sighed, "Don't be silly. We have to take him back with us. If what you've told me is right, then he's like a homing pigeon or something. If we drove off without him, he'd try to make his way back to your barn—and honestly, I don't think he has the energy to make it."

Dot nodded. "Right. I didn't think about that. Here, I have a pocket that zips." He handed it over and she sealed the furry warm creature in.

Ned shivered. "Let's get back. I'll drive slow so the wind won't be too bad."

He looked at her. She was looking back at North Mesa.

"What now?"

She shook her head. "I was just thinking. Maybe Duncan has been digging for his dwarf in the wrong place all this time."

Mort's Visit

Ruben Comal watched them approach, seeing the headlight from a mile away. He sat on the porch swing as they came into the driveway and stopped by the barn. It was too dark to make out the details, but it looked like Ned hugged his daughter, and then they drove into the circle of the porch lights.

"Hello Ned." It wasn't a friendly greeting.

The boy looked up sharply at his voice. He looked guilty. Dot gave the boy a shake of her head.

Secrets. Whatever they were doing out in the dark together, she won't tell me.

"Well, I'll see you in the morning, Dot."

Ruben interrupted. "I don't think that will be necessary, Ned. I'll be able to get her to and from school. Thanks for your help, but don't come by tomorrow. In fact, Dot won't be available for a few days."

Ned nodded, "Uh. Fine. Okay." He revved his engine and accelerated out towards the road.

Dot glared at him, stomping up to the porch.

"Dad! That was rude. Ned did nothing wrong. It took him a month to talk to me the last time you scolded him."

He got up from the porch swing. "Supper is waiting. We'll have to reheat it."

They ate in silence. He certainly wasn't going to cross-examine her about what she was doing out past sunset when they had long ago agreed that darkness was a perfectly reasonable limit on her activities. They lived in a wild place without a phone, in a land where anything from rattlesnakes to coyotes to Ned Kelso could leave her injured or worse.

She was quiet too, obviously refusing to volunteer where she'd been.

Once the dishes went into the sink, he asked, "Have you given any more thought to your aunt's invitation?"

The frying pan hit the plates a little harder than it should, but nothing broke.

She didn't look up from the dishes, as she added the soap.

"I don't know why I should go there. Seattle is rainy. You would have to feed Pokey, and he doesn't trust you. And besides," she faced him and shook a soapy spatula, "you haven't done your share of the dishes in over a month. Taking a trip would just leave the place a disaster area. I'd come back and have to spend all my spare time catching up whatever you've let slide."

He let her spew. She had more to say about his shortcomings, and then, "And I don't like Aunt Elizabeth! I don't like what she said about you, and I don't understand why you're even considering this!"

He closed his eyes. Some things just hurt.

"Maybe, maybe if June hadn't been angry with her father. Maybe we could have gotten her treated earlier."

Dot's lips were tightly compressed as she dropped the dish she was working on back into the sink and grabbed a towel.

"So, what you are saying is that in spite of everything you and Mom ever said, getting access to her family's money *is* the most important thing! And now you want me to swallow my pride and go begging for a few crumbs from their table!"

She tossed the towel to him. "You finish the dishes!" she said, and stalked out.

He picked it up, and slowly walked over to the sink.

All I ever wanted was a safe place for you to grow up, and now, not even Ranch Exit is isolated enough. He had laughed with Jake Cartulio when he had shared the story about what his boy had been up to with their family's new satellite dish. *And Ned is Bill Cartuilio's good buddy.* Ned had seemed a safe enough companion for Dot, but not now. *Not when they are out after dark, doing something too embarrassing to tell me.*

Elizabeth wasn't a bad person, other than a tendency to get hysterical. Once she'd formed the crazy idea that he had kept June from getting full-scale medical treatment for her cancer just to spite their family, she had seen herself as the rescuing angel, trying to save Dot from a life of squalor.

Well, maybe she can. Maybe Dot should go beyond the range of Ranch Exit and see what the world has to offer. A summer away wouldn't hurt her.

And when it's time to sell the ranch, she'll have something to look forward to.

In any case, his daughter deserved someone with a better future than Ned Kelso. She deserved better than any of the boys in Ranch Exit.

...

It was pitch black, but the mouse had no trouble locating the wrinkled old hand. The fingers twitched under its feet, but that was no cause for fear. It scurried up the arm and sat resting on the thin papery skin of a forehead. Long gray hair surrounded it in all directions.

He came awake with a sneeze, and that was enough to send the mouse back to the floor.

"What is it, Mickey?" He clicked a large switch next to his bed and pushed himself upright.

The lamp, for all its yellow weakness, was enough to bring the whole room into his view. Three brown mice, siblings he had raised himself, were circling, following each other's tails in a three-foot loop.

Clockwise. Someone has been poking around the old airshaft near the railroad.

He pulled himself out of bed and dragging himself across the floor by his hands, opened the closet and found a threadbare shirt to wear.

Good news indeed. Time to get to work.

He slipped shoes on his hands and headed out the door.

...

Dot felt odd without her motorcycle helmet. Her dad seemed cheerful enough as he drove her to school.

"I need to go into town today. How about I write you an excuse and you come along?"

The idea of getting to walk the aisles of the stores, and to eat at a real restaurant was immensely appealing.

He continued, "There are some times I just have to get out of this dusty old place and see some faces I don't know. Ranch Exit is an off-ramp to nowhere."

She stiffened. "No. I'm sorry, I'd really like to go, but I have a project due and I'm going to need the study time."

He nodded, his face dark. They pulled up to the school and he got out as well and went in ahead of her.

Dot was early, and half the kids hadn't arrived. Ned wasn't there, but that was normal. He usually pulled in as the bell rang. Dot nodded to Latoya Harris, who sat next to her. She was back in khakis and her orange blouse—the fancy suit saved away for the next excuse to dress up.

Ruben came out of the little side building that was the teachers' office. "I just called Mrs. Baker. She'll drive you home after school, in case I don't make it back by then. You won't have to rely on that boy. Can I get you anything in town?"

A little respect for Ranch Exit. And for me and my friends. "No ... the only things I can think of are too expensive, and with your eye for color, I'd hate to think what you might buy at the clothes store. But pick up some more apples and any other kinds of fruit you can think of."

He left and she immediately regretted not going. Town, any town, offered color and excitement—nothing better than her hometown, but certainly different.

Seattle wouldn't be better either. But no one who hasn't lived here even knows Ranch Exit exists.

Maybe that's what my proposal should be, some way to bring Ranch Exit some respect. But how?

Ned arrived at the last minute and they had no time to talk.

...

Ms. Carson called the older girls together. "We're going to have a visitor in class today. I want each of you to take some of the little ones in hand and keep them out of trouble while he's here."

Dot was quick on the draw and selected the Gibson twins and Duncan Bly and then held her breath while Ross the rock thrower was assigned to Latoya.

"Who's the guest?"

"You'll see."

They didn't have long to wait. The shiny blue Humvee pulled up to the parking lot shortly, looking like someone had taken a Jeep's big brother and squashed it wide.

Ms. Carson rapped the desk with her pointer.

"Class, I would like you to greet our neighbor and special visitor today, Mr. Ellis Mort."

The students were agog. In spite of living in the same valley, few had ever seen the man.

Some were disappointed he wasn't dripping with gold.

Dot marveled at his suit. The bald old man, looking like he was in his seventies, wore a nicely tailored business suit. At first glance it looked gray, but as he walked past her, she saw it flicker, as if the fabric was striped in a million tiny colors.

"Greetings class. Your teacher and I were talking on the phone yesterday, and she indicated that you might have some questions for me. Since I had never been to the school before, I offered a trade. You show me around the place, and I'll answer a few of your questions."

There were more hands raised than one per student. He pointed to Larry Samuelson.

"How much money do you have?" asked Larry.

He chuckled, "I don't know, and I don't care."

"No really! I bet you're a billionaire."

Mort pulled out his wallet. "Well I have enough to pay my bills and ... it looks like a little over a hundred dollars in cash and my credit card. How much do you have in your pocket?"

"Three dollars."

"No credit card yet?"

"No."

"You will. Next question."

Some kids asked about his signs and other odd displays.

"Artwork. Some people paint. My hands shake too much for that. So I put up signs."

Quad Brewster asked, "Can I go for a ride in your eagle?"

"Sorry, son. It only has one seat. But that reminds me, I was flying over the other day and I saw a big hole in the ground. What's that all about?"

There were a few giggles. Dot, who had been sitting with her charges took Duncan's hand and stood up with him.

"Hello, Mr. Mort. My name is Dorothy Comal."

"Yes, I know your father."

"The hole is Duncan Bly's project. Would you like him to show it to you?"

"Why yes, I would like that. Mr. Bly?"

Duncan, who talked little and stuttered more, just nodded and turned red.

Dot handed April and May over to Ms. Carson and appointed herself Duncan's moral support.

"We'll be back in a moment." The rest of the class were visibly disappointed that they weren't included.

The jokes when Duncan started his pit had faded away over time, but Dot knew making a public event of it would bring out the worst from the hecklers. *Duncan needs a little respect too.* She just hoped Mr. Mort wouldn't laugh.

They stopped at the edge.

"This is Duncan's project? How long have you been at it?"

Little shoulders shrugged.

"About three months?" she prompted.

"Yes."

Mr. Mort looked it over, getting his fancy suit dangerously close to the dirt. "A big project, Mr. Bly. What are you digging for?"

Duncan looked at Dot, desperate for a clue. She nodded confidently.

"Ah. There's a dwarf down there. I'm trying to rescue him."

Mort frowned, just for an instant, but then covered it quickly. "A dwarf? Have you heard him recently?"

Duncan shook his head. "Just a couple of times. People don't believe me."

The billionaire knelt in the dust beside the hole and looked at it again.

"You know, I know some things about dwarfs. When did you hear him—what time of day?"

Duncan's eyes were wide. "It was morning. Both times. Mom had dropped me off early and I had the whole playground to myself."

Mort nodded, "And were there any animals around?"

"Just critters."

"What kind of critters?"

"Little brown ones."

"Good. Good. Well, Mr. Bly, I think you are right on track. Sometimes dwarves can send messages through animals. He did call for help, and only you could hear it because you are special. But for now, other people won't understand, so don't even try to convince them."

Duncan nodded, "I know."

Mort shot a glance at Dot. She had been listening in amazement. Either Mort was spinning a tale for Duncan's benefit, or ... something.

She nodded to Duncan. "I can keep a secret too. But I've always known you were special."

Duncan smiled, and it seemed to satisfy Mort. He slapped the dust from his pants legs and they went back in.

...

Ms. Carson showed off her best students and was disappointed when Dot declined to give her proposal speech a few days early. Mort stayed for lunch, not glancing at the clock too many times, and then won a cheer from the students when he revealed that he had brought an ice chest of specialty ice creams to share for dessert.

Needless to say, after he left, the teachers had an interesting afternoon coping with a wholesale sugar rush. Even the older ones were bouncy.

After the final announcement, Ned asked, "Do I take you home?"

"No. Dad made arrangements."

He looked at his shoes. "Oh. I'm still in the dog house."

She sighed, "He'll get over it. I told him you didn't do anything wrong."

"Yeah, but you'd say the same thing if we had been out smooching."

A laugh bubbled up, hearing him say it out loud. "In your dreams ... but you're probably right. Just stay out of sight for awhile and Dad'll forget."

Ned nodded. "But what about the mouse?"

She had tried to forget about it, but Duncan's story had brought the strangeness of it all rushing back. And having a businessman speak of talking animals was a record oddity from a man known for oddities.

"We can't do anything until Saturday. I'm not going back there in the dark. And Dad will be watching me. We'll just have to see."

...

"Hello Dot. And Mr. Kelso. How has the photography been going?"

"Fine, Mrs. Baker."

"Would you like to unload the pictures now?"

The middle-aged lady walked with a spring in her step for someone so old. She led them to the office and Ned dug out the camera.

She removed the little memory card from the camera and burned the pictures onto a CD-ROM. Ned thanked her.

"Well, you could do me a favor," the photographer smiled. "I have been intending to hike across Salt Creek Wash this Saturday. The only problem is my car. If you could go out there with me, and drive the Jeep to the south entrance, I'd only have to hike it one way. I'll pay twenty bucks?"

Ned's eyes lit up. "I'd love to ... but I don't really have a driver's license."

She waved that aside. "We're just going to be on dirt roads. You're not going to crash my Jeep are you?"

"No way!"

"Then it's a deal. Come by my place early, so I can hike in the cool of the morning."

Ned looked an apology to Dot. Saturday was out for a mouse expedition. She understood.

...

"Are you going to be taking pictures Saturday?" Dot asked as Mrs. Baker drove her home.

"Of course. I take pictures all the time. I'll probably take several hundred on that hike."

"Wow. How much do they sell for?"

She laughed. "Most of them will never sell. If I can take one good shot out of a morning's hike, that would be a good day. If I can include it in a magazine article, it could earn me a few hundred dollars. When I'm really lucky, I can make poster prints and sell them at a gallery in Salt Lake. This isn't something you can get rich at. I just love doing it—and the hikes are good for my health."

Dot hesitated, "Um. I heard you took a picture of Mr. Mort's eagle."

Mrs. Baker looked at her with a huge grin. "One of my better shots."

"They say he paid you to not sell it."

"Not exactly."

"What do you mean?"

"Well, he offered ten thousand dollars for the picture, and I turned him down."

"Why?" Dot couldn't imagine that much money.

"Because I would then have to pay a big chunk of that money to the IRS in taxes. Instead, I opened up one of my photography magazines and pointed to a new high-end digital camera that I had been drooling over. He whipped out his credit card and bought the camera and a set of lenses over the phone, probably over twenty thousand dollars worth, and gave it to me as a gift.

"Since I really didn't sell him anything, and we never signed anything, it wasn't income and I'm not paying the taxes."

Dot couldn't imagine a camera that expensive. But she understood barter. "Sneaky. Do you think the IRS would buy the story?"

"I'm not telling them. I don't think Mort will either. Maybe it wasn't a sale—maybe it's blackmail." She laughed.

"But without something in writing, what's keeping you from taking another picture of it?"

The lady's grin faded. "He didn't have to ask. I'm afraid to."

"You're afraid of Mort?"

She shook her head, "Ha! No, I'm afraid of the picture!"

"The picture?"

Mrs. Baker turned into the Comal driveway and pulled to a stop. She looked at Dot with a sober expression.

"I haven't told anyone about this part. I hadn't intended to tell you as much as I have."

She paused. Then in a rush she said, "But I'll explode if I can't tell anyone. Dot, you'll have to keep this absolutely quiet. It's not a secret you can share."

Dot nodded. "I understand exactly."

"Okay," she looked in her rearview mirror, not that anyone would likely be around to overhear her.

"You've seen the eagle plane before?"

"Sure, dozens of times."

"You know it's painted like an eagle and the head of the eagle is looking straight ahead. It's symmetrical."

Dot nodded.

Mrs. Baker held her breath and then said, "When I look at my picture of it, the eagle's head is turned to the left, as if it is looking that way.

"But what's really strange is that if I take the picture into Photoshop and blow it up to see the details, the eagle's head is straight ahead just like it's supposed to be.

"But Dot it's the same picture file! Look at it normal, or at a printout of it, and the eagle looks to the left. But zoom in close, and it's looking straight ahead."

She shivered. "I don't understand it. I've been all through my software, and in all my decades of photo work, I've never seen anything like this.

"It's almost like ... magic."

Ruben's Rage

Ruben Comal was fifteen miles past the off-ramp before he realized he'd missed the exit.

He rubbed his eyes. *I didn't realize I was that tired.* The round trip to town was a long drive, and he missed having Dot with him for company.

The stars were blazing overhead when he finally pulled up to the house.

Dot bounced down from the porch where she had been waiting for him.

"Hi. Dad. Can I get a camera?"

"A camera? What for?"

As they unloaded the pickup, Dot gave him the story about Mrs. Baker—how she made hundreds of dollars on photos for magazines and sold her work in art galleries.

"Mrs. Baker is a professional," he cautioned. "She has expensive cameras and tripods and spends a lot of time at it."

"Oh, I know that, but Mrs. Baker says there is more to photography than equipment, and that with an inexpensive starter camera I can learn the basics of lighting and composition. She said she could teach me."

He nodded and listened to all that "Mrs. Baker says" for most of the evening.

"We'll see. Ask Mr. Filmore. See what they cost and we'll check the budget."

"I just wish I could afford a digital camera like Mrs. Baker loaned to Ned. That way I could take lots of pictures."

Ruben put his hand down on the table hard enough to shake it. "You're still talking to that boy?"

She nodded, startled at his sudden anger.

"Well, don't! I don't like him." He got up and left the room.

Dot just stared. *What has gotten into him? And what am I supposed to do now?*

...

By Friday afternoon, Ned had three sheets of paper covered with doodles. School was torture. He had a website to build, a wild animal mystery (he underlined INDIAN MAGIC!!!) to solve, gas to buy for his motorcycle—and on top of that, Dot warned him not to talk to her, at least where anyone could see them.

His own dad was as laid back as anyone could imagine. The idea that he would have to ask permission from Albert Kelso for anything didn't seem to connect with reality.

When he realized that Mr. Comal was another kind of parent entirely, it had shaken him up. The man was cold, and very, very polite when he thought Dot was in any danger. Ned was forcibly reminded of the rattlesnake that had climbed into his saddlebag a couple of years earlier. It too had been polite.

Ned followed the same tactics then as now. Wait them out and keep his distance.

But he really needed to talk to Dot about the mouse mystery. How could he manage that?

He scratched out the INDIAN MAGIC and wrote below it, GOVERNMENT SPIES.

...

Bill Cartulio sat down at the work table. "Hey Dotcom."

She looked up from her math papers. "Bill."

Which is the opposite and which is the adjacent?

"They're holding church over at my house this Sunday."

"That's good." Ranch Exit hadn't enough population to fund a church building, not unless Mort got religion, so services floated from house to house. Everyone came from different faiths, so the composite was an uneasy truce on everything except favorite songs and simple doctrine. With Chris Lee carrying his Book of Mormon, and Ruth Harris quoting from the Apocrypha now and again, Christian unity was a popular sermon.

"Are you coming?" he asked.

It was a valid question. Since her mother died, Ruben Comal intended to come every time, but in practice, it depended on how hard he worked the Saturday before and whether he slept late Sunday. And until he turned his daughter lose with the keys to the pickup, her attendance matched his.

"I'll try." She liked church. For one thing, the only community that existed in Ranch Exit was school, George Filmore's general store, and Sunday church. Some people she only saw at church.

Bill grinned. "That's good. My family and the Brewster's are having lunch together after. Would you like to come?"

The trig equations suddenly vanished from her head. Eating at someone's house was the closest thing to a date for Ranch Exit kids. Bill was asking her 'out'.

Her brain locked up. Bill was a year older than she was, and the idea that anyone would be interested in her just slid away when she tried to latch onto it. She wasn't interested in Bill. She wasn't interested in anyone.

Ranch Exit was too small to limit friendship to just the girls, but other than Ned, she didn't spend much time with the boys.

But Bill had just asked her a question. He was expecting an answer. What should she say?

Across the room, Ned stood up from his desk. He caught her eye, and then walked over to the library shelf, where all fifty or so books were arranged in alphabetical order. He tapped the 'D' tab, and then the 'A' tab, and then the 'D' again. As he walked back to his desk, she noticed a piece of paper stuffed between two of the books.

Dad! Of course.

"That's nice of you Bill, but my dad is old-fashioned about some things. I really think you will have to ask him about that."

Bill's smile faded, "Oh. Okay then. I hope to see you Sunday."

She waited as Bill went back to his books, not wanting to be too obvious when she picked up Ned's note.

But then Latoya hopped up from her seat and checked the library herself. When she went to the bathroom, the paper was gone from the shelf.

...

Latoya! She had been there yesterday when she showed up with her father, instead of Ned. She was listening this morning then she whispered the warning to Ned that they weren't supposed to talk. *She has spread the word. Everyone knows something is up now.*

Even April and May had asked her why Ned hadn't brought her to school. Denying that there was any problem meant nothing.

And now it appeared Bill had gotten the impression that she and Ned had 'broken up' and that he could move in.

Silly. Ned was never my boyfriend in the first place.

But now Latoya had her note from Ned.

There was only one thing to do. She headed for the bathroom.

It was an add-on to the original school building, just like the teachers' office, but at least the new bathroom had plumbing. Class legend had it that the one before was fifty feet away with no flush. Fifty feet in a Ranch Exit winter was frightening.

Dot's heartbeat was tripping when she knocked on the door. Latoya exited with just a nod of her head, and a grin on her face.

The folded sheet of paper was propped up before the mirror. Dot grabbed it. Ned's block lettering covered just a couple of lines. In blue cursive, Latoya had left her commentary.

...

"I saw your face when Bill came to talk to you. You looked panicked. Use your Dad to scare him off—works for me."

"Hey DC, I saw your face too. Practice it for Halloween."

"We have to talk about the mouse. He's making me crazy."

"Bill as a mouse!!! Ha. Ha. He does have a cute nose.

"But seriously, you two lovers need a better way to send messages!"

...

Dot felt her face burning. It was a disaster. Latoya couldn't keep a story to herself, not even if she explained the truth.

I'll never be able to live this down!

...

Latoya was whispering something to Hallee Cooper when Dot came back into the room. They straightened up and exchanged looks.

Dot tried to ignore them. Instead she walked to Ned's desk and dropped the paper in plain sight in front of him, and then returned to her math papers.

Ned picked up the paper, frowned as he saw Latoya's notes. He shot her an evil look.

But then when he saw Dot's message at the end, he nodded slowly and gave her a thumb's up from across the room.

Hallee and Latoya started whispering again.

Ned folded the paper and stuffed it into his pocket.

Dot really looks steamed. She shouldn't let silly chatterboxes rattle her.

Still her note to him was interesting, and it was certainly going to make it harder to deal with Mr. Comal.

"No help for it now. If anyone asks, we are a couple, but don't get cute! I'll meet you at church service, Bill's house Sunday."

...

The instant class was over Ned was out the door. The sound of his motorcycle's engine faded off into the distance.

Dot went to talk to the teacher.

"Mr. Filmore, do you sell cameras?"

She was barely into the listing of what she needed when Ruben Comal came in.

Something's wrong. What did he hear?

But her dad's expression softened when he entered and nodded to the shopkeeper.

"Howdy Ruben. Dot tells me she's going to get into photography."

"If the price is right."

"Oh, I've got all kinds of prices. Come on over to the store and we'll take a look. Anything I don't have in stock I can order."

The store was close, easy walking distance, but they drove.

"Dad?"

"Yes, Dot." His smile had faded by the time left the school.

"I can't stop talking to Ned. It just doesn't work."

"Hmm." He seemed focused on his driving.

"People now think we are boyfriend/girlfriend, and it's all your fault for making a big deal out of it."

He glanced at her, but said nothing.

They went into the store, following George Filmore as he unlocked the door and flipped over the CLOSED sign.

"What's wrong Ruben?"

Her dad looked at Dot and then at Filmore. He sighed, "Aaron Locke has been arrested."

"What?"

He nodded, "Yes. He was on the interstate and was pulled over for speeding. The story I've heard is that he lost his temper and tried to slug the officer."

"Aaron did this?" Filmore was incredulous.

"I don't believe it either. Do you think he might have gotten drunk?"

"Not Aaron. I don't think I've ever seen him drink, nor raise his voice either. Not in all the years he's been here."

Dot only knew Mr. Locke as the man who worked with her father, but the news had upset him. She was sorry she had griped at him about Ned.

"Something had been eating at him," commented Mr. Comal. "He worked with me on Mort's crop circle. I heard him muttering about something that day. I didn't think anything about it. He was just acting strangely."

The last sentence cut right through Dot. 'Strangely', like the mice and the coyotes? What if this mental instability was going to affect other people too?

Shortly, they got back on the subject of cameras, and settled on a disposable that already had film loaded and included pre-paid developing for the pictures.

"That way you know the cost up front, and if you run out of things to take pictures of, you won't be out the cost of an expensive camera. Just be cautious. You only have twenty-four shots, so plan them carefully."

...

Old Man Wanekia sniffed the air as he came into the store.

George Filmore looked up from his shelves. "Good afternoon, Watson. Can I help you?"

He wrinkled his old face. "Craziness in the air. You can smell it."

"You may be right there. Would you like more cornmeal?"

"No. Give me a flashlight."

George laughed, "Now Watson, I've heard you claim you can see in the darkness. What do you need a flashlight for?"

"I can see in the dark. I can sneak up on rattlesnake and swipe the fangs from its mouth. I can speak to the hawk and charm an egg from his nest.

"But the flashlight isn't for me. It's a gift."

"Well, then. We have several kinds. How much do you want to pay?"

...

Pokey's whinny of terror had Dot running from the house in a flash.

"Dot! What is it?" Her father called out from behind her.

But she was already up to the fence line. Pokey was running, his tail high in the wind, and in the fading sunset, she could see two dark shapes chasing the horse.

"Dad! Help! Coyotes are after Pokey."

She dashed to the barn and grabbed a rake. Her father raced past her.

She charged up hill, but the dark shape of her dad was bearing down on the animals. Barehanded, and with a bellow of rage that caused all three beasts to turn their heads, Ruben Comal had his arms wide and his hands stretched like claws.

Pokey cut left and headed for the fence line. The coyotes spun to the right, and Ruben was right on their tails.

Dot couldn't believe her eyes as Pokey jumped the fence. There was a crack, and her heart lurched in her chest.

Please, please, please don't let Pokey be injured!

She raced for the fence, and climbed over in a flash.

Dad said we'd never be able to afford a big vet bill. He warned me. Please God! Don't let it happen. I don't want him dead.

...

She found Pokey shivering down by the dry creek bed. At first, he wouldn't let her get close—not until she put down the rake, and with the coyotes at large, she was afraid let loose of it.

Setting it on a rock, she called to him. He came, favoring his left rear foot, but he came on his own power. In the failing light, she couldn't see anything wrong with it. At least it wasn't broken.

She retrieved the rake and headed back to the house.

Where's Dad?

By the porch light, she saw that Pokey was scraped. He must have kicked the fencepost as he jumped over. It was easily treated. Soothed and cooled down, she locked him up in his stall for the night.

Dad was still missing. *What do I do now?*

"Dad!" she called out into the night, but there was no answer.

The keys were in the pickup—no one locked anything out here. She fired up the engine and turned on the headlights. Dad had given her driving practice, but night driving was different.

She pulled past the outer fence line. Dad had gone to the right. Shifting to low gear, she pulled off the road and started following the fence line at slow speed, honking the horn every twenty seconds.

Motion in the distance caught her attention, and she turned the pickup that way, going slow to avoid bushes and rocks.

In the distance, she saw him, approaching with his hand up to shield his eyes from the headlight. She dimmed to the parking lights, stopped the engine and got out.

"Dad, are you okay?"

He moved slowly. "Just wait there."

He joined her and took the passenger seat. "You drive."

She got in, and by the dome light, she saw a dark stain on his shirt.

"Dad, you're hurt!"

He slapped away her hand. "No. It's not me." He was breathing heavily. "Just get me home."

Her mind was racing with a dozen horrible thoughts, but she had to drive. She had to concentrate. Carefully, she turned the brights on and eased around toward the house.

"Dot," he said after his breath settled down to normal, "I want you to write a letter to your Aunt Elizabeth telling her you accept her invitation."

"But Dad...."

He cut her off. "Do it! Do what I tell you. It's important. Believe me."

She opened her mouth to complain, but his breath had gone ragged again.

Not now. Not tonight.

Underground Invitation

When the morning sun lit her window, Dot got up. It was Saturday, but she hadn't slept well, and she was unable to sleep late. All night long, she could hear her father moving around. He had run the washing machine, and the image of the bloody stain on his shirt repeatedly invaded her half-dreams.

In the barn, Pokey seemed to have shaken off his close call. While he wouldn't let her touch his scrape, he no longer favored the leg while walking. The fencepost was much worse for the experience. It had snapped off close to the ground and was only held in place by the wires. She would have to fix that soon.

Her father joined her for breakfast. He looked tired and worn out, and the blue uniform was jarringly out of place.

"Are you working today?"

"Mort wants his landing field mowed. Aaron was going to help me with it, but I'll have to do the job myself."

"Just mowing? I could help."

He shook his head. "Against Mort's rules. You don't have one of these spiffy blue uniforms. Besides, this being a Mort project, it isn't a simple mowing job."

"Oh?"

"Yes, his airstrip will look like a lace-edged handkerchief from the air when I'm done. He's even ordered a load of white-blooming flowers to seed the place with."

"Ought to be pretty, if anyone ever sees it."

I wonder if I could ever pull off advertising Mr. Mort as a tourist attraction.

"Pokey looks in good shape. I thought I would take my camera and ride him a bit today."

Her father looked down at his plate, not saying anything.

That made her mad. "In case you're wondering. Ned has a job today, driving Mrs. Baker to Salt Creek Wash."

He nodded, picked up his dishes and put them in the sink. "Don't forget to write that letter to your Aunt Elizabeth."

...

Pokey tolerated the saddle. Dot felt in the mood for a long ride, so she packed the saddlebags with her lunch and apples for Pokey, and filled the large canteen. She read the instructions on the camera again and headed out to find something scenic.

The railroad grade, being higher than the surrounding terrain, and very flat, made for a tempting route, at least to start with.

She took a picture of their ranch, and another of the long straight grade itself. It was still morning when she started, and the rugged land around Ranch Exit seemed more grand and friendly before the heat of the day struck.

Pokey soon accepted that it would be a long walk and eased into a reasonable pace, for him.

She had gone less than a mile when she noticed turkey vultures circling overhead.

No, I don't want to see it. She deliberately focused on the way ahead and rode on.

Something had exploded in her father last night. He was like a wild beast himself, tackling the coyotes on their own ground and, from the looks of things, killing at least one of them.

Dad has always had a temper. He hid it well, most times, but sometimes it seeped to the surface. Ned in particular could sense that he was dangerous to cross.

But he had never been violent.

What has changed?

...

The satellite carrier dropped out, and Ellis Mort hit his fist on the mahogany surface of his desk as his Internet connection vanished.

"Not now!"

He rushed to the floor-to-ceiling bookshelf that made up the whole east side of his large office. He moved the ladder in its tracks and pulled a worn old bound notebook from a shelf of nearly identical volumes.

"Orbits, orbits, orbits. Aha."

He set the book open, to show a large diagram spread over several pages. He pulled materials from a well-equipped art shelf and began to draw. In mirror image, he duplicated the diagram on the page and then closed the book. He stared at the sheet of paper, folded it and tossed it into the trash.

His Internet connection came back up.

...

"DOUBLECROSSROAD" said the sign in the distance. She stopped and dismounted.

I should have brought the mouse. But it hadn't been afternoon, and so she hadn't checked the grain barrel.

Pokey snorted and backed up a pace.

There was a mouse standing there on the road grade with them.

It's a different one. She couldn't put a finger on what was different. One brown field mouse looks a lot like any other brown field mouse, but she was sure this was a different individual.

But looking at the ground opened her eyes to something else.

Next to some motorcycle tracks, Ned had scraped an arrow in the dirt with his foot.

So, this is where we came back up. Ned marked the direction to the glowing rocks.

Dot ignored the mouse and walked over to the arrow. Staring across the rock field, she saw a white patch.

"Come on Pokey. Let's find an easier way down this time."

The white patch was a pile of paper scraps, each smaller than her little fingernail. She picked up one. There was a fragment of printing on it. The same was true with all of them.

Someone has shredded a whole book. Why would anyone...?

A mouse poked its head out from between the rocks, and deposited another white flake on the pile.

Oh. It was another message from the mice: Here is the place.

Propped up against a rock were a shovel and a crowbar—evidence that Ned had come to the same conclusion. A rope was coiled beside them. Ned must have come out here yesterday to dig.

There were ruts too, where he had spun his wheels. She looked closer. There were fresh chip marks on the rock.

He was trying to move this one boulder.

But it had been too heavy for him. Even using his motorcycle, he couldn't budge it.

Dot looked at Pokey. He was slow, but he wasn't feeble.

She analyzed the situation before attaching the rope. Pokey would never be able to drag it, but if they pulled off at an angle, it might roll.

Pokey's girth was slightly loose so she fixed it. She secured the rope to the pommel and attached the other end as high up on the rock as she could manage.

"Haw! Pull!" She urged, and Pokey strained. The boulder rolled free.

She paused to praise the horse, but stopped in mid-phrase.

A dozen mice were swarming over the white pile. She unhooked the rope and patted Pokey on the side. "Stay here."

The mice were picking up the scraps of paper and taking them into a large hole now exposed by the shifted boulder.

She knelt down, near the opening, and tried to see how deep it was.

Come in.

She blinked. The opening was a little more than three feet across, with heavy traffic of mice coming in and out.

She shook her head, "I'm not going in there."

Help me. I can help you. Come in.

The voice wasn't actually a voice. It wasn't something she was hearing with her ears, and it wasn't like thoughts in her head either.

It was like the memory of a voice. She shivered, although the daytime temperature was climbing.

The pile of paper scraps was dwindling. It had done its job, and now was a danger to him.

Dot shook her head again; her thoughts were being mixed up, contaminated with something else.

Who was 'him'?

Help me. It is safe. Come in.

Dot leaned down, trying to let as much sunlight in as was possible, hoping to see what was in the hole.

In the deep black, there was a single reflection. Something square.

Come in.

She burned with curiosity. *But I'm no stupid hick.* If she were trapped inside, no one would know where to find her, not until Ned returned from his drive with Mrs. Baker.

She walked over to Pokey and rummaged through the saddlebag, looking for a piece of paper.

Her fingers closed around something round and hard. She pulled it out into the daylight.

A flashlight? Where did this come from?

It was new, and a click showed the batteries were fresh. Perhaps Dad had put it there, or maybe Ned?

She put it in her pocket.

Paper and pencil were in the saddlebag too. She scribbled, "At DOUBLECROSSROAD on the rail line."

With the note in the saddlebags, and Pokey only restrained by promise of a treat, she took the apple, the flashlight and her camera and turned back to the hole.

The mice were still coming and going, but they kept to one side. She got down on hands and knees and climbed in.

Come in.

"I am. I am. Be patient."

...

The landing strip was less than mile from his main house. Mort checked his watch. There was no sense in flying a search pattern too early. If the sun wasn't at the right angle, trees, rocks, or anything else wouldn't leave a distinct shadow, and even eagle eyes wouldn't notice it.

But today he was having the landing strip's resonance enhanced, so he might as well go down there and check it out.

He unlocked the console of the Humvee and pulled out his logbook. He had last run a search flight Wednesday. He'd been lucky, discovering a sensory echo like that. The little dirtball didn't have any idea what he was doing. It almost made it worth getting close to all those ... peasant children.

But if he could detect one or two more echoes with the same resonance, he should be able to calculate the nexus.

"And not a minute too soon," he mumbled.

The airfield had two hangars, one for each plane, and a big grassy field carefully leveled three years ago.

The Beechcraft had been sitting idle for months. Once his office building in Los Angeles had been sold, he had no need for frequent commuter flights.

"That'll change, once I get...."

He put on the brakes. A large green and yellow mowing tractor was on its side, one wheel still turning. A patch of blue in the grass wasn't moving.

He picked up his satellite phone—there was no cell phone service out here—and called George Filmore.

"George, there has been an accident. Get Ruth Harris over here immediately. I think Ruben Comal is unconscious—tractor accident."

Mort got out, and headed for his downed worker.

I hope he's not dead—with both of my people down, word will get out and I won't be able to hire anyone. Of course if he's badly injured, I'll have to fly him to Salt Lake City and that'll really mess up my schedule.

...

Ned blazed down the Kelso Express line, sure that he knew where Dot would be.

Sure enough, she was at the DOUBLECROSSROAD sign, coiling a rope and attaching it to Pokey's saddle.

Dot looked up as he arrived, a very remote look in her eyes.

"I thought I would find you here."

"Yes. I found your tools." She touched the shovel, on the ground next to her.

"Fine. We'll talk about the mouse later. You've got to hop on now. Your dad's hurt."

"What?" She dropped the rope.

"A broken leg, maybe more. He's overturned a tractor. It's lucky he's not dead. Come on, I'm supposed to bring you back. They've got him over at Ruth Harris's house."

"I'll ride Pokey. I can't leave him here on his own."

Ned shook his head. "We don't have time for that! Pokey is a slug. You need to come now."

Dot didn't argue. One foot in the stirrup and she was up. She whispered something in the horse's ear, and he was off, at a gallop.

Ned was so startled that he stood there, just watching them recede in the distance. *What's gotten into that horse? I've never seen him run. I've never seen him walk fast.*

He revved his motorcycle and began the chase.

It wasn't as easy as he thought it would be. With a head start, Pokey was hard to catch. They were already at the Comal house by the time he had to ease up on the throttle.

Dot and Pokey sailed over the fence, and pulled up to the barn. She whispered something else to the horse, and he tossed his head, like he understood. Dot pulled the saddle free and sent Pokey off into the field.

"I'm ready."

"Then get on. And what got into that horse?"

"Later. Let's move."

...

Ruth Harris worked while she talked, but since everyone had heard it all before, no one was listening.

"I'm a horse doctor, not a people doctor. I'm not licensed for this. I can't just keep patching you all up forever."

She turned her tongue on Ruben, "And you! You have a compound fracture and it will never heal right if you don't go into town and have it treated immediately."

"I can fly him to Salt Lake City. We can have an ambulance waiting there and get him into the hospital in an hour or two at most."

Ruben shook his head, gritting his teeth whenever something moved wrong. "No need. It's bad enough I wrecked your tractor. The clinic in Green River will be fine, and Luke Samuelson can take me there."

Mort looked at Mrs. Harris and sighed, "Okay, but have them call me about the bill. You were working for me at the time."

The sound of a motorcycle approached, and a minute later Dot came in. "Dad!"

Ruth warned her to be gentle. "There are several bone fragments in there."

"Dad? What happened?"

He winced. "Carelessness. Going too fast. Turned too sharp I guess. I don't really remember.

"Dot, can you handle yourself for a couple of days. Luke is going to take me into town and get this fixed up."

"I'm coming too!"

He squeezed her hand. "No. It will be easier on me if I know you're safe at home. It's going to take two days at the very least and getting you a place to stay is just one too many things for Luke to deal with. Okay?"

She blinked her eyes. Every time his voice caught from the pain, she could feel it too. "Okay, but ... let me do something."

Dot placed her fingertips on the right side of his temple, and tapped three times. She then pushed hard into the bundle of tendons on his right wrist.

Ruben sighed, "I don't know what that is, but it helps."

"Dad?" she whispered, "do you remember what happened last night?"

His eyes were closed, and his face was relaxed for the first time since the accident. "No. Something about coyotes?"

She looked up as Ruth Harris came closer.

Ruth said, "Latoya and I will look in on you. But Luke has arrived and we need to get your dad into his Suburban."

Four men carried him out, with Ruth doing her best to keep the leg immobilized. Amazingly, Ruben seemed to be tolerating the jostling fairly well.

When the dust from the departing vehicle settled, Latoya asked, "Do you want me to take you home? Mom said Ned brought you here?"

Dot looked at the innocent expression on her face.

"No. I've got to go get Dad's pickup. Ned will run me over there. I appreciate the offer."

Ned overheard and headed for his bike.

She climbed on behind and put her arms around him.

"I'm not wearing my helmet. Go slow."

"Gotcha." He revved the engine and spun gravel.

Dot leaned her head against his back.

Let Latoya look. Right now she would rather be with Ned than anyone else. Her world had been shaken to its roots even before she found out her father was hurt. Now she needed something stable to hang on to.

The Man Under the Mountain

"You don't?" whispered the dry voice.

*"No, a friend of mine, Ned Kelso, believes in magic, but I don't."
Sitting in the darkened tunnel, talking to someone who never came
within reach of her flashlight was frightening. Her only defense was
bravado.*

*"So mice that make voices in your head—that isn't magic?" asked
the whisper.*

*"No. I don't know how that works, but it isn't magic. There's no
incantations to spirits, no sacrifices to demons, no alignment of the
planets—it has to be something else."*

*The voice laughed. "I like you, little one. What did you say your
name was?"*

*It occurred to her that giving your name was dangerous when
dealing with magic, but she couldn't back down now.*

"Dot. People call me Dot."

"From Dorothy, I suppose?"

"Right. Or Dotcom."

"Dotcom? I don't understand."

"Dorothy Comal—Dotcom. An Internet joke."

"Internet? What's that?"

...

The pickup was parked next to the landing strip. At least on this side, the edge of the field was cut in curving swaths.

"Okay, now tell me."

Dot rubbed her forehead, "Tell you what?"

"Everything. How did you get Pokey to run so fast? What did you do to your dad? What did you find out at the mouse place?"

"I spoke to him."

"Who? Who did you talk to?"

Dot blinked against the sharp headache that was growing by the minute. "Duncan's dwarf, I think. I didn't see him. He was in the cave."

"What cave? The mice have a cave?"

"I pulled the rock aside. There's a tunnel or a cave. It opens up, but it's dark. Without your flashlight, I wouldn't have gone in."

"My flashlight? I don't have a flashlight."

She winced, as the headache grew sharper. "Well, someone left a flashlight for me.

"The headache is getting bad. He warned me."

"That's enough. Start at the beginning."

"I opened the tunnel and the mice told me to go in."

"The mice told you?"

"Well, sorta. He explained it. He can talk through the mice, just like he told Duncan to rescue him."

Ned shook his head, "Just keep going."

"Once inside, he talked to me."

"With the mice?"

"No with his voice—but he hid in the shadows. He claimed to be a wizard, but I told him I didn't believe in magic. We made a trade. He gave me a charm, and I promised to bring him an apple pie."

"You didn't! Don't you know anything, Dot! You don't make deals with demons."

"But he wasn't a demon, I told you that."

"But ... what was the charm?"

"He showed it to me, on a piece of paper. When I looked at it, something went click in my head. It was like when your ear pops, or when your sinus drains all of a sudden. Something went click in my brain and I could see things differently."

"Like how differently?"

"More real. Like Pokey. Remember when Mr. Wanekia said Pokey was sick? I knew Pokey was healthy because I took good care of him.

"But when I came out of the tunnel, I could see it. Pokey's mind is sick. When I said the right words, the haze in his head was pushed aside and he was suddenly strong and powerful, and could run really fast. I know it won't last, but it's something I can work on."

"So, you talked to your horse? What did you say?"

"Ah... You know, I don't remember. It was like horse language ... but I remember saying it, but I don't remember what I said. Maybe it's this headache.

"And your dad?"

"Oh that was easy. I could see the lines of pain running up to his head. I just smoothed them out."

"Lines of pain? What did that look like?"

"Ah ... You know—lines, sorta."

Ned could see lines on her face, wrinkle lines as she scrunched her face against the headache. "Are you going to be able to drive?"

She nodded, and then changed it to a shake. "I don't think so."

"I'll drive you. Give me a minute to get my bike up in the bed of the pickup.

"What else could you see different?"

But she just walked over to the passenger side and got in. Ned backed the pickup into a ditch and eased the bike up the tailgate. He spun the pickup's wheels, but got out of the ditch with no real trouble.

Dot was curled up, leaning against the window with her eyes closed, but mumbled, "Tell me about your drive this morning."

...

"Mrs. Baker has a nice Jeep, but she has so much camera gear that it filled the back seat. And by the time she'd loaded on her backpack and strapped on the tripod and slung two cameras around her neck, not to mention that awful floppy hat she wore—well, she looked a sight! I was worried she was so loaded down she'd never make the hike. But she was determined.

"I drove around to the other side of the trail and waited for hours before she arrived. I was never so bored! But she eventually made it, looking happy with three hundred and some pictures. I've been on that hike, and I've never seen anything worth wasting film on. But that's what she does, I suppose."

Dot whispered something.

"What? Oh yeah, 'A trained eye'. Photographers need that, I suppose."

...

"We're here. Dot?" Ned shook her arm, but she was deeply asleep.

He left a skid mark in the bed of the pickup as he jumped his bike out the tailgate, but even that didn't wake her up.

She's breathing okay, but she won't wake up. I can't just leave her here.

But he couldn't carry her in to her bed—that wouldn't be right.

He settled for bringing a blanket from her house out and tucking her in where she lay.

Ned's face was in deep frown as he started his motorcycle and headed off at high speed for the railroad grade.

...

Dot had covered the tunnel entrance with a few cut bushes, but Ned knew right where to look. He pushed them aside and crawled in on his hands and knees.

I need Dot's flashlight.

"Hello," came a dry voice, disturbingly close.

Ned froze. He strained his eyes to see by the faint light reflecting in from the outside.

"Who's that?"

"Surely Dot has mentioned me?"

"What did you do to her? She won't wake up!"

"Your name is Ned Kelso?"

Dot! You don't tell names to demons!

"Maybe. What did you do?"

"Ned, I have some questions, too. I'll make a trade. Question for question. Is it a deal?"

Ned had read all three of the fantasy novels in the school library, and he had seen one movie when his family had gone into town about a year before. He was well aware of the dangers of making any deal with magical forces. But he was worried about Dot.

"Okay, but I go first! What is wrong with her? She had a terrible headache and fell asleep. Now she won't wake up."

The voice laughed, but it wasn't a sinister laugh. "The little lady is well served to have a friend like you. But you don't need to worry. This was expected. She will wake up shortly. Her mind needs the time to ... words fail me ... re-energize areas that have been over-exerted. Like a muscle that aches from over-use. No harm has been done."

Ned frowned. "But what happened? She talked to her horse, and made her dad's pain go away—it was like magic. How did she do that?"

"Ah Ned, that is another question. Explain something to me first. What is an Internet?"

...

It was near sunset when Ruth and her daughter arrived at the Comal ranch. Dot was on the porch, peeling apples.

"Hello Dot. We thought we'd bring you supper, but maybe you've already eaten."

"No I haven't. Thanks Mrs. Harris. Whatever you brought has to be better than what I'd planned."

Latoya was looking around, and when she realized Dot was watching her, flashed a smile. "I expected to find Ned here."

Dot thought as much. "Come on in."

Ruth Harris took pains to reassure her that her father would be okay. But Dot had seen him herself, when "her eyes were open" as the man in the tunnel had said. The leg was something that a doctor could set on the course for recovery. But the cloud in his mind would take a different kind of healing.

Which was why she had to go back to the tunnel. If anyone knew what had affected her father, if anyone had the knowledge to heal him, she could find him there.

And that is why she had to bake the apple pie as soon as possible.

"You bake often, Dot? Latoya doesn't seem to have much interest in cooking. Do you, honey?"

Latoya glared at her mother and said nothing.

Dot shook her head, "I don't bake often. I just wanted something nice on hand for when Dad gets back."

"Good idea."

They shared the cheese casserole, and then they left.

Dot watched them drive off and then went back to the apples.

...

"I need help. My food stores have run out."

Dot sat in the darkness—she had turned off the flashlight to conserve batteries. "How long have you been down here?"

"Too long," the voice faded even quieter than before.

Dot dug into her pocket, "I've got an apple. Do you want it?"

"Oh, an apple! Hold it out where I can see it."

She reached for her flashlight.

"No, don't turn that on. There is plenty of light for my old eyes.

"Mm. It has been so long since I've had an apple. My mouth is watering just from the scent of it."

"You can have it then."

The sigh he let out was long and heartfelt. "No. It would do no good. My teeth are gone. About the best I could manage is applesauce."

"How about a pie? I could cook you an apple pie."

"An apple pie! With sugar, and soft baked apples, and a flakey crust—oh I would give anything for a taste of an apple pie!"

"Then you'll have it," said Dot, "if you can just let me know how you can get the mice to work for you and carry your messages!"

...

Ned could see him, at least the vague outline of his shape. He gestured with one hand as he talked.

"When I was your age, computers weren't machines, they were people; young ladies who sat at desks all day long making calculations. But by the time I ran the department, we had one of those machines. The very idea that one of those giants could be sitting on anyone's desk—that's magic to me."

Ned said, "Your kind of magic is what's interesting to me. I thought it might be Indian magic at first, but you don't talk like Mr. Wanekia. You speak with a different kind of accent, I don't know..."

"New Jersey?"

"Maybe. But that's my next question. How does your magic work?"

"That's too big of a question. It's taken me decades to learn, and I can't tell it to you in an instant."

"You gave Dot that charm. She could do it instantly."

"Ah, but that's just a trick. She doesn't understand it any better than you do. Have you ever seen the trick where you stare at a black star for a few seconds and then when you look at a blank wall, you can see a white one?"

"Yes. Only the one I saw was a flag shape."

"Right. That's what I did for Dot. You push a few patterns into the mind and one of the old filters drops for a few minutes. For just a little bit, you can see with your eyes wide open. Once you can do that, this 'magic' you are talking about is simple obvious stuff."

Ned nodded, "Well, then show me how to do that."

He laughed. "Oh, no! I gave her that as a trade. What can you do for me?"

...

It was dark out when Ned left. He started the motorcycle and eased up the grade. He wasn't very far from his home, and there was no need to hurry.

This is important stuff. If he really has discovered secrets of the mind, then Ranch Exit could be famous. He'll need help—he says so! I can be his assistant!

There were still doubts. The eerie voice in the dark didn't really convince him, but Dot had. Pokey had run like the wind. Mr. Comal had been in intense pain until she soothed it away. And it was just Dot! His Dot. She didn't even believe in magic.

So it's up to me to do my part. I'll get food for him, and anything else he needs. And when I get my charm, then I'll be able to see what else needs to be done.

His parents were both home, which was no surprise. His mother had a few friends in the valley, but she spent most of her time tending their garden. His father rarely left the living room.

He went to the pantry and surveyed the canned goods.

"Hey, Mom, what's good when you can't chew?"

"D'you got a tooth ache?"

"No. I just want to take some food to a friend."

"An she got a tooth ache?"

Ned smiled down at his mother, "No, it's not a girl. I just met an old man, and he's hungry."

His mother crossed her arms. "You take my food, that I grew and canned myself and give it to some bum?"

"No, Mom. He isn't a bum."

"But he got no food for his own? He can't buy some?"

"Mom, it's complicated."

His dad's voice echoed from the living room, "What's going on out there?"

Ned rolled his eyes to the ceiling. "No problem, Dad."

"He wants to give food to a bum!"

"Both of you, come here."

Albert Kelso sat in his rocker, his crutches propped to the side where he could grab them. The television faded to black as they came in.

"Yolanda, the boy wants to give food to the needy?"

"To a bum."

"Ned, who is this bum?"

Ned shook his head. "He's just a man I met, here in Ranch Exit. He's pretty much living off the land right now. But his teeth are mostly gone and he can't chew."

"Is he traveling through, or does he intend to stay?"

"Ah, I think he is planning to stay."

Albert Kelso nodded sadly. "I've got no problem with sharing a meal with the needy. Ha. If anyone knows people need help it's me.

"But we can't take on a new mouth to feed. We've got this land free and clear with the Workman's Comp settlement, and the Social Security check barely pays for the electricity and propane. With your mother's hard work we have food on the table and clothes on our backs.

"You know how it is. I've only been able to give you my old motor-cycle—the gas has been up to you. There's no extra money.

"Your mother will help you pick out a couple of jars for your friend, but that's it—no more from our pantry. If you want to keep feeding him, you'll have to earn the money to do it on your own."

...

The Man-Under-the-Mountain, Carl Stellman, waited until the motorcycle sounds were long gone. The insects were calling, and for the first time in decades, there was a way outside.

Are the stars still shining? When he had left New Jersey to take this assignment, the city air was getting so contaminated by smoke that he could barely see the constellations. Perhaps after all these years, the problem had gotten worse and all of the clear skies were gone.

He pulled himself up the tunnel passageway. *How many times have I come this way?* Only to be blocked by the final boulder, able to feel the air from outside and to hear the desert noises, but able to see nothing.

The kids had left the opening covered with branches, as he had requested. Those he could handle.

He pushed aside the twigs and pulled himself through the opening.

The cool evening air hit him and he shivered. He looked up and froze at the sight.

There were more stars blazing overhead than he ever remembered from his youth. He couldn't see the constellations, not because they weren't there, but because the minor stars were so bright that there was no contrast for the major ones.

He took a deep breath. *Free. I'm free.*

He closed his eyes and absorbed the fragrances, the different plants, the flowers, even the tang of mouse.

But there was another scent on the air.

He looked around. The brightness of the sky made the surrounding hills plain by their darker silhouette.

The pad of a foot was loud enough for him to hear, against the insect chatter.

The coyote approached quietly, but confidently, as if it knew he couldn't escape.

Carl watched carefully as the predator checked him out. The beast felt a surge of anger, and its muzzle showed teeth.

"Sisss", Carl replied. With no teeth, some of the words he would have liked to say couldn't be spoken, but the coyote paused.

Carl growled quietly and pawed the dirt with his left hand.

"Yip," came the reply, and the coyote moved away.

Carl frowned and with a last sorrowful look at the stars, he crawled back into the tunnel and secured the opening.

On Her Own

Dot wore her best blue dress, the one with white lace trim, and drove to the Cartulio ranch for church. *The more people see that I can take care of myself, the less they'll be inclined to come check up on me.*

Besides, she'd told Ned that she would be there, and in spite of all that had happened, they hadn't changed their plan.

Other than a prayer for Ruben to heal well, the service was the same as it always was.

Afterwards, Ruth Harris was insistent that she eat with them, fending off the Cartulio's invitation. Dot realized she really didn't have a say in the matter.

Mr. Samuelson was there, and she asked about her father.

"Your dad is doing fine, but the clinic insists that he stay for a few days to make sure the bone sets properly. Mr. Mort is covering all the expenses, but I'll be going back on Tuesday to check out how he's doing."

He handed her a letter from her father.

...

"Dot, I need you to visit Mr. Mort and get my last paycheck. Have it made it out to George Filmore, then take it to George and apply it to our credit line there. You should be able to get whatever food and supplies from the store you need until I get back.

"I called your Aunt Elizabeth and explained the situation. She will be arriving at the end of your school year.

"Honey, I won't be able to take care of you until my leg heals, so this is for the best. You can have a nice summer and once I'm back on my feet, everything will be fine.

"Thinking of you. —Ruben, Dad."

...

Dot was crying inside, but she blinked her eyes hard to keep from making everyone feel sorry for her. As it was, she could see Ruth Harris and several of the others watching her.

Don't send me away! I'll be good. You need me to take care of you.

Almost as if by instinct, people clustered around her, talking cheerfully about nothing at all.

Her eyes lit on Ned, keeping his distance. He tapped his wristwatch and held out four fingers.

She gave a slight nod, and he acknowledged. He was gone shortly thereafter, his distinctive engine catching several people's attention.

...

As people drifted off after church, Dot looked around for Ruth Harris. She spotted Latoya talking to Mr. Samuelson, so she drifted that way.

The magical sight she had felt yesterday was almost gone. She was back to normal, except for a little insight that stayed.

Latoya said goodbye to Mr. Samuelson and then stared at the ground. It was the final piece of the puzzle.

"Hi, Latoya. Any news from Roger?"

The stricken look on the girl's face lasted only a second, but it confirmed everything. "No."

Roger Samuelson was a year older than Latoya and had left for a school in California on an academic scholarship. Now that extra insight brought it back to mind, Roger and Latoya had been a couple for as long as Dot could remember.

"Well, if I had a boyfriend, and he didn't write me every day, I'd sure let him know I didn't appreciate it."

There was a sad smile on Latoya's face. "He used to write, but for the last month, there's been nothing. He doesn't even call his parents. They call him, or do without news altogether."

Latoya sighed, "I knew it was a lost cause. He's older than I am, and there are thousands of girls on his campus. It's a different world. He saw what was out there, and he'll never come back to Ranch Exit."

Dot held her hand. "If you could get a scholarship, would you follow after him?"

She nodded, "But Momma doesn't have the money. We've applied for every grant and scholarship in the book, but nothing is working. Ranch Exit is such a tiny place, we have no band, no sports, no honor society, no nothing! My list of accomplishments is pathetic."

Dot could only stand there and be sympathetic.

It was so frighteningly real.

Roger was a nice guy. If he promised to wait for Latoya and California caused him to forget, then what would happen to her in Seattle? Would she even be the same person?

"At least you two are the same age," said Latoya, obviously talking about Ned.

"No. We aren't like that. It's not ... kissey-kissey with us."

The older girl shrugged, "Maybe not yet."

Ruth waved at them. It was time for lunch.

Dot glanced at her watch. Surely she could shake off her well wishers by four.

...

"I can smell it from here!" His voice came from deeper in the tunnel.

"Dot, could you hand the pie to Ned and let him bring it closer?"

Dot hesitated, "Ah, sure." It had been hard to carry the pie in through the tunnel on her hands and knees, but she had wrapped it well. She removed the foil and stuffed it into her jeans pocket.

Ned took the pie with a puzzled look. Dot gave him the flashlight too. He walked twenty feet deeper into the tunnel.

"Set it on the table." The voice was very close.

Ned aimed the light and located the table. It was an old, but very recognizable folding table—very much like the ones at the school. But this one had its legs cut down to less than half size.

Ned leaned down and set the pie carefully on the table, then added the two jars of preserved beets.

"I'm really sorry that's all I have today. I'll find a way to get you something better. Do you have any requests?"

"Ned."

Instinctively, Ned aimed the flashlight at the voice, and caught him in the eye. The face winced.

"Oh, sorry." He averted the light.

Ned had the vivid image of a man's face, full bearded, with a heavy mop of gray hair.

"Ned, for more years than you've been alive, I have been trapped down here eating stale army rations. For the past three years I have been limited to tasteless crackers sometimes dipped in mouse broth. That plus a few stale vitamin tablets have been all that has kept me alive.

"Can you imagine the utter joy I felt when I saw those glorious jars of beets?

"Ned, any food you bring me will be welcomed beyond measure.

"Now, I can't help myself. I am going to eat one small piece of that apple pie, but then if you two could stay, I have something I need to talk to you about."

Ned nodded. "Sure. But just out of curiosity, why don't you want us to see you? And why did you have me bring you the pie and not Dot?"

There was a long silence, and then a sigh.

"Okay. Shine the light on the table, and not directly on me."

He came out of an opening in the wall where he'd been hiding. Ned recoiled as he saw the figure. And then he made out the details.

He was a man, but with both legs gone at the hips. Dressed in a worn laundry bag, he walked on both hands, dragging his torso behind him. Moving quickly and deftly, he pulled himself up to the table and picked up the fork.

He looked at Ned, "I'm sorry, but I'm just not ready to eat in public yet." He lowered his head. "You can understand why I didn't want the little girl to see me like this?"

Ned nodded, and went back up the tunnel.

...

"And you baked this yourself? It's marvelous. I could barely stop myself from eating it all in one sitting. But if I did that, I would kill myself. I've been on a miniscule diet for years now. I've calculated exactly how many bites I had left from the stockpile, knowing that when it was gone, I would die from starvation."

"What kind of a place is this Mr. Stellman? A fallout shelter?" asked Dot. She had insisted on knowing his name.

"What's a fallout shelter?"

"You know. A place to go when a nuclear bomb explodes."

He gasped, "So! They actually did it. Atomic bombs had been in the fiction magazines, but I didn't think they could ever actually do it. When did this happen?"

Ned stared off into memory, "Ah, I think it was at the end of World War II. 1945 or something like that. The United States used the bomb to end the war with Japan."

There was a moment of silence.

"Kids. Could you please get me a history book? These shocks aren't good for my heart. My world, since shortly before that war, has been the ruins of this underground base. I know nothing of the world you take for granted."

"I will, but what exactly is this base? Why were you here?"

"Dot, Ned, I'll tell you, but you have to keep it secret. Maybe this is all old stuff in the modern world, but I swore an oath to protect these secrets, and it is important that I do so. Do you understand?"

"Yes, Mr. Stellman," Ned agreed. "I promise to keep it secret."

Dot added, "Me too. I'll promise."

...

"In the 1930's, the US government was worried about the wave of communism and the successes it was having in Europe. Then a new group, the National Socialists in Germany started using the same public persuasion techniques to gain power there."

Ned said, "The Nazis. You're talking about the Nazis."

"You've heard of them—I really need that history book. But anyway, a research facility was established to try to understand how the human mind works, and why certain kinds of persuasion work on people.

"I was a lead scientist in the effort. After a time, the base was deactivated and when it was closed up and buried, I was trapped here. They must have thought I was dead.

"But there was a stockpile of food, and a well of fresh water. There was just a trickle of electricity, using thermocouples, which could power a few lights.

"But it was the secrets of the mind, my research, that let me stay alive. Otherwise, I would have gone totally insane long ago."

Ned looked at Dot and twirled his finger near his ear. She frowned back at him.

"Mr. Stellman, there's no sign of your base, other than an abandoned railroad grade across the valley."

"It was tunneled into the mesa, with the cover story that it was a mine. Not many people lived in the area back then."

"Not many people live here now. We're both rancher's kids."

"I thought you might be. Maybe you can tell me something. Last night, I went to the tunnel exit, and I was almost attacked by a coyote. He acted strangely. Have you seen anything like that?"

Ned and Dot exchanged glances. "You go first," said Ned.

...

Ned took Dot home full of questions.

"He's crazy."

Dot frowned, "Why do you think that?"

"His story doesn't hold together. Did you get that he was a major scientist in the mid 1930's? That would make him over a hundred years old—unless they were recruiting boy scientists back then. And while he is in really bad shape, he doesn't look that old."

"You saw him then. I saw a look on your face...."

"Yes." Ned debated silently and then told her what he had seen.

"The poor man."

"Yes, he's been run through the mill, but that's what I'm saying."

"What do you mean," Dot crossed her arms, "that just because someone's been injured that they're crazy?"

She didn't think Ned was so closed-minded, but she had been surprised before, disagreeably.

Ned knew what she was thinking. "Don't look at me like that. Just listen.

"Have you met my dad?" She shook her head.

He looked at the road, trying to find the words.

"He was different before, back in Las Cruces, back before the accident. He was a big man, he built houses, laughed a lot, and had lots of friends.

"The accident changed him. He's still the same great guy. He's still my dad. But he lives in an easy chair and watches TV. The most excited he gets is when the clouds come in and he can pick up distant channels. Did you know we've got the tallest TV tower in all of Ranch Exit?"

Ned sighed. "Dad's not crazy, but he's different. He thinks differently.

"And all I'm saying about Mr. Stellman is that we would be crazy to pretend that losing his legs and being trapped underground for however long it's been hasn't changed him. He said it should have driven him crazy, and he should know."

Dot nodded. Her dad's leg should heal, but it was something else she had to consider.

"Is that why you haven't looked at your charm yet?"

Ned took the folded paper out of his pocket. "No. I'm just not ready yet. I know it works, I saw what you did. I just don't want to waste it. Besides, I have homework to finish for class tomorrow. I'd hate to be extra sharp and aware just for homework."

She knew exactly how he felt. When she realized Stellman was going to let Ned take his charm with him, she asked for the one he had given her.

"It only works two or three times, that's what he said," she agreed. "I've already used up one of mine." She touched it in her pocket, just to confirm it was still there.

And she was facing homework too. There was no fairness in a world where people expected you to do homework when your whole life has been turned upside-down.

...

There was something perverse in the pleasure of being able to drive herself to school, Dot decided. She didn't have a license, but she hadn't seen a policeman in Ranch Exit her whole life. When they made a trip to town, she would occasionally see one zip by on the interstate, but her valley was like a kingdom unto itself. Outside laws were ignored more often than not.

But she hated to gain the privilege at her dad's expense. The road branched as she passed the store, with the interstate access to the left.

She gripped the steering wheel harder, fighting the impulse to go find her dad. A glance at the gas gauge told her the pickup would never make it that far. She would have to go back to the Cartulio's and buy gas, but she didn't have the money, and there would be questions, and there were always the highway cops who might think she looked too young.

The impulse passed the second it was born. She took the right and pulled into the school's parking lot. Latoya noticed her arrival and gave her a thumbs up. Ned obviously hadn't appeared yet. The little kids never noticed. Dot was beaming as she went into the school building. Driving herself was satisfying.

...

Nora Baker was pleased to have four students around her computer table, although she was aware that computer graphics wasn't the draw. Ms. Carson had reminded the class that a failed student's proposal project could only get a higher grade if they assisted the winners with their projects.

"Which kind of picture is best for a web site?" asked Ned.

"Pretty girls." Larry Samuelson grinned.

"Behave, Larry, or I'll tell your father." Latoya grumbled from her status as eldest.

"That's not what I meant." Ned said, frustrated. "I was over at Bill's house, using his computer, and the first thing the software said was that pictures had to be GIF or JPEG. Which one is best?"

Mrs. Baker nodded. "On a webpage, most of the time you want the picture to show up fast, and to look good. This isn't an art show we're talking about. You're trying to send a message, and the picture is just part of that message.

"If the page loads slowly, people will just click over to somewhere else. If the picture looks crude, you give a poor impression, and that undercuts your message.

"Ned, what is the message of your page?"

He looked uncomfortable. "Ah. Just that Ranch Exit is a cool little place, I guess."

"And you took pictures of real scenes with the digital camera, right?"

"Yes."

"Okay, then you need to use JPEG."

Hallee Cooper asked, "Why?"

Mrs. Baker said, "Let me show you. Ned, you have the CD with your pictures?"

He handed it over and she brought up the first one, showing the Ranch Exit highway sign with the rocky hills in the background. With several practiced mouse-clicks she made two pictures—a GIF and a JPEG.

"As you can see, the JPEG looks more lifelike, even though both pictures take up about the same size on the disk. That's because a GIF image saves space by throwing away color information, and because it's a real image, the missing colors make the image crude and dull."

Hallee then asked, "Then why even bother with GIF?"

"Because in certain circumstances, it works great."

Nora cropped off everything from the image except the sign itself and made it into a GIF.

"See here, with all this solid green and white, GIF only needs a few colors, and see, the file is really tiny compared to the JPEG, so it loads fast and looks great. Use GIF for things like this sign—lots of solid colors.

"But for real life scenes, with all the complexity of real life, use JPEG."

She hesitated, and looked across the room where Dot was working on the proposal speech she had to give the next day. Nora Baker turned back to the students at her table.

"But there is something else you have to be careful with when using JPEG. The people who designed JPEG were able to get the file size to shrink down by throwing away certain information. Instead of throwing away color information like GIF, they realized how the human mind sees images and threw away the stuff the brain ignores. JPEG can make compressed pictures that look perfect, but only when it's the right size."

She had their attention. On the computer screen she zoomed up the size of the JPEG image of the sign until the 'R' of Ranch Exit took up the whole screen.

"Look at this ugly blockiness around the edge of the letter. It's not like that in real life, is it Ned?"

"No. Not at all."

"So, if you are going to blow up an image, make sure you do so before you compress it. JPEG tricks the mind, but it can't do so if it's the wrong size."

After the demonstration, Ned took over the laptop while his 'assistants' went back to their desks to do some web design with pencil and paper. They would decide which ones were best and Mrs. Baker would help them write the HTML code.

There were twenty-three pictures, and he started looking at them one by one. Mrs. Baker suggested that he take the best six or seven and use them, rather than overload the page with too many pictures to appreciate.

He looked at the picture of him on his motorcycle, standing before the sign. It was a nice picture, but it wasn't the best of Ranch Exit.

The next image was of a bear, heading away in the sage.

What's this? I never took a picture of a bear. He hadn't even seen a bear around the valley in over a year.

He blinked his eyes. The image was slightly blurry.

How did she do that zoom? He found the control and zoomed in closer, too fast and too close.

The image blown up on the screen was the back side of a man's head. Ned would recognize that felt hat anywhere.

This is Old Man Wanekia. That's the wrong picture. He remembered Dot snapping that picture, when she took a huff at something he had said.

Ned stared at the toolbar of the image program. *How did I switch pictures?*

He found the way to shrink the image. Click. Click. Click.

The bear was heading away.

He hesitated over the mouse button. He zoomed in one click.

Old Man Wanekia was heading away through the brush.

He zoomed out. Now it was a bear.

It's the same picture. Dot took a picture of a man, and the camera captured a bear.

Mrs. Baker smiled at him from across the room, he waved back.

I can't tell anyone about this. Dot laughed when I said Indian magic, but this proves it.

Healing and Hurts

Ruben Comal gripped the nurse's arm.

"Sir, you're hurting me."

He tried to lift himself up in the bed. "He's after my daughter! I've got to stop him!"

His grip was strong, but she had experience. She shifted to the side, where his arm had no leverage, and peeled his fingers off. The doctor was just down the hall.

"Mr. Comal has gotten violent again."

He frowned, "The same thing?"

"Yes. I tried to talk to him about it, but he gets these spells where he just isn't rational."

"We'll just have to increase the dosage to keep him calm. I'll be glad when we can release him. We're just not set up to handle disturbed patients here."

...

George Filmore's store was older than he was, as were a few of his items of stock. Hanging from the bare rafters was a hand scythe, from back before the era of mechanical harvesters. When he bought the place, he had thought it was rustic decoration, but one long winter when there was little else to do, he had gone through the old books and found where the long curved knife had been purchased as stock from Sears and Roebuck back in the early 1900's.

Buying stock was a special art. Having just what your customers need, when they need it, is the only thing that keeps them spending their money at the local store instead of going into town. But buy too many of the wrong things, and all your profits end up being mistaken for rustic decorations.

George looked up from his books and watched Ned carefully walking the aisles. Food items—not what his favorite young motorcyclist usually bought.

"Can I help you?"

The words pushed Ned to make a decision and he brought his selection to the counter.

"Three jars of baby food and one medium jar of peanut butter." George rang up the sale and took the twenty-dollar bill.

As he made change, he asked, "Running errands for Mrs. Brewster?"

"No. Mr. Filmore, can I have a job?"

Every year several students asked that question. Most he had to turn down.

"Well, Ned, what can you do for me?" That was the question. He did his own purchasing, stocked his own shelves, and manned his own cash register. As much as he enjoyed seeing the light of joy on young faces as he handed out the weekly wages, his finances couldn't handle it.

With the part time teaching, he could use someone to keep the store open at odd hours, but he couldn't justify taking a student out of school just for that.

Ned was thinking, too. "I can drive."

George nodded. "I have a few deliveries in the valley, but not many of those could be carried on your motorcycle."

Ned brightened up. "I can drive a car. I drove for Mrs. Baker."

"But I can't supply one, Ned. Not only do I need my own car, but I couldn't get insurance for an unlicensed driver."

"What if I get a driver's license?"

George nodded, "If you get a license, and if you can show not only a good safety record, but an excellent safety record, then maybe I can use you for supply runs too. But you need a license before we can do anything."

...

"Dot? I'm ready to close up now."

She closed the newspaper she had been staring at for the last fifteen minutes. "I'm done, Mrs. Baker."

All day long, she had been supposedly doing the last minute research for her speech tomorrow. In reality, her thoughts never stayed on one track more than a few minutes.

Driving the pickup on the road past the store, her thoughts drifted back to the things that had worried her all day long.

Her speech was important, more than just for the grade. Here was her chance to make a difference to Ranch Exit. With her father injured, and Aunt Elizabeth expecting her for the summer, conditions were ripe for something dreadful to happen—like the adults in her life making decisions for her own good.

What were the chances she would still be in Seattle when the new school year began? What if all of her friends, her horse, her home, and her whole life were taken away from her?

Certainly that's what Aunt Elizabeth had in mind. That's what she wanted all along.

And without her father to defend her, what chance did she have?

Dad. What has happened to you? She could understand his despair over the broken leg and not being able to make a living for them, but what about that cloud in his head?

It was like the demons in the Bible. Something had latched onto him and made him act crazy. He snapped and ran off into the night to kill a coyote. And for some reason, he was angry with Ned. What if he snapped and attacked Ned?

Was there some trick Mr. Stellman could work, from his tunnel, to heal him, to make the cloud go away?

And what could she do about the 'dwarf'? What could anyone do for a hermit with no legs and no teeth, and who wanted to stay hidden more than getting help with his own health?

Was he crazy too? Ned thought so. But she couldn't deny the hour or so of clarity that the funny little diagram on a piece of paper caused.

Was that magic? She didn't believe in magic—except Bible magic, of course. And Mr. Stellman was no apostle.

She shifted gears as she made the turn towards her house.

A face flashed right by her open window.

Dot slammed on the brakes, and skidded the pickup into the ditch.

The engine chugged to a halt, and she sat with her hands locked to the steering wheel, breathing so fast she was wheezing and dizzy.

Did I hit him? Did I kill him? Dozens of possible disasters raced through her head.

A hand on the door shook her out of the silent panic. She shrieked and jumped away.

The old Indian face smiled at her. "Well, if it isn't the girl with the horse. Did this one get away from you?"

"Oh! Mr. Wanekia! You scared me to death!"

"Calm down little one. Close your eyes and listen to your heart."

Amazingly, she did as he said. Her heart was surging along in a panic, like Pokey when he had been chased by the coyotes. She just listened, feeling the rhythm slow. In less than a minute, she realized the panic was gone. She opened her eyes.

Mr. Wanekia was still there, watching over her. He nodded.

"Got a good run for yer money, eh?"

"Are you okay? I never saw you! I could have killed you."

"It'll take more than a young girl in an old pickup to run me down!"

He stepped back and looked at the pickup again.

"See if you can move it."

Dot started the engine, and was relieved when it rumbled to life. She looked in the rear view mirror, and then shifted into reverse.

The engine revved high, but the pickup didn't move. She shifted into low gear. Again, she didn't move.

What's wrong? She pushed in the clutch and let it out again. Still the engine growled and nothing happened.

"It's out of balance," Mr. Wanekia said.

"What?"

He shook his head, "I don't know machines. But your pickup is out of balance. I can feel it."

Dot knew a little, but she had never gotten whole-heartedly into machines like Ned had. As long as cars and telephones and computers followed their predictable paths, she could use them with no problems. When something got off the track, she was lost.

"What do I do now, Mr. Wanekia?"

He laughed, "You get out and heal it, I suppose. You are a healer, after all."

A healer? "I don't know what to do." She opened the door, and when she stepped out, she realized how tilted into the ditch the pickup was.

He shrugged. "Why don't you get out your flashlight and look underneath? Maybe you can see something. It's always better to act on what you can see."

Dot nodded, fished the flashlight out of her bag and started walking around the vehicle, shining her light at the problem.

Ah. One of the rear wheels wasn't quite touching the ground. *That's what he means—out of balance.* One of the tires had no traction, so it spun freely. The other had traction, but the first was draining off the spin.

I need to get them back in balance.

She located a couple of large flat rocks and wedged them under the tire that wasn't touching the ground. *Now they both have traction.*

"Stand clear Mr. Wanekia."

She started the engine, put it into reverse, and with her face scrunched up in sympathetic effort, applied power.

The tire spun half a turn, and then gripped the rock. Very quickly she was back on the road.

"Whoa, that had me scared. I would have been embarrassing to have to walk back to town to get help."

The old Indian just smiled.

Dot turned her head. "What brought you out here this evening?"

"Why, little one, I came to talk to you."

...

Ned set the baby food jars and the peanut butter down on the low table. Mr. Stellman hadn't answered when he had called out at the tunnel entrance. But this time he had been prepared, and brought his own flashlight.

The tunnel to the surface was just an air shaft. Once he passed the table, the place appeared to be made of full height rooms. Unhindered by a host, he turned his lights on the walls and ceilings.

This is certainly not like the movie. Instead of a vast cavern carved out of a mountain, this was a plain little room, with white plastered walls and a tiled floor.

Dust had settled over the years, but little wheel tracks and the odd trail the man made when he dragged himself along the floor had swept a path clean.

"Mr. Stellman?"

Ned went to the open doorway. It joined a hallway that led deeper into the mesa. There was less dust, and he had to look harder for tracks.

There were other doors, with simple numbers to identify them. Only the doorway to the entrance tunnel was opened.

I could get lost in here. And I haven't been invited.

He turned back, but he resolved to bring paper and pencil next time, and more batteries, in case he needed to explore. *A map would be good.*

...

"The valley is sacred. My people were here long before your kind came over the mountains."

Dot had invited the man to sit in the pickup, but he declined to enter the 'machine'. He said he was much more comfortable sitting on Mother Earth. Dot preferred the cushion, but she kept the door open.

"As it was in the old days, the people have taken it into their hearts to protect the valley. Good sometimes attracts evil. Evil drew me here."

Dot asked, "You think there is evil in Ranch Exit?"

He smiled at her. "What do you see?"

She had seen her father chase down and kill a coyote in a senseless rage. She had sensed a cloud in his mind, just like she had sensed something in Pokey.

"Animals are acting strangely. Some people are becoming enraged over nothing."

He nodded. "Even the valley itself is hurting."

Dot asked, "What's causing this?"

The old man shrugged, "Men usually. My kind or yours. This valley has strong magic, and long ago it drew wizards here. Two of them battled and shook the ground with their spells. It has been quiet since," he shook his head, "but the land hasn't been at peace."

Dot asked, "And now it's getting worse? You warned me my dad might be caught up in a wizards' duel. Is that what's happened to him?"

"It could be. When wizards battle, many are caught in the magic that is released. Power draws to power, and when a wizard is on the scent, anyone and anything can get in the way."

Dot put aside her objections to magic. She'd seen enough strangeness with her own eyes. Call it magic for now and understand it when she had the time.

"What can you do about it? Ned said you were a shaman."

He chuckled, "The young rider. He'll go far, once he decides which direction to travel. I think he sees dragons when a lizard crosses his path."

"I'm just an old man, with no power left in me. I can't stop this."

He pointed a gnarled old finger at her.

"But you are a healer! You love this place, just as my ancestors did. Heal the valley!"

...

Ned saw the Samuelson's pickup in front of his house, but didn't think anything about it until he walked in the front door.

Mr. Samuelson was in the living room, talking to his father. They both looked up as he walked in. From the expressions on their faces, he had been the subject of their conversation.

"I'll see you later, Albert."

"Bye, Luke."

Ned went on into the kitchen and set his books on the table. There was no sense in heading for his room if his father was just going to....

"Ned, come in here for a minute."

Mr. Samuelson was gone.

"Yes, Dad?"

Mr. Kelso clicked through several channels of static. It wasn't a good day for television. He shut the set off.

"Ned, have you been seeing Dot Comal?"

"No, not today. We were both at school, but we were both in different sessions. We didn't even talk."

"Well, I don't think you should be talking to her at all, not for a while yet."

Ned frowned and sat down. "Why Dad?"

His father sighed, "Luke Samuelson just got a call from the hospital. Ruben is agitated over Dot and you. For now, it would be better if you stayed away from her."

"But that's not fair! We haven't done anything."

Albert's voice notched up. "Ned, they've had to sedate the man! He obviously thinks something is going on!"

Ned clenched his fists. He forced his voice to be calm. "Do you think I've been ... messing with Dot?"

Albert looked away. "I don't know. When I was a teenager ... at that age, things can happen."

Ned asked, "And if something happened, would you have lied to your father about it?"

More than anything, it hurt having his father believe the worst of him.

Albert sighed, "No. No, I wouldn't have lied to him."

"And neither would I! Dot's my friend. She's my best friend. And if I had a girlfriend, it would probably be her. But we're not into that. Nothing has happened. Her dad has just gotten a bug in his head."

Albert nodded. "Okay, Ned. I believe you. But it doesn't change anything. He's her father. He's concerned about her, and helpless. We can't do anything to make that worse.

"Leave Dot alone. Don't talk to her. Not even in school. And most importantly, don't meet her anywhere alone. This is a small place, and everyone knows something is going on. Every eye will be on you, and on Dot. She's alone, and there can be no hint that you are in any way taking advantage of that."

"Dad, it's not fair. We're just friends."

"Son, it has to be this way. Promise me."

Ned stared at the floor. "Dad, she's my friend."

"It won't be forever. Ruben should be home soon. You say there's nothing to his worries. Well, when he's no longer helpless, he'll likely think differently. Until then, you have to make sure a bad situation doesn't get worse. It's your responsibility. Promise me you'll keep your distance."

"It's all a mistake. Besides you don't give up friends like this."

"Take it up with Ruben, but for now I need your promise."

Ned took a deep breath. "Okay, I promise. But only until I can talk to him."

Homecoming

It was a big day, and Dot spent more time than usual fixing her hair for school. For one thing, she would be driving herself and wouldn't have to deal with the wind and the helmet. She checked her closet and shook her head over the limited selection. Time for the red blouse and her white skirt.

Dad might be coming home today, and she was happy about that. After school, she would have to get Dad's paycheck like he asked. She should have done it yesterday, but staying late at school, and then that very strange run-in with Mr. Wanekia, had ruined that plan.

And, of course, today was her proposal speech.

She had no hope that it would be good enough.

I'm just going to stand there, talk about the flowers, and take my 'C' with good graces.

At least with a failed proposal, she could sign up to help Ned with his website. Dad certainly couldn't object to working on a school project.

She smiled into the mirror. The smile was fake, and she knew it. She straightened her collar nervously.

Today was her only chance to do something important for Ranch Exit, and she was unprepared.

In the morning light, she saw that her accident had left a mark. The right sidewall was scraped where it had hit the side of the ditch. It was no worse than the other scrapes the pickup had acquired, but it was fresh.

Dad won't worry about that. Not after all he's been through. Will he?

She drove to school at a slow pace, watching the road carefully. The ruts in the ditch seemed to scream at her, "DOT COMAL'S ACCIDENT".

I'm just being paranoid.

...

Luke Samuelson took the paper envelope with the three pills in it.

"This will keep him calm for the rest of the day. But honestly, if these fits continue, call the number I gave you." Doctor Loomis pointed to the sheet of paper.

"The state mental health people?"

"Right. It's not something I would wish on anyone, but sometimes getting a potentially violent person under professional care is the best choice for everyone. You say he has a daughter at home?"

"Right, but Ruben has called an aunt to come get her. I think he was afraid something like this was going to happen to him."

...

Ned gave his progress report. The website was up and registered with the search engines. He had the homepage with the Ranch Exit off-ramp sign and another page of text making his claim for the smallest school. He had more picture pages and a history page yet to complete.

He sat down, and realized that he hadn't looked at anyone in the room the whole time he had talked. That would be points off. Ms. Carson had talked more than once about making eye contact with your audience.

But he couldn't worry about that now. Dot was fussing with her papers, and looking depressed—and he wasn't allowed to even talk to her.

Twice she had looked his way, but Ned couldn't return the look. This off-limits policy was impossible, but he had promised his father.

I don't know what I'll do if Mr. Comal doesn't listen to reason. Not speaking to Dot was bad, but if Dot's evil aunt came to take her away, what then?

Ned looked around the room. There was Larry and Bill, and even Latoya and Hallee—maybe a couple of the older young ones. Other than Dot, those were all the friends he had.

For the first time, he felt the boundaries of Ranch Exit close in on him. *I've always expected to live my life here.* Each year Dad gave him a little more responsibility and control. He would learn to ranch and turn their idle land into a way to earn money. Odd jobs and cattle—he had always expected to make that work.

But he couldn't make it without friends. Maybe Larry would stay, but Bill had his eyes on another world, one with neon signs and shiny cars and more faces than you could ever recognize.

Latoya would be off to California as soon as she could find a way. Everyone knew that. Hallee was questioning everything. Ned didn't think there were enough answers in Ranch Exit for her.

April Gibson noticed him looking around, and stuck her tongue out at him. May noticed her sister and joined in the attack.

"Girls!" Ms. Carson raised her voice. April and May snapped back face-front with their best angelic looks.

Ned smiled. In ten years, those two would be interesting. But the smile faded. Could he survive ten years here without Dot?

...

"Dot Comal, are you ready to give your presentation?"

No, not at all.

"Yes, Ms. Carson."

Dot picked up her papers. She had copied several garden layouts from the magazines. The photographs had looked glorious, and part of her ached to grow a garden like those.

But she knew how much effort it would take to make a community garden for Ranch Exit. Who would pay for the water, supply the land, buy the plants and seeds?

Ranch Exit people got by, but not because they had any money to spare.

She set her disorganized collection on the podium, looked up at the faces, and stalled out.

Everyone waited. The silence caught the attention of even the people who didn't care. The teachers in the back gave her encouraging looks. Bill smiled, satisfied now that he was done with his ordeal and entertained by hers. April and May looked worried. She could feel support radiating from Ned.

"Uh." She looked down at her papers, and shifted them with her fingers. The pressure to run away was building by the second. She had thought about having a written script, or at least an opening line, but she had never gotten around to it.

"Dot?" Ms. Carson asked.

"Excuse me." She shuffled the pages, as if she had accidentally gotten them out of order.

A folded, yellowed piece of paper came to the top of the heap. It wasn't part of her presentation, but she knew instantly what it was.

Her fingers moved by their own accord, and she unfolded the paper.

A diagram appeared before her eyes, with a large circle and several patterns nested within.

Her mind clicked, like a pressure was released.

Oh.

She looked out at the audience. There were twenty-six distinctly different pairs of eyes. She looked at each and there was a story behind every one of them.

Oh, Ned, I'm sorry. It's okay you can't talk to me now. We'll work it out.

Ms. Carson was gripped in fear that Dot's stage fright proved that she was a failure as a teacher.

Mr. Filmore was worried about his store.

April and May were afraid she was sick.

Latoya was hurting for her, remembering her own stage fright last week.

Bill was looking at her breasts.

Dot absorbed everyone's stories. There was a single gold thread that connected them all. She took a deep breath, and smiled.

...

"Ranch Exit is a town just like every other small town in this nation. We are a community. We pull together, partly because we have to. But partly because we have become something a little grander than a community.

"We are a family.

"And like a family, we have new arrivals and some will depart. Of course, we have newborns, but more often people come here for their own reasons. Many have come out here to the edge of civilization to prove themselves as storekeepers or ranchers or artists or teachers. Some have come here for no more reason than to be with their loved ones.

"And some will leave, many to find their place in the wider world.

"But for those who stay and those who go, we all share this place. Ranch Exit has touched our soul. No one, not the most eager to go, wants to sweep this place under the rug.

"And so I propose that Ranch Exit celebrate this community that we are all a part of. We should hold an end-of-school town fair—the Ranch Exit Roundup."

She went on, the dream growing and sending out roots with every spontaneous word she spoke.

Enthusiasm broke free from her, and spilled out among the audience. No one could break free of the spell of her words.

Dot spoke to the heart of Mrs. Baker, a scene of her prized art photos out among the people, where everyone could see them and appreciate what her trained eye had seen.

To Mr. Filmore she spun the idea of his store as the centerpiece of a commercial fair. To April and May, she described in bright colors a booth populated by their fancy dolls. To several of the boys, a shooting gallery with prizes caught their imaginations. Every student proud of mother's cooking imagined blue ribbons.

"Every one of us has something to be proud of, something we could sell. Imagine signs along the interstate for a hundred miles in either direction bringing traffic here for the first time.

"I imagine quite a few travelers might be just a little bored and hungry by the time they get here."

There was a titter of laughter through the room.

"Let's take half of everything we sell and use it to prove how much we care for those who will be leaving us.

"I propose that this annual fair be dedicated to creating a scholarship fund for the outgoing senior class."

...

By the time she was done, the room spontaneously shifted into a free-ranging discussion on how to make it happen. Her sketchy ideas were immediately fleshed out. New booth ideas, new ways to advertise it, new possibilities for fund raising were bubbling out of people.

Latoya walked over.

"Dot, I don't know how to thank you."

With her enhanced perceptions, Dot was well aware of what the gesture meant to the older girl.

"We haven't raised one penny yet," she cautioned. "Could you get with Ned and see if we can't start advertising on his website?"

"Me?" Latoya was puzzled.

Dot nodded. "Irrational parents. We can't talk directly for a while. You can pass on the request for me?"

"Sure."

Ms. Carson approached her. She was glowing with the dream of what this 'Roundup' would do for her career. It had been her idea to have the student proposal speeches, and if a whole community could be inspired in such a way, it was a firm validation of her ideas and her teaching skills.

"Dot. This is a wonderful idea, but you know you have to hit the ground running? This was your proposal. According to the rules, it's your project. You have to organize it, recruit the workers, and make sure it all comes off.

"And the end of the school year is almost upon us. I'll try to help you any way I can, but expect to be busy from now until the fair closes. Good luck!"

The rest of the school day was a blur, as everything was dropped in favor of working on the Roundup. A day was set. Mr. Filmore pledged the support of his store, and Mrs. Baker made use of the telephone to rush order a supply of her nature photo posters.

By the time Dot headed home, word had spread throughout the town and everyone was looking forward to Ranch Exit's first town fair.

Ms. Carson never thought to hold the vote for Dot's proposal.

...

Elation battled with a growing headache as she headed home. The speech had been everything she could have hoped for, although the details were fading from her memory.

Will Dad be home? Mr. Samuelson had said he might. *He'll be proud of me.*

At the driveway, she saw Mr. Samuelson's Suburban and her heart pounded. She parked and dashed into the house.

Luke and Carol Samuelson were there waiting for her.

"Is Dad home?"

"He's asleep." He nodded, and Dot was still able to read details from his tired smile.

"What's wrong?"

"Have a seat dear."

Luke Samuelson gave a plain unvarnished report. "The leg is the least of his troubles," he finished. "I don't know where these rages are coming from, but he is just on the edge of being out of control."

He paused and looked at his wife for support.

"Dot. Ruben gave me a paper that authorizes me to commit him to the state hospital if he gets too violent."

"No!"

"Dot, he was clear of mind when he wrote it, and he was terribly concerned about you. This thing, whatever it is, scares him to death. You know about Aaron Locke?"

Dot was feeling the horror, compounded by the after effects of the charm. She nodded.

"Ruben is afraid he will go the same way, and voluntary commitment is a better situation than being arrested for assault. And it is so much better than hurting someone you care about."

The headache was throbbing. If it was anything like last time, she would be unconscious soon.

But she wouldn't let them take her Dad away!

"I'm not convinced. He's not violent now. I want to see him." She was insistent, and she was still alert enough to know the right words to say.

The Samuelsons went with her to his bedroom. At first glance he looked peaceful and healthy. There was a wheelchair next to the dresser.

But she could see deeper. In addition to the complex of injuries that surrounded the leg, she could see the demon in his head.

It was nothing so melodramatic as a red glaring face with horns, but the cloud of wrongness was no less fearful.

"He's drugged," Dot said.

"Yes. The doctor gave me these pills. There are two left. He should have one every twelve hours. It keeps him calm. After they are gone ... we will have to consider other options."

Dot put her hand to her head. A wave of weakness threatened to overcome her.

"When is the next pill due?"

Carol said, "I will stay here with you tonight. I have the schedule the doctor gave us for his care."

"No. I will take care of him." She had to get them out of the house.

"It's no trouble Dot."

Dot shook her head firmly. "I've taken care of him for years now. He's been sick before. He's my dad."

She looked up at them. "I understand the problems. I can handle it! And if he is worse than I believe, I can get to your place in ten minutes."

It took more argument, but she got them to leave, with a promise that they would be back in the morning.

"There's no help for it Dot," said Carol. "Taking care of him is more than any one person can handle. And you still have school."

Dot nodded. The pain in her head gave her no chance to talk anymore.

As they drove off, she looked at the schedule, but the words were blurred. She barely made it to her bed before she collapsed.

...

"I expect you to wear the blue uniform every time you are out in public working on one of my projects. Do you understand?"

Greg Cooper nodded. He scratched his gray stubble beard. "I've seen 'em. They look hot."

Ellis Mort shrugged. "Prepare for hot days. Make sure you have plenty of water. Are you up to the job?"

"Sure. I'd rather be working for a salary than for my niece."

Mort looked puzzled. "Your niece?"

"Little Hallee. She came home from school this afternoon all fired up about the fair. 'Sure as anything, she'll rope me into this,' I said to myself. I'd been meaning to come by here, but now I figger'd I'll need an excuse in a hurry."

"What's this fair? I haven't heard about a fair."

Greg pushed the brim of his sweat stained cowboy hat back a bit. "The Ranch Exit Roundup—never heard of it either. It sprung up all of a sudden.

One of the kids at school thought it up and now everyone's all hep for it. A scholarship thing, I hear. Money-raiser. Get some of those tourists on the interstate to stop and buy some barbeque."

Mort nodded. "A scholarship. I can understand that." He frowned and looked back towards his house.

"Mr. Cooper, I'll order the uniform and get you to work immediately. You say you can repair the tractor?"

"Sure. Anything with wheels."

"Get started on that immediately."

...

Crash! The noise startled Dot awake.

Dad! She struggled to shake off the sleep and rushed to his bedroom.

The light switch showed him half off the bed and the wheelchair fallen over on it side, collapsed.

"Dad! Hold on!" She rushed to his side.

A hand gripped her wrist. "Where is he?"

"Where is who? Dad, let me help you back onto the bed." She carefully moved his cast-bound leg back onto the mattress.

"I know he's here! He's after my daughter!"

"Dad! You're hurting my arm!" The grip was strong. The look in his eyes was intense, and yet he wasn't seeing her. She struggled to break free.

"Dad! I'm Dot. I'm right here. Look at me!"

But his grip was iron. No matter how hard she pulled, she couldn't pull free.

"Help me!" he pled.

Dot felt herself slipping toward panic. It was the demon she was seeing in her father's eyes. She had to get through to him.

She pushed her other hand onto his face—not to push him away, but to make contact. His face was clammy, sweaty.

"Dad! You're hurting me! I'm Dot. You're hurting me."

He blinked, "Dot?"

"Yes Dad. I'm right here. My arm. You're holding on too tight."

He breathed in sharply. "Dot?" His maniacal grip loosed. She slipped free.

He sagged back to his pillow. "Dot. I've had a bad dream."

"I know, Dad." She knew the demon would be back, soon. It was growing. She had to do something, before it destroyed him.

She found the pills and gave him one, while he was still docile.

Twelve hours. One pill left.

She looked at the clock. *Three in the morning.*

No time to spare.

She moved the wheelchair out of the bedroom, and turned out the lights. She dressed for the night quickly.

The night air was cool, and the stars above were only slightly washed out by the moon.

"Pokey. Come here boy."

The horse snorted and showed his puzzlement at these nighttime activities, but by flashlight she saddled him.

"You've got to hustle tonight, boy. I don't have much time. There's only one person who can help me, and I have to see him tonight."

Get Well Card

"Mr. Stellman!" She waved her flashlight around in the chamber. "Mr. Stellman, I need to talk to you!"

She went through the first door, and down the corridor. It was a long walk. She flicked the light on the tile, making sure she could still see the strange tracks.

What's that? She clicked off her flashlight. There were lights in the ceiling, glowing dimly, giving just enough light to navigate by. *Save my batteries.*

There was a noise, like a whisper of cloth or something else. "Mr. Stellman?"

A mouse darted across her path. She jumped back, just barely stifling a shriek. *It's just a mouse.* Her heart hammered. *But I can follow it.*

She picked up her pace, following the little furry messenger. In the darkness it was nothing more than an obscure shadow on the floor.

It turned at a branch in the corridor. She followed.

One of the walls became a handrail. She looked over the side. *It's huge.*

Easily ten stories deep, there was a central cavity a couple of hundred feet across, surrounded on all sides by corridors and doors. The light was a little stronger here.

She counted. *I'm on the third floor down from the top.* She looked back. *Which corridor did I come out of? And which door?* Panic started to build, but she put it down.

Follow the mouse.

One ramp down and on the next wall facing, she heard an answer to her calls.

"Mr. Stellman?"

"Dot?" the voice was hoarse. "Don't come in here."

"I have to."

"Don't. Don't look."

She opened the door wider. In the dim light she could see motion on the bed.

"I can't see you, Mr. Stellman, but I have to talk. I need your help."

He coughed. It didn't sound good.

Dot asked, "Are you sick?"

"I'll survive." He didn't sound strong.

"What's wrong? Can I help?"

"The pie. I ate too much."

Dot felt relief, and guilt. But at least it wasn't too serious.

"I should have known better, but it tasted too good. That pie was enough food for a month. My digestive system has shrunk over the years. I ate two pieces, and it nearly killed me."

Dot sat down on the floor by the door, unwilling to infringe any closer on his privacy.

"My father is being taken over by a demon. I need help to save him."

...

Pokey ran. The dawn's glow lit the way. Dot was crouched down over his neck, feeling fear and hope.

The horse tossed his head towards the barn, just visible in the distance. She gave him his lead and he cut off towards home.

"Good boy." She removed the saddle and gave him a minute's worth of grooming. It was all the time she could spare.

"Dad?" She was grateful to see he hadn't tried to get out of bed again.

"Hmm." He appeared to be asleep. How much could he understand through the drugs?

"Daddy? Can you hear me?"

He tossed his head from side to side, struggling to wake up, or struggling with something else. "Uhh. What?"

His eyes opened, and she could see the rage struggling to fight its way to the surface.

"Look what I made you, Daddy. It's a get-well card."

She showed him the paper. Inside a valentine heart, there was a complex spiral that blended from one texture to another. Below, in her handwriting, "Get Well Soon Daddy".

His eyes tracked onto the card, and she could see the rage fade.

"Dot?"

"It's okay Dad. I'll be off at school today, but if you start to feel bad, just look at the get-well card. Can you do that for me?"

He nodded and closed his eyes. "I'm so tired."

"Just sleep when you can. You have to heal."

She waited while he struggled. She could see him shiver. When his eyes opened, she couldn't see any sign of the insanity.

He coughed. "How have you been doing, Honey, while I've been gone?"

She relaxed. "Fine Dad. I've got a big project at school. We're going to hold a fair."

"A fair? At Ranch Exit?"

"Yes, the 'Ranch Exit Roundup'. It's my project and everyone is excited about it."

He smiled. "Your project? Well, good luck."

She straightened his sheets. "You just get some rest and look at the get-well card. Okay?"

He nodded and drifted off to sleep.

She set card on the dresser next to the bed where he could see it easily.

It is so nice to see him act normal.

She had fifteen minutes to shower and get ready before the Samuelson's arrived. It was going to be a long day.

"He is doing much better," Dot told Carol. "He is sleeping a lot. Maybe the drug is doing that."

She pointed at Dot's wrist. "Did he do that?"

There was a bruise where her father had gripped so tightly.

Dot shook her head. "No, I had a tumble with Pokey. It should have started to fade by now."

Mrs. Samuelson didn't believe her, but she said nothing more.

Dot picked up her books. "Mrs. Samuelson, there is only one pill left, and I would rather hold off using it. He really is doing much better! If he seems agitated, tell him to look at the get-well card I made for him. It seems to help."

"I'll do what I can Dot."

"Thanks so much for helping Dad. You don't know how much I appreciate it."

...

Carl Stellman pushed himself on his home-made wheeled platform down the corridor.

The girl didn't understand when I said the gor-spiral was temporary. I could see it slide right off her mind.

With every push of his hands, there was a squeak in the rear wheel. How many wheels had he worn out over the years? Oh, well, there were still plenty of office chairs to scavenge new ones from.

Could this Mort be Dwight? His description is close—and who else would even know about iconoplaks?

Carl had questioned Dot about her father, and this demon she was seeing. His first thought had been that the seeing charm had damaged her, but it took just a few questions to put that idea out of his mind.

If Dwight is alive, and putting up iconoplaks all over the valley, there could be more at risk. If he knows how to do that, then at least some of the other research notes could have survived.

A pit of bitterness aggravated his stomach ache. He paused to burp. It was painful, and something his shrunken and streamlined digestive system hadn't had to do in a long time.

For years, the spark of pride that he had saved humanity from this danger had given him peace of mind. He had needed it to continue living his trogladite existence. And it was all a lie.

Carl could see the base lights brighten ever so slightly as the sunlight on the surface warmed the buried thermocouples and increased the voltage for the lights.

Day and night and the seasonal changes—they had all been filtered down to slight changes in his lighting.

But something bad is happening outside, and I can't get out there. It's too dangerous. He was little more than a hothouse slug. The sun alone would kill him in minutes, blistering his unprotected skin. There was the desert dryness, the predators, the cactus thorns. Even the roughness of bare rock would do him in.

But who can stop him but me?

...

Ms. Carson had just put away a video copy of Marilyn Monroe's "How to Marry a Millionaire". She had accidentally let it play all night. Her trailer was parked just a few hundred yards down from the school. It was close enough to walk every day, but just far enough away so that students wouldn't be tempted to follow her home. Filmore had arranged utilities for her, but live television was out of the question. It felt like she had seen the movie a hundred times, but it was still one of her favorites.

The phone rang. She sighed and put the player on pause. Which parent was it this time, so early in the morning? These country folk never understood business hours.

"Ms. Carson?"

She fumbled the phone. "Why yes, Mr. Mort! What can I do for you?"

"I'm sorry to call you so early."

"Oh, no problem! A teacher's job is never really over when the door closes."

Mort's voice resonated within her. *Such an honest man.* The idea just popped into her head.

"I just heard about the fair you're planning."

"Yes, the Ranch Exit Roundup. It looks to be the biggest thing to hit this community in a long time. Would you like to be a part of it?"

There was a long pause. Doubt touched her through the silence.

"Well, I appreciate the offer," he said. "However, I must confess to a fear that it won't come off. Ranch Exit is so far from everywhere. There can't be a very big turnout.

"Ms. Carson, these are poor people. Proud but dirt poor. I had heard some of the plans they are making. Some families are going to go bankrupt over this.

"I called to ask you to re-think this plan. I know it's supposed to be a fund-raiser. If you could see your way clear to cancel the event, I would be willing to write a couple of checks, one for the scholarship, and another to you to handle the administration of the fund. Just tell me the amount, and we can save these people from hurting themselves out of misplaced pride."

Her stomach twisted. She ached to tell him 'Yes!'

"I am so sorry, Mr. Mort." Her mind raced to think of some way to please him.

"The problem is that this fair was never my idea. Dot Comal came up with the idea, and it was an instant hit. I don't think I could stop it if I tried. Some ideas just take on a life of their own."

"Hmm." There was a deep disappointment in that sound. "Well, can I count on you to be the voice of reason with these people? As an outsider, you can point out the folly when it threatens to get out of hand. They are my neighbors and I care about them."

"I totally agree with you, sir. I will do my best."

...

The Store, it had no other name, had been built in an era when glass for windows was an extravagance. It did have a wide and shaded open porch, and some decades it had been filled with hard-goods, like barrels of nails, stacks of tubs, shovels and picks, barrel staves, and round tins of gunpowder. There was still some of that gathering dust on the porch when George had bought the store, but it was all gone now, replaced by six wooden slat rockers, a half-sized refrigerator and one adult-sized school chair.

The rockers were popular, the only real public place for adults to gather in Ranch Exit. There were drinks in the refrigerator, a coffee pot and an open cash box on its top. Only one week out of twelve years had the honor box failed to pay for what was consumed. That was the week Jerry Kline left town for good. George chalked it up to community service and resisted the impulse to increase the prices.

The school chair was his favorite. Especially when the dawn was clear. The red-tinted glow gave him a view of the valley from the porch—a promise for a glorious day. Like the students he would teach later in the day, he had his homework spread out on the curved, L-shaped table built into the chair.

He flicked through his organizer and checked the delivery date. *RurlGo should have gotten here by now.* Demand for everything from sugar to crepe paper had skyrocketed as people were experimenting with their Ranch Exit Roundup ideas. *It'll be a hundred times worse by the end of the week. I'll have to boost my orders.*

His call to Western Oil had worked out better than he had expected. If the Roundup came off as big as everyone hoped, then dozens of cars, maybe even a hundred, would be arriving from places far down the interstate and when they got ready to leave, they would all need gas. Jake Cartulio and he had already talked it out. Jake couldn't handle the traffic. It was up to him to resolve the problem.

George had ordered two tankers and Western had them already outfitted with filler hoses. He could handle regular unleaded, a half-load of premium and a half-load of diesel. He could rent the tankers for a couple of weeks and get a credit for any unused fuel. It was expensive, but with luck, he could break-even on the deal. It was something that had to be done.

But it was just one more expense item on a budget already over-stressed.

Motor noise intruded on his calculations. He could hear it long before he could see anything. Most days, he could even hear the occasional big rig on the interstate, in spite of it being over the hill and out of sight. But this one was inside the valley.

It came into sight, finally. *Red—the Kelso pickup.* He knew every vehicle by sight. There weren't all that many of them.

Yolanda and Ned pulled up in front of the store. Ned was driving, he noted.

"Good morning!" He always liked having the first word. People felt more at ease when the ice was broken.

"Good mornin', George." Yolanda Kelso was short, wide and always walked at a quick pace. As she approached, he felt like an infantryman watching a tank.

"What can I do for you this morning?"

"Ned's going to get his driver's license today. I figured we could tell you and not have to wait for school to start."

He nodded. "Good thinking. It looks like it'll get hot today. I'll pass the word."

He turned to Ned. "If you could handle an errand for me, while you are in town, I'll consider you already on salary."

"Great," Ned said.

George also got a nod from Ned's mother.

"Good. Give me a minute to write up the order."

...

Latoya knocked at the door, and was surprised when Carol Samuelson answered. "Come on in, girl. We're all having breakfast. Want some pancakes?"

"No. I was just checking on Dot."

Dot waved a fork. "Pull up a chair. Mrs. Samuelson makes 'em better than I do."

Ruben, sitting in his wheelchair, defended his daughter's cooking, "I've never had any complaints."

Latoya shook her head. "I just came by to offer a ride to school."

"Sorry. I am really appreciating this chance to drive myself. Dad's leg will be healed soon enough and I know what will happen then."

Latoya nodded, "But you could get a hardship license. I've heard Ned is going into town today to get one so he can work for Mr. Filmore."

At the mention of Ned's name, the Samuelson's and Dot looked at Ruben. He seemed to be ignoring it, looking over at the get-well card. A spike of tension seemed to bleed away, but Latoya had seen it all and knew her mistake.

Ruben shook his head. "I don't think it makes sense. Dot will be leaving for the summer in just a few days. I don't think we could get the paperwork done before then."

Dot's smile faded a notch. "Well, then I'd just better enjoy it while I can then. But Dad, you will need me to be able to drive when I get back. Don't think you can keep me locked up here all the time!"

He smiled. "I know. Hadn't you girls better get off to school?"

They left shortly, Dot leading the way in the pickup.

Luke Samuelson wheeled Ruben to the front porch. "It is really good to see you doing so well. I was worried."

Ruben looked at the morning landscape. "Luke, hang onto that piece of paper I gave you. I am better, but I don't know what caused it, and I don't know why it went away. Something like that, when your mind betrays you— it leaves you unsettled. I can't really rest until Dot leaves with her aunt."

He sighed. "I just wish I knew what had happened."

...

Mort scowled at the bank balances on the screen. Under five different names, they all told the same story. He was running out of money again.

No plan, no success. I knew that. But these just have to last me until I go to the next phase.

That stupid Ranch Exit Roundup was definitely throwing off the timing. He had been sure that that teacher was someone he could work with. He laughed at the memory. She sniffed at the bribe like a hungry dog after a bone.

No guts. She's too scared to actually scuttle the fair. What does she think the townspeople will do? Lynch her?

He sighed. In the old days, he had people working for him that would risk even that. Say the word and old Gaylord would put his head on the chopping block. But it took time to cultivate good servants.

Once the wards were up and he was secure, he would have the time to work on that. Until then, just play the eccentric and smile when they laughed at his amusing road signs, never realizing that there were such things as iconoplaks.

Let them have their fair. There would be too many ripples if I erased the town too soon.

But until then, I need more cash.

He closed the bank window web page and navigated to a new car dealership in Los Angeles. The site was designed for browsing, and he put together an order for a top of the line Corvette. One of his names was already in the system—he had done this many times before. He clicked the GET QUOTE button and only had to wait a few minutes before his phone rang.

"Hi, Ed. I was expecting you." Mort checked his notebook to make sure he was playing the correct role. With so many false names, he had to keep good records or he could trip himself up.

"No, it's not for me. It's a gift."

The salesman was in an extremely good mood. He had dealt with this customer before and he smelled big money.

Mort nodded at his suggestions. "Yes, that sounds good. I want all the extras. It will be just like the one before. Once you're done, deliver it to the parking garage at Central ... yes, the same place as before.... credit card."

Mort read the number, one digit at a time, off the plastic card. It always gave him a thrill of satisfaction to try to remember the number. He always came up blank.

Extracting a promise that the car would be delivered today, Mort finished the call and turned back to the computer.

A programmed keystroke brought up eBay and navigated to the sell window.

"Metallic blue Corvette, brand-new just off the lot, all papers, full-warranty, loaded." He put a quick-sale price on it at three-quarters of what he had just paid and filled in the other details.

He was barely done when Greg Cooper knocked on his door.

"Ah, Greg. I was just working on your paycheck. Is it done?"

The old cowboy in the blue uniform was damp with sweat and he held his cap in his hand. "Yes, sir. All the way around."

Of course Mort had not lived as long as he had by taking people's word. He drove over to the landing strip and took the eagle up.

Below, on the broad pastureland of his ranch, the landing strip appeared as the sharpest feature in view. The lace-like resonance pattern that surrounded its perimeter wasn't visible, but its effects were.

Excellent. No matter what happens now, I have my escape hatch.

He banked over towards the northwest. The abandoned rail line cut through the rolling hills and up to the mesa lands. Somewhere down there, he was sure, was the treasure to end all treasures.

Go Postal

Ned folded the temporary driver's license carefully and slipped it into his wallet next to the credit card with his father's name on it.

"I'm trusting you to be careful with this," Albert Kelso had said. "Everything you buy with the card costs more than if you paid cash, because of the interest charges. Now that you'll be earning a salary, I still expect you to buy your own gas, but I want you to have this in case of an emergency."

Ned put his wallet away and turned the ignition key. "Where do we go next?"

His mother pointed, "The jail. I want to check on Aaron Locke."

The officer at the desk shook his head. "He is no longer here. A psycho—that one. The judge had him sent to the Salt Lake state hospital."

Yolanda frowned. "Aaron Locke? You can't mean that. He is a simple, good natured man. I've never heard a word of anger from him."

The officer snorted a laugh, and held up his arm. "You know why I'm riding a desk today. See this cast. Your 'good natured' friend fractured my forearm. He exploded like a grenade. I still don't know what set him off. All I know is that we couldn't handle him here and he needs serious mental help."

He looked at his paperwork. "But while I've got you here, where did you say you people live?"

Yolanda said, "Ranch Exit."

He laughed again and set the paper aside.

His mother stiffened and asked, "What's so funny, young man?"

Ned had heard people laughing at the name of their town all his life, but the officer quickly realized it was no joke to her.

He held up his hand in peace. "Nothing, Mrs. Kelso. Nothing at all."

...

George Filmore's order filled two large crates that Ned strapped carefully into the bed of the pickup. This was his first real delivery and he wanted nothing to happen to it.

His mother slept most of the ride back, enjoying having someone to drive her for a change.

Ned was alone with the road and his thoughts.

Aaron was a quiet guy. He had seen him occasionally. *If he went crazy, could the same thing happen to Mr. Comal?*

The interstate through Utah had many stretches where there was nothing but scenery. Rest areas with picnic tables, bathrooms, spectacular rocks and mountains tempted him, but it was nicer today to be on the road, keeping pace with a tandem trailer US Post Office long-haul truck. Ned's right foot was sorely tempted by the long stretches of vacant road, but one ticket would stick his job in the mud.

Dad had told him, "Your mind gets used to the whine of your engine, and without a cruise-control your speed creeps up. We don't have a cruise-control, so follow someone who does."

The Post Office truck was doing the job, but Ned kept an eye open for someone to pass them. He would willingly trade up another couple of miles per hour.

He glanced over at his mother. It would be nice to take Dot on a drive. The worst part of riding the motorcycle was that it was hard to talk to her.

If Dot ever talks to me again.

...

Ned's eye caught the line of table-top mesa land to the north.

That's not right. He checked the odometer, and did the subtraction.

"Mom? Mom, wake up. I think I've passed the exit."

She blinked awake. "Hmm. What did you say?"

"I think I missed the Ranch Exit turn-off."

"That's okay. You're doing fine."

He looked at her. She seemed awake, but her words were a little spacey.

It definitely wasn't okay to miss the road home. He checked his rear-view mirrors and waited until a convenient crossover presented itself.

There was a sign, "Authorized and emergency vehicles only", but he wasn't about to drive another hundred miles waiting for a turn-around.

He eased down and made the turn. No sirens. Only a couple of trucks, and they didn't seem to care. He increased his speed.

Ten miles later, he blinked. *I know that creek! Have I passed Ranch Exit again?*

His mother had gone to sleep again. He clenched his teeth, checked the traffic, and found another place to turn back.

Okay. Play close attention. Never lose track of where I am.

He stared at the road, straining to see any signs off in the distance. The speedometer read fifty, and he watched the odometer carefully. The turn-off had to be somewhere in the next ten miles.

The scenery in the distance looked very familiar.

"That's North Mesa." He put on the brakes.

Almost as if it appeared out of a heat haze, the large green "Ranch Exit, No Services" sign appeared.

He sighed and made the turn. A noise caught his attention as a delivery truck made the same turn after him.

But this was his territory now, his roads. He pulled up to George Filmore's store, and so did the delivery truck.

George was already out there to greet them.

The delivery man with the clipboard was already walking up to George.

"Mr. Filmore, I'm sorry I'm late, but I missed the turn-off, not once, but four times!"

...

Ruben Comal woke from his nap. *What time is it?* Dot said she would be late getting home from school. He reached for the wheelchair. *I'd better get used to doing this for myself. Dot will be gone sooner than my cast.*

He managed to get into the chair and wheeled himself out into the hall. The windows were open to get a breeze through the house. Air conditioning was much too expensive. The wind shifted and the bedroom door slammed shut. The get-well card flopped over and slid behind the dresser.

...

School was chaos. Dot felt her face freeze into a permanent grin about three PM. The Cartulio's had set up several open tents outside the schoolhouse. From the far left, she could hear familiar voices from church try their luck at singing country and western standards. The painting crew were hard at work in another tent, putting together the road signs. One in particular caught her eye.

Free

Ranch Exit

Your Off-Ramp to Fun!

That's my slogan. She had paraphrased what Carl had told her about the magic marketing words.

"Use 'Free' and 'Fun' as much as you can, and pretty girls to imply 'Sex'. These have nothing to do with your message. They exist only to attract the eye and make your target mentally receptive."

Nora Baker's photo gallery was half populated with various desert and mountain scenes. The rush order of her most popular photos hadn't arrived yet and she was fearful she would have to re-hang everything at the last minute to fill the gaps in her display.

"Dot! Come over here!"

She changed direction. It seemed a lot of people wanted her. Ms. Carson had told people it was Dot Comal's project, and although people were going to do what they originally planned anyway, they at least wanted her to bless their decision.

All it does is slow everything down. If she hadn't been so certain Ms. Carson was enthusiastic about the fair, Dot would suspect she was doing it to put a drag on the efforts.

Everyone is here. She had seen Mort make a brief stop at the school. All of the students and almost all of the parents seemed to be hard at work. She even caught a glimpse of Mr. Wanekia watching the activity from a distance.

I wonder what he thinks of this. Is the Roundup a 'healing' activity for the valley?

...

"Ned, take this over to the Brown house." George Filmore handed him a small paper sack.

"Right!" It was just what Ned had been hoping for.

He had spied the shaman watching the town, and just for an instant, he had seen the bear.

That's enough for me. There's just too much weirdness. With a bag this small, I can take the bike, use the shortcut, stop by Carl's and still get back here before anyone notices I'm gone.

When he left, worn out mufflers signaling, half the town looked up. Dot's smile dropped a notch.

I wish I were out of this madhouse and hanging on tight behind him.

...

The delivery was quick and smooth. Mrs. Brown even hesitated and gave him a fifty-cent tip. Tips were practically unknown in Ranch Exit. Ned had heard of them and was quick enough to accept it with a smile.

He headed up the railroad grade.

It's nice driving the pickup, but I wouldn't know how to get to the tunnel by car. It's all steep grade.

The motorcycle navigated the route quickly.

"Carl? Are you there?"

"Ned! The mice heard you coming. It's good to see you."

He got down to business.

"Carl, who can do this mind-bending stuff, other than you?"

Stellman rolled his wheeled platform to the wall and slid off. He could move faster on his board, but it wasn't stable and leaning against a wall was much more comfortable.

"I suspect that the person you know as Mort may be using old research notes of mine. With those he could do quite a bit."

Ned nodded. "I suspected that, what with all his funny signs. But is there anyone else?"

"No one that I know of. But then I don't know many people. Who would have access to my old notebooks?"

Ned shook his head. "I don't think that's it. You see, for years there has been an old Paiute shaman in the valley."

He told Stellman everything he knew or suspected—the strange disappearances, the digital photo, and the bear. Ned knew how other people reacted when he started talking about Indian magic. There was the amused smile, the carefully worded disbelief.

The light was very dim in the tunnel, but he could see that Carl's face wasn't smiling.

After a long pause, he said, "What does he look like?"

Ned did his best, he painted the picture of the frail old man, the felt hat, the walking stick.

"Hmm. That's unbelievable."

Ned asked, "What is?"

Carl looked him in the face. "I met a man with that description in this valley back before the base was shut down. A crackpot, I thought. We talked, and I remember trying to translate his talk about the sacred valley into the concepts I was working on. The idea that the Indians had long ago codified certain elements that I had just discovered was not something I was ready to accept."

"But it's true? Wanekia's magic is the same as your stuff?"

Carl shook his head. "Maybe they are related. That's all I'm ready to accept." He laughed. "If the Paiutes knew what I know, then there would be no white men west of the Rockies, and no one would even suspect this land exists.

"But what's unbelievable is that he could be the same man."

"Why?"

Carl waved his hand, "Because I thought he was an old man back then. That would make him a hundred and fifty years old now."

Ned laughed long and loud. "But that's what I thought about you. How old are you? Near a hundred?"

"About that. But that's not surprising is it? Moses lived to about a hundred and twenty. What's the modern record? That and more I'd bet. I live a dull and safe life here. If a limited diet and keeping out of the sun can extend your lifespan, I'll end up older than Methuselah!"

Ned considered it. "What do you make of his warning to Dot? That Ruben was in danger, working for a wizard?"

"Tell me more. What did Mr. Comal do for Mort?"

Ned told him more about the signs and the crop circle.

"And he makes him wear a blue uniform?"

"Yes. Is that important?"

Carl was angry. If he had legs, he would have been pacing. As it was, he rocked on his hands.

"That callous idiot!"

"What's wrong?"

Carl tried to explain. "One of the first things my project learned is the effects of uniforms on people's minds. A blue uniform is particularly insidious. People work harder in blue uniforms. But they are also more susceptible to rages. Without precautions, they could lose all control and strike out at the people around them."

"They go postal." Ned nodded.

"What?"

"'Go Postal'. It's an expression. Every so often some postman will go crazy and shoot people."

"Do postmen wear blue uniforms?"

"Yeah, I think so."

Carl sighed. "It's worse than I thought. But you see, when working with iconoplaks and other patterns, the effect can be magnified. And Mort knew that! He knew the dangers and deliberately put his employees at risk just to get more work out of them."

He pulled himself back on his wheels. "I've got to make a counter pattern, but it will take some research."

...

Dot made her excuses. "I've got a couple of errands to run, and then check on my father. Will you need me to come back later this evening?"

Nora Baker shook her head. "Probably not. We still have Thursday and Friday to get it all ready. Try to get some rest, dear."

Dot drove to the Mort ranch gateway.

He's been at it again. There were two tall pillars with wings at the entrance. At first glance she had thought they were Indian totem poles, but those weren't animal faces on the body of the pole, but rather abstract patterns. There was a sequence of smaller poles following the property line. She got chills looking at them.

Driving up to the main house, she saw yellow and green. *There's the tractor.* Through the grapevine she knew Hallee's uncle was working for Mort now.

Ellis Mort's house was huge, boasting three stories with a main building and two wings. She couldn't even guess how many rooms it contained. Other people who had seen it compared it to English manor houses, but for her, there was nothing in its class. It was a palace in the desert. All it lacked was a suitable garden around the grounds.

Dot remembered the time when a steady stream of construction trucks passed through town, stopping at the store for food and supplies. Some of the men had lived in temporary trailers while the house was built.

But when it was all done, there had been no open house, and many in the valley had never driven close enough to look at it.

Mort opened the door at her knock.

He was in the same fancy coat that he had worn to the school with the shimmering colors. The doubts and suspicions about him that had been building in her mind over the past couple of days vanished in a feeling of well-being.

"Yes, Miss Comal. What can I do for you? Come on in."

She held out the letter her father had given her. "Dad told me to get his final paycheck, and if possible have it made out to George Filmore."

He perused the letter and nodded. "Come with me to my office, and I'll fix you up."

The inside of Mort's house was impressive, if sparsely furnished. Some rooms looked empty, but the ones in use were fabulous. The ceilings were higher than in ordinary houses, and the wooden furnishings made her want to stroke them. His office was huge. Her jaw dropped at the bookshelves. The school library could be shelved in the gaps and lost entirely among the volumes he possessed.

She caught herself before she asked the stupid question, "Do you read all of these?"

Mort pulled some ledgers from his desk and checked the entries. Dot looked at the drawing table and glanced at the old books laying on them. One was open. An elaborate diagram was partially visible. It looked strangely familiar.

"Miss Comal?"

She turned back to face him, "Yes?"

He held out a check to her. "I hear you are responsible for the fair this weekend."

She took the check. "I suppose so. I suggested it, at least." She laughed. "Everyone else is doing all the hard work. Would you like to have a booth? There is room, and Ranch Exit wouldn't be what it is without some of your signs. Mrs. Baker has a booth for her scenic photographs, and Mrs. Bly has scented decorative candles, and Mr. Brewster has metal sculptures of windmills and locomotives and things he makes with his welding. Your artwork would fit right in."

He nodded tolerantly, "Maybe some other year. I have a rather large project underway right now and I couldn't spare the time."

She glanced at the check. It was for a thousand dollars, much more than she had expected. "Thank you for all you've done for my father."

He escorted her out to the front porch.

"What is this?" he exclaimed as several hundred mice scurried across the driveway.

"Whoa!" she agreed. "I've never seen that many mice in one place before."

Mort just watched them go.

Dot said goodbye and drove away.

...

In the cockpit of the eagle, Mort pulled out a leather-bound photo album that contained a set of intricate patterns. He opened the first, labeled 'Eyes' and absorbed the link.

The plane leapt into the air as if it were alive. His hands operated the controls, but all he could see was the valley below, with the sharpness of eagle's eyes.

Carl Stellman is alive. This is proof. No one else had his way with the lab animals.

He toured the valley, and it was clear that the whole area was alive with mice. They were moving in waves, acting together like mice never did.

Locate the nexus. Sunset is just an hour away. I'll never get a chance like this again.

The fair was alive with people and they reacted when a wave of mice passed through. Mort laughed. They were all mice—pocket-sized ones and people-sized ones.

The railroad grade, cutting straight down the valley always caught his attention, and this time was no different.

But looking again, something appeared significant. The mice seemed to be moving evenly on either side of the line. It was if the railroad were the center.

And a single human figure was positioned on the road grade. A shimmer of power radiated from that spot.

Carl. It has to be him. I'll never get a better chance. Mort flipped the album to the page labeled, "Talons".

...

Ned raced along the grade. *I spent too long with Carl. I'll have to have some excuse for George if he asks what happened.*

He wondered what Carl was doing. He had vanished, gone to 'do research', whatever that meant.

The old bridge near Dot's house came into view. *Some day, I'll fix that ramp.*

He eased the throttle, and turned towards the well-worn rut that took him around the bridge.

The crack of a rifle and the puff-flower of dirt just a foot from his front tire took him by surprise. He jerked the handlebars and went flying.

Hidden Landscape

Dot heard the shots. *Oh no!*

Up on the railroad grade, she saw Ned weaving. Another shot rang out and he went sailing off the edge.

She turned into the driveway at high speed. There was her dad in the wheelchair, rifle aimed, and taking shots at Ned.

She plowed through the fence line. Her father turned the rifle toward her. She read the blind rage in his face for less than a second. The rifle cracked. The far rearview mirror shattered into pieces. The windshield cracked on that side.

With a hard twist to the steering wheel, she slung the pickup to one side and jumped free.

With the unmanned pickup lumbering off to the right of him and Dot running up from the left, Ruben was momentarily distracted.

Dot plowed into him. The rifle went sailing through he air and the wheelchair overturned.

"Aiee!" her father screamed with pain.

Dot rolled away, keeping clear of the grasping claws of the man. "Dad! It's me, Dot!"

The chair. She grabbed up the collapsed wheelchair and dragged it with her as she searched for the rifle. The pickup chug-chugged until it hit the side of the barn and stalled out.

"Dad, stay calm!" She shouted at him, but she knew in her heart that nothing but the card would bring him down from his rage. *Did he shoot Ned?*

There! Grabbing up the rifle, she left the wheelchair on its side in the dirt. Tossing the rifle against the wall, she dashed into her father's bedroom.

Where is it? The card wasn't on the dresser where she had left it.

I've got to see if Ned is hurt. He could be up there bleeding to death!

She raced to the kitchen, looking everywhere, and then back to the bedroom. A corner of white behind the dresser caught her eye. *The card!* She pushed the dresser aside and grabbed it.

"Dad!" She ran toward him, holding the card out where he could see it. "Dad, look at the card!"

The Samuelson's Suburban pulled up into her driveway and Carol hopped out. Dot got to him first.

There was a moment's puzzlement in his eyes. And then he reached for the card, staring at its contents as if it were water to a man parched for days.

"Dot! Get back. Stay clear." Carol raced up and grabbed her away.

"Ned! I've got to check on Ned."

Carol went white. "Oh, dear God no. I heard shots. Did he...?"

Dot heard the stuttering to life of the motorcycle with relief so great she could hardly stand. The motor revved and in a cloud of dirt, she saw him regain the crest of the railroad grade.

The figure waved, and she could read volumes into it. *"I'm okay, but I'm not coming any closer."*

She waved back. *"I'm so glad you're okay, but do stay clear."*

Carol Samuelson said to Dot, "Come with me. We've got to get my husband."

In a voice weak, and raspy from exhaustion, Ruben said, "Yes. Go get Luke." His eyes never looked away from the pattern on the card.

...

Ned was throttled down to less than ten miles per hour. Getting shot at was unsettling. Trying to duck down and get off the top of the grade, he had sailed off the edge and landed hard. He was lucky he hadn't bent the wheel—or broken his neck.

I won't be talking to Dot any time soon.

It seemed hopeless. He did nothing wrong, but every time he turned around, something got worse. Life had been so much simpler before magic was unleashed in Ranch Exit.

The ground shivered up ahead.

What now? He slowed even more.

Mice, several waves of dozens were crossing the grade.

He stopped to let them pass. There was no way to continue without running them down.

"That's it!" he shouted to the sky. "No more weirdness, please!"

Nothing made sense anymore. He had driven this route so many times he could do it blindfolded, and now, he couldn't even get back to the store with being shot at and barricaded by rampaging mice.

"What's going to happen next?"

He sat back on the seat, just waiting. He put his hands in his pockets, and touched paper.

The charm. That's another thing. More weirdness. He pulled it out and considered tossing it to the winds.

But, maybe not. This thing was supposed to open your eyes, to make you see reality.

I need a little clarity right now. What could it hurt? Maybe someone will shoot at me, again?

He unfolded the paper. The pattern was crisp and clear. In his head, there was a pop, like something had been locked up and had now come free.

He looked at the valley below him.

Tiny movements of uncountable rodents created patterns that he could see.

Ah. So that's it. The entire mouse population of the valley had been triggered into a bound migration. Starting in lock step, the mice formed waves of living flesh moving back and forth across the valley. But every time they encountered obstacles, the orderliness of their progress was altered. The waves of mice themselves held information about everything they touched.

It's Carl. He needed to research the valley, and our descriptions weren't enough. He couldn't go himself, so he sent his mice.

The mice made a holograph or sonogram, not out of light or ultrasonic sound, but out of themselves. Back near the tunnel, there was a dead patch. *The mice go underground there—reporting back the information they carry.*

Below this surface motion, millions of years of geology crystallized in his head. The layers of rock, the branching drainage channels, the natural ones, as well as that area to the northeast that had been created and disguised to look natural, everything about the land was clear to him.

I can see it now. Part of the secret underground base had been tunneled out of the rock, but there were signs of other activity. He could see where the old railway had gone, where the explosions had disturbed the land. He could see subtle differences in dust deposits that told where ventilation shafts had been cut.

As plain as a map, he could see the boundaries of the underground complex. Amazingly, most of it was under his family's ranch. How many years had he walked across it and never sensed anything?

He looked back along the railroad grade, back toward where Carl's tunnel entrance was. He blinked.

Something dulled that place. *A spell. Some kind of protection over the entrance. Carl had opened it up for Dot and me, but I'd bet it's still hidden from Mort.*

He opened the throttle and raced back in the direction of the tunnel. The old bridge appeared, but without a thought and without a built-up ramp, he bounced through a dip and a stray boulder and sailed the gap easily, landing on a part of the trestle that he *knew* was solid.

Feeling a high from the jump, he turned around and raced back, sailing over the bridge using the pile of rocks he had stacked months ago, finding by instinct the path of stability that he had never been brave enough to test.

This is great! He could feel a rush of power unlike anything he had sensed before. The seemingly endless line of the railroad grade called to him and he raced towards the store at top speed.

Even the bike's engine talked to him. When he got home, he knew exactly what changes to make to the motor to enhance its power. The rumble of the road below him told him volumes about how to tune the suspension.

I could live like this forever. I could solve any problem, understand any mystery.

But off to the side, two hundred yards from the path, a cloud of darkness flashed past his sight. He acted instantly, turning completely around at high speed on a narrow path.

He sailed off the edge, touching down lightly with hardly a bounce. Swerving through the sage he approached the darkness and pulled to a stop next to the body.

...

Dot held the Samuelson's phone to her ear. "Hello, Aunt Elizabeth?"

"It's so good to hear from you Dorothy!"

The lady sounded nice, but Dot could think of nothing but her father, hands bound by his own choice, waiting in Jake Samuelson's Suburban for a trip to meet the hospital's ambulance half way. He waited while she made the call, holding the card in his fingers where he could look at it any time.

"Hmm. Dad said I should call you. Ah. He's had a relapse."

"Oh! Is anyone hurt?" She sounded worried.

"No. No, everyone is fine." It was a lie. Dad was hurting. Her stomach was tied up in knots. Who knows what Ned must be thinking?

"It's just that before he leaves for the hospital he wanted to confirm that you would be coming to pick me up."

"Of course, Dorothy. You will have a home with us for as long as you like. Should we leave now?"

"No. No. I still have the rest of the week. I am needed for the community fair we are holding this Saturday."

That sounded important enough. It was another lie, of course. No one needed her there. The Roundup had quite enough momentum on it own.

Aunt Elizabeth promised to be there for the event. "It will be so nice to have June's daughter in our family circle."

I am Ruben Comal's daughter, and I won't let you forget that.

She closed the call as politely as she could, and walked out to say goodbye.

With his hands bound, she had to crawl into the seat beside him and do the hug herself. Head to head, he whispered, "Take good care of yourself. I will die if anything happens to you."

She could only nod. She flicked the card with her finger. "Hold onto this. It's important."

"I know. I know!" It was a whisper more intense than a shout.

Carol asked, as Dot watched them drive off, "Would you like to stay here tonight, or with Ruth?"

Dot shook her head. "No. I'll be fine." She looked at the valley around her. "I have a lot of things to take care of."

...

Ned led George Filmore and Chris Lee to where the old Indian sha-man's body lay broken on the hillside.

"The police said to leave him where he is. They will be here in an hour or so." George looked at the sky, where it was very near sunset. "I'll need to be back at the store to lead them here. Will you need any help, Chris?"

The smaller man shook his head. "No, I just need to keep the animals away, although it looks like we're a little late on that score."

Ned had seen it before. The old man's shirt was torn, and large claw marks raked the skin.

Chris shook his head. "From the looks of him, my first guess would be that he had been hit by a car. Those animal marks didn't bleed much. They probably happened afterwards."

Ned looked around, but there was no sign that Mr. Wanekia had been dragged. There weren't even any footprints.

His rush of insight was fading fast under a horrible headache.

George was saying, "I'd like to keep speculation about what happened here as quiet as possible until after the Roundup is over. It's probably im-possible, but I'd hate to undercut the celebration."

Ned nodded. "Mr. Filmore, I don't feel well."

"Of course, Ned. Do you want me to drop you by the house."

"No. I can drive myself, but I'd said I would help you this evening...."

"No. Go on home and get some rest, Ned. We can handle this."

Ned started up his motorcycle and for the first time he could remem-ber, the noise hurt!

He put on speed, heading for Carl's tunnel.

I have to tell him. There's something wrong about Mr. Wanekia. He couldn't put it into any clearer thoughts than that.

Driving took all his concentration, and he almost passed the DOU-BLECROSSROAD sign. The trail down to the tunnel entrance did him in.

The front tire hit a boulder at a bad angle and he went sailing off. The motorcycle bounced riderless a couple of times before falling on its side in the sage. Ned landed hard in the other direction. It was the last insult. The headache was blown out of him with his breath and he faded into unconsciousness.

...

George should have known better. The police car with its flashing lights pulled up to the store. Everyone noticed. Practically the whole town was there in the midst of the tents, lit up for the night by strings of Christmas lights and utility lights and Coleman lanterns. In seconds, all of Ranch Exit was abuzz with the mystery of Old Man Wanekia's death.

"It has to have been the coyotes."

"No. I saw the body myself. Those were no coyote bites."

"It doesn't matter anyway. He died from a broken neck. He probably fainted and fell wrong. He was an old man."

"Sorry, it has to be a murder. Or at the worst manslaughter. He's always stumbling out onto the road. Someone ran him over, panicked and dumped the body out where no one would see it."

"But you didn't see those claw marks. It was like nothing I've ever seen!"

"Has anyone contacted the Paiute Tribal Council? He probably has relatives somewhere."

Mort watched the events, hearing the scratches of the policeman's pen taking notes. He left quickly, driving his Humvee up the road toward North Mesa in the dark.

Less than an hour later, all of the conversations paused for a moment, before starting up again.

The coroner's wagon had arrived and already departed. Officer Lakey was still collecting notes.

"Who did you say discovered the body?"

George frowned, trying to pull a memory that was no longer there. "Umm. Let's see, Chris and I went out to see the body. I don't remember which of us had spotted it first."

Chris shook his head. "No, I don't remember either. We've been all over this valley getting ready for Saturday."

The detective checked his notes, scratching out the one saying that Ned Kelso had discovered the body, because that line was clearly unintelligible gibberish.

Yolanda Kelso walked from one tent to the next. There was no reason she had come here. She wasn't going to bring her home canned foods up to the Roundup until Saturday. Still it was nice seeing all her neighbors making their preparations.

The Browns were heading home, and she waved. Something twisted in her stomach as she saw the children. She wished she had a child of her own ... no, that was an unprofitable thought. The sickness in the pit of her stomach tightened.

As Mr. Mort's Humvee passed on the way back to his ranch, she headed back to her pickup. The lights were going out, and even the policeman had headed back out of town. She took one last look at the store, but there was no one ... nothing there for her.

...

Ned woke up with a bad scrape on his arm and every muscle in his body sore.

It's night. Stars were bright overhead. He shivered from the cool breeze and a slight touch of dew.

Where am I? He pulled himself upright. A spike of pain in his arm made him look. Even in the starlight, the black streak was obviously blood.

He put his palm on his forehead and pushed. *Why can't I think clearly? Did I hit my head?*

An accident—it had to be an accident. He was riding on his bike...

He could smell the exhaust in his memory, and see the boulders. But why was he here? Where was here?

There was a trail. He followed it up the side of the railroad grade. Step by painful step he made it up to the top and then he was going downhill again. He followed the trail past some brush in the gully and then it petered out into a pile of rubble.

I don't want to climb this stuff in the dark. But what choice did he have. Carefully he crawled ahead, making sure in the starlight that he had a good handhold before moving.

After a few minutes, he was back at the brush at the bottom of the gully. *Did I turn around in the dark?*

An hour later, the truth gradually forced itself into his exhausted brain.

Every path I take leads me right back to where I start. He slumped down, resting against a boulder with fewer edges than the rest. *There is no other place to go to. I'm alone here.*

...

Dot groomed Pokey.

"Once I'm gone, you are going to live with Ruth Harris. I want you to be a good horse and don't try to fight with Buster. He's bigger than you and sometimes there's nothing you can do."

Her eyes blurred, and she put more muscle into the grooming brush.

Events were too big for her.

"Last night, I thought I had a solution. I can remember thinking I could do something this morning. But it must have all been a dream.

"Dad has gone crazy, and I don't know why. Aunt Elizabeth is coming to take me to Seattle and I'll likely never see ... home again.

"Everybody wants to help me, but no one knows what to do. I wish..."

She could feel something, just at the edge of her brain. She strained to remember, but it eluded her.

Pokey poked his nose at her pocket. She rubbed behind his ears.

"You're my best friend, you know that. I can talk to you about anything even when I can't talk to ... talk to ... anyone else." She frowned.

Who else should she be able to talk to? Her school friends? Latoya was older, and sometimes mean. None of the boys. Hallee was never interested in the same things. April and May were fun, but they were little kids.

Neighbors? Mrs. Kelso was nice, but not someone she shared confidences with. Ruth Harris, the Samuelsons, her teachers—they were all people she liked, but not one of them was close enough to cry with.

And not one of them could save her from losing her father, and her home.

Dawn was erasing the stars one by one. She remembered her strong desire to take a ride before she had to leave for school. It was important to her yesterday. But was there a reason for it today? Why not find Pokey another apple and give him more long overdue grooming?

Pokey loved the attention. She tolerated him nosing into her pocket. There was nothing there, but let him have the fun.

The horse thought he had something and almost pushed her over as he struggled with her wide pocket.

Then with a triumphal snort he pulled a piece of paper out of her pocket and tossed his head.

"Hey, give me that, Pokey! What do you have there?"

He held it out of reach, making her grab for it. She laughed and grabbed at his halter.

"No you don't. Paper isn't for horses."

Big flat teeth grinned at her, holding the folded paper by the corner. Dot couldn't remember what it was, but it wouldn't last long if Pokey had his way.

She grabbed a handful of grain from the barrel and held it near his head in her open palm. His ears swiveled and his head turned to get a better look.

Grain was better than paper any day. He dropped his prize and messily took his reward from her hand.

Dot wiped her palm on her overalls and grabbed up the paper. It had teeth marks, but not too much slobber.

What is this? She unfolded the sheet and looked at the pattern by the light of her lantern.

There was a release in her head, just slightly, as if something had tried to click but hadn't quite made it.

But a thread of memory came rushing back.

Ned! How in the world could I have forgotten you?

Imaginary Friends

Am I the only person in the world? Ned shifted his seat to keep the sun out of his face.

The evidence of his eyes was clear. He was the only person in a tiny world no more than a thousand paces in any direction. He had no memory of anyone either.

It didn't feel right.

"Why can I talk if there is no one to talk to?"

...

Dot pulled Pokey to a halt. From her vantage point on the railroad grade, she could see the Kelso ranch. One part of her brain told her that only Albert and Yolanda Kelso lived there, a childless couple. Another part of her knew Ned existed.

The valley was still sleepy, not ready to tackle the morning. *Much better to scout on horseback. The pickup would wake everybody up.*

Besides, this might be the last chance she got to ride Pokey.

"Let's go, boy."

Pokey turned his head and started heading farther down the grade.

Dot was ready to say "No" and pull the reins, but she held off. Why was Pokey going that way? Wouldn't Ned be at the Kelso's house?

But the horse headed confidently northward.

"Okay, boy, I don't know what I'm doing, but if you do, let's go."

...

"I thought we had him safely secured." Will Blake shook his head. The nurse was six-eight and over three hundred and fifty pounds. He had a reputation for gently putting any of his patients to bed, no matter how hard they struggled. His face was lined with distress. He tried to make sense of it for the doctor.

"I read the chart. I knew his history of rages. I made sure the straps were secure."

He looked up, "But somehow, he got one hand free. He choked himself to death with one hand. How can anyone do that?"

Dr. McCormick shook his head. "No matter how it happened, there will be an investigation. Have we contacted the family yet?"

Dr. Suhn looked at the folder. "There appears to be a problem. No phone number is listed, just a cryptic entry for the home address—'Ranch Exit'."

"Let me see that." The doctors looked at the form.

McCormick picked up the phone. "Sandra, could you check yesterday's admissions? Look for someone from 'Ranch Exit'."

He paused a moment, listening. "Okay read the symptoms."

He looked at Suhn. "That's what I thought. We have a second subject from 'Ranch Exit'. He also has violent rages. He also has no previous history of problems. It's an identical case, from the same place.

"Blake, I want you to personally take care of ... Ruben Comal. Have him scrubbed down. Remove all personal effects and treat them as hazardous materials. Get full blood screening as soon as possible. If this is an infection or environmental poisoning, we have to know immediately.

"I don't believe in coincidences. We have lost Aaron Locke, but there will be no excuse, no excuse at all if we lose Ruben Comal!"

...

Ned was hungry, and he didn't recognize anything that was edible among the hardy scrub vegetation and the insects that lived among them.

I'll need food and water, and shelter from the sun when it gets higher. Otherwise this little world is going to be uninhabitable.

He steeled himself to go searching again for a way out. *This is not how it is supposed to be!*

...

The mice woke Carl. Thousands of tiny sharp mice toes crawled over him in waves. The patterns of sensation wrote a map of the world above into the far reaches of his brain.

It was a poor excuse for seeing the world with his own eyes, but he needed some way to see what was going on with more precision than the tales of one untrained boy. The mice didn't know what they were seeing either, but they reacted in large numbers, and that was something he could understand.

But something very strange had happened while he was in his receptor trance. The world had changed half-way into the process. He was getting two streams of information—one from a large valley in an even larger world, the other from a small world so reduced as to be unbelievable.

And yet it was the small world that his conscious brain told him was the real one.

If he weren't Carl Stellman, he would be seriously confused.

Someone has warded me off. Someone outside of my current gestalt. Some-one I won't be able to reach.

If an area is warded, no one outside the wards exists for the people inside, and vise versa.

I'll have to modify my gestalt. Changing his world-view was something he had done many times before. He had spent his life learning how. The seeing charm was just the simplest of the ways he had discovered.

Another dozen mice appeared, their pace suggestive of their path through the larger world. Some wards were cross-species, the better ones. This one obviously had a flaw.

Carl picked up one of the wild mice, already confused and upset at what it was doing here in this underground place so far from its nest in the fields. His hands, strong and rough from having served double duty as feet for so many decades, were yet gentle enough to soothe the tiny beast.

In a tiny, high-pitched voice, Carl began to talk to it.

...

Dot patted Pokey's neck. The horse was confused about where he was supposed to go and had stopped high on the railroad grade where the route markers were thickest.

"It's okay, Pokey. I don't know what I'm doing either. Ned is somewhere, I know it, but I have no idea where."

She looked at the sun. School would just have to wait! Dad was gone to the mental hospital. Aunt Elizabeth was on her way to take her away from her home.

And Ned was some kind of ghost she remembered, but wasn't really supposed to exist.

Maybe they will drag me off in the ambulance too. Am I going to start shooting at people next?

She leaned over Pokey's neck and hugged him. "You don't think I'm crazy do you?"

Should I go on? Something in her said 'no'. This place where the markers were thickest was the right place to be.

Pokey moved a step towards the edge of the grade, but then stepped back.

Dot looked up. *Did I hear a motorcycle?*

It was strange, not a real sound at all. *Some people hear voices in their heads. I hear motorcycles. Ned's motorcycle.*

But it wasn't real. She knew that. Everyone imagines they hear things, every now and then. This was just an imaginary sound.

Except, it kept on, fading and getting louder, just like when Ned played with his engine.

Dot fought down the impulse to call out. *It's just in my head. I can't start talking to imaginary sounds, or I really will be crazy.*

But it was Ned's motorcycle. With Ned's hand on the throttle. She was sure of it.

She clamped her teeth together, fighting the urge.

The sound stopped.

"Ned! Ned, can you hear me! Where are you?"

The morning breeze, the distant call of a hawk, her own beating heart— these were the only sounds she could hear.

So, it was my imagination after all. I am going crazy.

...

Ned killed the engine reluctantly. The motorcycle felt like a part of him, and he had been overjoyed to see it among the rocks. It was bent and scraped, but nothing major.

The problem was that in the whole world, there was no place to go.

A bird called in the distance, for an instant it sounded farther away than the edge of the world, but that was just his imagination.

...

Carl raced as fast as his hands could push towards the tunnel entrance. The wards still held his gestalt under restrictions, but the sound of that motorcycle was unmistakable. *Ned is here.* The fact that he could name him, see him in his memory, meant that Ned had to be within the bounds of the wards too.

He reached the opening and tugged at the obscuring branches. Sunlight was out there—as deadly to his pale skin as ever.

"Ned! Ned, can you hear me? This is Carl, at the tunnel."

...

Dot heard Ned in her imagination.

"Carl? Wait a minute. I remember now. I'll be right there."

What did that mean? She frowned. Was it a memory? And who was Carl?

"Oh Ned, I wish I could talk to you. Things are so mixed up right now."

"What do you mean? I can hear your voice."

"Ned! Can you hear me?"

"No, just some birdcall in the distance."

...

Ned opened the tunnel entrance. Carl was just a dim image in the shadows.

"Something is wrong with me Carl. I can't remember anything. I couldn't even remember you until I heard your voice."

There was a pause. "Ned. My mind is affected too. An enemy has done this, but if we can work together, we might be able to clear it."

"Sure. I'm ready to do anything. This place is spooky."

"Okay, first of all. We are not alone. Dot is nearby, and she can hear your voice."

"Dot?" He strained at an almost memory. "I can't ... I can't remember who Dot is."

"Don't worry about that now. She is our only hope, but unless you can relay what I say to her, we are lost. Can you do that?"

Ned shrugged. "Sure."

"Okay, repeat what I am about to say."

...

Dot's stomach twisted as she heard, *"I can't remember who Dot is."* But it could just be her imagination, finding new ways to torture her. Then his voice started again.

"Dot Comal. Can you hear Ned's voice?"

She shouted, "Yes, yes I can hear you, Ned!"

"There are two of us here, Carl and me. Can you hear Carl's voice?"

She struggled to listen, but there was no other sound.

"No. I can hear you, but it's like a voice in my head, not real."

"Well, I can't really hear you at all, unless you are that noisy bird. Carl can hear you, and he tells me. It's a bit crazy."

Hearing Ned's voice, the old familiar way he talked, comforted her.

"Okay. I understand. This Carl can hear me. You can hear Carl and I can hear you. What do we do?"

"Carl is the expert on these things. He asks what you can see from where you stand."

"Well, I'm not standing, I'm on horseback, riding Pokey, but in any case, I am on top of the railroad grade, where all the markers are. All I can see is the mesa off to the north and the Kelso ranch off to the southeast."

"Weird. I have a ranch? And what is horseback? Is 'horse' an animal? Oh... Carl just told me not to get distracted. No, you should repeat what she says word for word. I need to hear it. Okay. I'll keep my comments to myself.

"Okay, Carl says to describe the markers."

It was confusing, with Ned's imaginary voice talking to an imaginary Carl as well as to her.

"Okay." She took a hard look at the markers. She had just accepted them before. They felt familiar, natural, like the sagebrush.

"There are about a dozen of them, evenly spaced along the north side of the railroad grade, right in front of me. The one in the center is about eight feet high and marked with a bunch of colored lines. The others are shorter. Some about six feet and some four. They all have the lines, but each pole has a different pattern. About twenty feet back was a roadsign that said DOUBLECROSSROAD."

"Look at where the poles are stuck in the ground. Are there signs that they have been freshly planted?"

Dot frowned. "Fresh? Haven't they always been here?" But she looked, looked hard.

She blinked. "You know, these poles are brand new. Shiny, not weathered. The dirt around them has been freshly disturbed. I never noticed that."

"Carl says we may be in luck. Can you knock the poles down? If you can, toss half of them off one side of the grade and the other half off the other side."

Dot nodded to the invisible voice. "I'll try."

She dismounted and walked up to the nearest one. Hesitantly, she grabbed the pole and pulled. It was firmly buried. She put her weight into it, pushing and pulling as hard as she could.

"It's shifting." It took several minutes, but her exertions were widening the hole. Finally, she gripped firmly and pulled. Inch by inch, it lifted. After shifting her grip a couple of times, it fell over. She dragged it to the edge and pushed it over.

"One of them is done."

"Good. Carl says he can tell a difference. I'm not sure I can. How long will it take to get the rest of them?"

She looked at the long line of poles. It was just her imagination, she was sure, but the markings on them looked like evil eyes daring her to move them.

"I don't know. That one was hard and took a lot out of me."

"Carl says to concentrate on the biggest one."

Dot looked at the monster. The pole was twice as thick as the first one. *I can't even lift that on a good day. I'm not that strong. I'll need help.*

Pokey whinnied. She looked him in the eye. "Of course."

"What did you say?"

"Hang on. I'm working."

She mounted the horse and gently urged him to put his shoulder against the central pole. "Push. Come on Pokey. This is just another fencepost. You hate them. Come on, push."

The horse strained against the pole, urged on by her gentle hand.

"She's doing it. I can sense it." A strange voice sounded in her head. She ignored it, whispering encouragement to Pokey.

With a crack, the pole fractured, and the horse powered it over.

"Hey. Dot! I can see you." Ned's voice—and no longer imaginary! She looked off the edge.

Ned waved at her.

Below the Surface

They all retreated underground where it was cool. It had taken Dot, Pokey and Ned another thirty minutes to bring down all the poles, and by that time they were sweaty. Pokey seemed content to wait in the shade of the rocks.

"So," asked Dot, "I could hear Ned because the seeing charm had just enough juice to let me. Ned could hear you because you were both inside the wards. But you could hear me—because why?"

Carl smiled, "Because I am experienced with these things, and I had already started absorbing the wider gestalt from the mice."

Ned shook his head, "Give it up, Dot. It's just magic. Leave it at that."

She lowered her head and shook it. "No. Magic is just an excuse for people too lazy to understand things. My life is being ripped away from me and I am not too lazy to understand why!"

Carl sighed. "Dot, I would love to explain these things to you, but you don't even know the words. It would take years, and we don't have the time. We have an enemy out there who will destroy this valley, and maybe the whole world, unless he is stopped."

Dot felt like Pokey, pushing hard. She had to make them understand. "My dad is the highest priority. He's already being destroyed, right this minute! I can't worry about some vague threat to the world when my father is being driven out of his mind!"

Carl looked at Dot, and then at Ned. "Okay. I'll try to explain, but you don't have the words. I'll make a crude analogy, and it's the best I have time for.

"Imagine the real world is a bucket full of rocks. The rocks are real things, but the way you look at the world depends on how the rocks are stacked, one on each other. Shake up the rocks and science is real, and you treat diseases with antibiotics. Shake them again and the only real way to fight disease is with prayers. Shake them again and the world is round. Again and it is flat.

"Each pattern of rocks is a gestalt. The number of possible gestalts is nearly unlimited. Putting up those wards changed the gestalt and people no longer could even think about what was on the other side."

Dot shook her head. "Maybe I understand that, but I forgot that Ned existed even before I saw the wards. How can that happen?"

Carl fought with impatience. He relished having Dot and Ned as friends, but he was used to no other minds but mice. And mice never argued.

"Okay. Think of the bucket of rocks as half full of water. You have a bucket. Ned has a bucket. Everyone in the world has a bucket.

"And the rocks under the water line are all the same for everyone. You look at the world a little differently than Ned because of your life experiences, but below the water line, that part of the gestalt is the same.

"If I took a stick and stirred the rocks below the water, it would change the world for everyone. The range of effect for things like these wards is wide. This isn't simple hypnosis we are talking about—not some clouding men's minds with telepathy. It is changing the reality of the whole world."

Ned nodded. "I understand. Dot, it's like a background file transfer on the Internet, downloading telepathically to everyone, even though you don't see it happening while you are browsing or viewing you email or whatever. Flip a switch and all the Republicans become Democrats and vise versa."

Carl shook his hand, pained by the analogy, "Something like that. I can't say. One name for the rocks below the water line is the 'collective unconscious', and my research proved that something very like telepathy is constantly working to keep everyone the same. Key patterns of lines or shapes or sounds, even certain smells can change your individual gestalt. Certain very dangerous ones can change the gestalt below the water line, for everyone.

"The man you know as Mort is using techniques we discovered back when the research was a government project seeking weapons. I saw the pattern he used on the ward you knocked down. It proves to me he is using the research notebooks as a cookbook. They are exactly the same as the ones I invented."

Ned asked, "These were weapons?"

Carl nodded. "The military was enthusiastic about the wards, at first. They could imagine surrounding militaristic Germany with wards to keep it isolated. In reality, such grand plans would fail. The bigger the area enclosed, the harder it is to keep it stable.

"You, Ned, you knew there was something wrong when the world was so small, but without Dot's link to you and the effects of the seeing charm, no one would notice if a few acres of desert vanished. Warding off a large area could be done, but it would take much more effort than a few marked poles.

"So can you understand why Mort is such a danger? He knows where this base is located. He suspects that there are more powerful 'spells' down here, and he is ruthless about what means he uses to posses them."

Ned nodded. "He has already killed one man."

Dot asked, "Who?"

"Old Man Wanekia."

...

They each had their task. Carl thought he had enough information about the work Ruben had been doing for Mort to construct a cure for him, now that enough of the mice had returned.

"But it will take time, kids. At least several hours. Ned, you say those digital pictures are instant—that they take no development time? Can you get me images of the iconoplaks that Mort has put up? And anything else odd that he has built.

"Dot can you find out what you can about the man? Rumors, speculation, anything—I need to have some idea of what he is up to."

...

It was nearly ten AM by the time Dot mounted Pokey and Ned pulled up beside her on his motorcycle.

"People are still suspicious of me. We'd better not meet up at school. I'm still not supposed to talk to you until I get your dad's permission."

He looked down at the ground. "I had to promise Dad that I would avoid you. I knew it would be impossible."

She nodded. "Do you have your truth badge?"

He patted his shirt pocket. "Yes, but I'm not going to use it until I have to, and never with my father. I won't lie to him. It scares me that I could lie to people, flash this little piece of paper, and they would always believe me."

Dot agreed. "It scares me too. Mr. Wanekia told me not to trust either of the wizards. It looks like both of them are dangerous people. I believed Mort. I now believe Carl, but how can I trust what I believe?"

Ned had no doubts. "Yes, but you have to judge people by their actions, not by what they say or by their power. Carl has done nothing but try to help us. Even if we give him the benefit of the doubt on Wanekia and your father, Mort has never helped people. Think back for the last couple of years. He has hired people to work for him, but he uses them hard. Say 'philanthropist' and no one will respond with 'Mort'."

"Maybe." Dot remembered what Wanekia said to her. She was a healer, and that's what her priorities had to be. *I'll work with Carl, and be grateful for any help he gives my dad, but trusting him has to wait.*

...

"Blake, how is Mr. Comal?"

The large man shook his head. "It's been downhill all the way. He was almost normal when he arrived, calm but possessive of a get-well card from his daughter. I had to struggle to get it from him, and he was frantic to get it back.

"By the time we had him scrubbed down and settled in, the rages started coming, sometimes directed against me, sometimes against other people he knew. It's scary how his rages come on so similar to Locke's. I've got him under constant observation."

Dr. McCormick nodded and looked back over the blood work reports. There were plenty of signs Comal was under stress, but nothing that he could identify as a precursor.

What was causing the rages?

...

Ned drove home to clean up. Sleeping outside on the rocks had left his clothes grungier than usual.

His father knocked on the bathroom door.

"Come on in." Ned steeled himself. The truth badge was still in his shirt, lying on the floor.

Albert Kelso leaned his crutches against the door sill and took a look at his son. Ned was washing a long, blood-encrusted scrape on his arm.

"Here, I can help with that." Holding onto the sink for support with one hand, he took the washrag and started working on the parts Ned had missed.

"Dad, before you even ask, I had a little accident, and it was Dot who rescued me. I didn't seek her out, but she is my friend, and I'm not going to run away from my friends."

His father said nothing, picking up a towel to dry off the arm.

"Dad, Dot is in trouble—but not the kind of trouble everyone seems to be worrying about! Her dad is gone. She is going to be hauled away from her home. She needs help, and I am going to be there for her.

"I'm sorry I made that promise to you, and I'm taking it back."

Albert reached for the iodine and began painting the scrape. "I know she has troubles, Ned. I just don't know what you can do about them. Are you sure that you won't just be making it harder for her? It's not a good situation, no matter how you look at it."

Ned waited until he could talk without gritting his teeth from the sting.

"Dad. I *can* make it better. You will just have to trust me on this."

...

George Filmore looked up as Dot drove her pickup to the gas trucks.

"Hey, Mr. Filmore, can I get a fill up?"

"Hello, Dot. Aren't you supposed to be in school?"

"Probably, but in case you haven't heard, my aunt is coming to pick me up the day after tomorrow. I've got a lot of packing and stuff to do. I'll get to school as soon as I can."

He reached for the filler hose. "Okay. You aren't going to run away from us are you?"

"Mr. Filmore, believe me, the last thing I want to do is to leave Ranch Exit."

...

The policeman was waiting for him when Ned arrived at the store a few minutes after Dot had gone on to school.

"Hello, son. I would like to ask you a few questions."

Ned looked at George Filmore who nodded. He had a solemn look on his face though.

"Ah, sure. What can I help you with?"

The policeman looked at his notes. "I was here yesterday about Mr. Wanekia and it seems I neglected to talk to you. Mr. Filmore tells me that you are the person who first noticed his body. Tell me about it."

Ned tried. He could remember the events, but he couldn't really remember what he was thinking at the time.

"I was on the railroad grade. I ride my motorcycle there. It's a shortcut. I cut over to where the body was..."

"What made you go that way? Could you see it?"

"Ah, no. I just knew something was wrong over that way and went to see what it was." Ned knew it sounded lame, even though it was the truth.

The policeman frowned and looked at his notes again. Ned tried to remember whether he had put the truth badge in his fresh shirt. Did he leave it on the floor?

"Is everyone in Ranch Exit psychic?" Lakey checked his notes again. "You didn't see something, or smell the body, or something like that?"

"Not that I can remember."

The policeman shook his head. "I've driven past this place for years, and never even realized there was a town over here. And now within the space of a couple of days, I have people going insane and two deaths to explain, all from Ranch Exit."

"Two deaths?" Ned asked.

The policeman looked over at George Filmore. George shrugged, "Might as well tell him. The story will be all over the valley within another ten minutes anyway."

"Well. You know about Aaron Locke?"

Ned nodded.

"I received word that he has committed suicide overnight. The hospital is worried that the two cases they have received from Ranch Exit might be related, considering they have the same symptoms.

"I came out here again just to check. Can you think of anything that might relate these events?"

Ned knew, of course. Ruben Comal and Aaron Locke both worked for Mort. Everyone knew that.

But he couldn't open his mouth to say so.

The policeman asked George, "How about you? Do you know of anything that might connect them?"

George frowned, as if thinking, and then shook his head.

Ned opened his mouth. *Mort. Say 'Mort'.* He ended up yawning. No word came out. Somehow that information was locked up.

...

Latoya raised her eyebrows. "I was wondering if you were going to show up. Everyone was guessing where you and Ned were this morning."

Dot was too tired to rise to the bait. "Yesterday was a very long day. I don't know where Ned is. Fill me in. What has happened while I was gone?"

School was over, as far as grades were concerned. Ms. Carson had caved under the flood of requests from parents to let their children assist with fair preparations. This was a ranching community. Work requests were always granted. She announced no more tests, and set the remaining older ones to baby-sit the little ones.

Mrs. Brown was mad at Mrs. Cooper for making Prickly Pear Butter to sell. Mrs. Brown claimed Old Aunt Judith gave her the recipe ten years before she gave it to Mrs. Cooper.

Dell Bly broke his arm falling off the booth he was building for his uncle.

Bill Cartulio ran over and interrupted Latoya's rumor report.

"Hey Dot. Is it true your dad shot Ned?" He was wide-eyed.

She blinked. "Ah, no, I don't think so."

"Harry Beal claims he saw Ned go home with an arm all bloody. He says your dad caught you and Ned in bed and chased him away and shot him as he ran."

Dot's hand stung from the slap she laid on Bill's face. She had exploded before she even thought to react.

She fought her pounding heart. "You tell Harry he'd better watch his back for telling lies about me! I don't care if people think I'm kissing Ned. I like Ned. But my dad has a temper. And when he gets back from the hospital and finds out who's been lying about me, he just might get angry!"

Bill's had his hand on his cheek, where she struck him. He nodded and left, in a hurry.

Latoya watched it all with fascination. "I was going to get to that rumor too, but I'm glad I waited."

Dot was still seething. She could feel her eyes watering and turned her head. Rage screamed to get out. *Listen to my heartbeat.*

This temper had better be something I inherited normally. If it's a side effect of Carl's spells, I'm doomed.

She gripped Latoya's hand. "I need to walk. Will you stay with me? I need a little moral support."

"Okay, but we need to drag Duncan along. He's in my charge."

Dot's racing heart settled quickly. Wanekia had taught her the trick, and she used it.

Out on the yard, she asked, "What do you know about Mr. Mort? He paid Dad's medical expenses, and I'm thinking about making some kind of thank-you award to give him at the Roundup. What do people know about him?"

...

Ned loaded the boxes into the pickup. Larry rushed to help him. "Can I come along?"

Ned shook his head. "Against George's rules. It's an insurance thing. I'll be back from the delivery pretty soon." He was lying on both counts. He needed to be alone to take some pictures, and it would probably take longer than even George would be happy with.

Larry whispered, "Is it true you got shot? My mother won't say what happened, but Harry said he saw you bleeding." He mentioned the other details of the story as well.

Ned grabbed Larry's shirt under his chin. "I don't have so many friends that I can afford to lose them, but I won't put up with dirty lies about Dot! You can go tell Harry he is on my list!"

Larry held up his hands. "Calm down. It was just a story."

Ned gripped Larry's shirt even tighter. "'Just stories' and sick imaginations have made my life a nightmare for days now. For your information, Dot's my best friend in all the world, but I haven't even kissed her, not once! But that won't stop me from bloodying up a couple of foul mouths."

Larry saw something in Ned's eyes, and he realized this was different from all the other times his buddy and he had traded blows.

"Ned, cool it. I apologize. I didn't mean it."

His friend released his shirt and turned back to the pickup. "Just keep Harry out of my sight."

Ned drove off, breathing heavily, trying to cool down.

Shake it off. I've got pictures to take.

...

Her questions turned up much more on Mort than she had imagined. Mrs. Baker knew about him from before he had come to Ranch Exit. He had been a real billionaire, one of those people talked about in the financial newspapers. His corporation had collapsed shortly before he had bought his ranch, but his name had never been associated with the scandal. He had other companies, land holdings in California and New York. Mort was never slow to spend money, as her encounter over the eagle picture proved.

Still, of all the people she questioned, none mentioned philanthropy as a characteristic. His local spending had helped the people in the valley, but not as much as people had hoped. Other stories of millionaire ranchers usually had them operating the place as a business, taking the ranching losses against taxes. But not Mort. His ranch was large enough, about a half-million acres of what used to be Bureau of Land Management holdings, but he treated it all as a big back yard for his ranch house. If he had attempted ranching, he could have hired half the population of Ranch Exit to keep it running.

To a couple of the men Dot chatted with, it was still a sensitive topic. None of the locals had been hired to work on the house. And the promise of ranching prosperity, with it continually delayed, had kept some families from putting more effort into their own projects. They were always looking over to Mort's ranch in the hopes he would finally start hiring.

Ms. Carson was the most glowing in her praise of the man, and she was instantly in favor of awarding the man a plaque.

"Has he done anything for the Roundup?"

"Oh yes, haven't you heard. He is handling the advertising. He has promised radio spots, and is hiring a crew from Green River to put up our signs all along the highway."

Dot was intrigued.

That's strange. The last time I talked to him, he was against the whole idea of the Roundup.

Duncan Bly ran up to Dot, and tugged on her sleeve.

"Yes?"

He looked cautious eyes at the teacher and tugged again at Dot.

"Sorry, it looks like I'm needed, Ms. Carson. We'll talk some more later."

...

Duncan pulled her toward the fence line. Latoya noticed and started heading her way.

Latoya watched as Dot and Duncan knelt down to peer at something on the ground.

Dot looked up, "Good, I need to go now. Duncan, stay with Latoya."

"What...?" But Dot was jogging towards the parking lot.

Latoya looked down at Duncan. "What was that all about?"

He pointed to the ground near the fence. She saw a blur of brown.

"The critter told her she had to go meet the dwarf."

"Oh." Latoya watched Dot drive off, and Duncan go back to the swings. *Tomorrow. Tomorrow, I have to ask what this is all about.*

Pocket Magic

Ned made his delivery, and took two dozen pictures on the digital camera, snapping signs, the giant apple relic, Mort's property with the landing strip and all the poles he had near his entrance gate. He knew of dozens of other signs, but it would take all day to visit them all.

He returned to the store, did a couple of smaller tasks for George, and then slipped over to the school.

The place was deserted, but Mrs. Baker's computer and printer were still there. Cautiously, he unloaded the pictures from the camera and used her photo software to print out the images, four to a sheet.

I don't really know what Carl wants. I hope this will do.

...

Dot paused before mounting Pokey.

Something is wrong. She tried to put a finger on it. It was something inside her. *What I'm doing isn't quite right.*

But what was it?

I'm not doing my part. Her priority was getting her dad healed. That was as it should be.

But she was making demands on Carl. As strange as the circumstances were, as dire as her need was, she wasn't raised to be dependent on anyone.

Carl was working hard to help her rescue her father, and all she had ever done for him was to give him a pie that almost killed him.

I know what to do. She turned back towards the house.

...

George called out, "Delivery!"

Ned stashed the pictures in his motorcycle's saddlebags and trotted over to the store.

George handed him a small sack. "For Mrs. Cooper. Jar labels."

Ned was grateful. He could take the bike and drop off the pictures.

The Cooper ranch was one of the oldest in the valley, well past the Cartulio's place. Unfortunately, it would be a wide loop to visit there and Carl's tunnel as well. It was nowhere near the railroad grade.

The road went up and down, and curved back and forth through the easiest notches in the hills. Speed hadn't been an issue when the road had been cut for horse-drawn wagons.

When the ranch house came into view, he saw Hallee drop her gardening tools and run into the house. *She's taking the day off from school, too, I see.*

Mrs. Cooper was there at the door when he walked up on the old boarded porch, in the shade.

"Howdy, Miz Cooper. Here are your labels."

"Thank you Ned." She opened the screen door and took the package.

He knew in an instant that something was wrong. The lady's face was lined and worried.

"Are you selling your canning at the Roundup?" Not that he cared. His mother did that kind of stuff and it had lost its fascination years ago.

"Yes. There is still a lot of work to do." She smiled politely, and closed the door. Now wasn't the time to talk.

Ned nodded and turned to go.

Through the front window, a mirror over the fireplace caught the reflection of Hallee hiding behind the door. In one fraction of a second, he saw her face, and her black eye.

He rode out slowly, looking for Greg Cooper's old blue Ford, but it was nowhere in sight.

Another one. I heard he had started working for Mort, but I didn't know the rages started so quickly. I've got to get to Carl's immediately.

Luckily, Ned knew every road, trail and footpath in the valley.

I'll cut across the next hill, and go through the fenceline at the gap Feller-man has never gotten around to fixing.

Ned leaned into the ride. The motorcycle had springs, and he used them. The road turned into two ruts, and then faded away altogether. He followed the fenceline, the poles whipping by too fast to count. A treeline marked an old spring and its watercourse.

Over the hill, the land turned into a broad meadow.

He let off the throttle.

Every time he had passed this way before, there had been a shallow bowl over a mile across, filled with grass that was sculpted into drifting waves by the breeze.

Now it looked like a giant clock-maker's blueprint. Circles of all sizes were carved into the grass, stacked and overlapped. It was an elaborate pattern impossible to completely view from ground level.

Dot mentioned her dad worked on a crop circle. Is this what he was talk-ing about? Or had Greg Cooper been hard at work. *Aaron Locke worked on the first one, too.*

Ned turned uphill and tried to find the best overlook.

He snapped photos, ten or more in an effort to encompass the intricate panorama. *There's no time to go back to the school to print these.*

He cut to the north, hesitant to drive across the pattern. Whether it was his imagination or the result of having *seen* the valley with the charm, he could sense the power here.

I'm not getting any closer.

...

"Mr. Stellman? Did you call for me?"

Dot tugged at the folded wheelchair, and finally managed to pull it through the opening.

"Yes, Dot." The voice was close enough to startle her.

She stood up straight when the ceiling allowed. "I brought you something." The wheelchair widened out to full size under her pull, and she locked it open.

"I saw your skateboard thing, and I wondered if you would like to try this."

...

Carl was in awe of the gift, but he refused to open the second package— some used clothes of her father's.

"Not until I have cleaned myself up. Washing clothes down here takes days—my water reserves are limited to what the spring can produce.

"Dot, I can't even tell you how much this means to me."

He climbed into the chair and practiced moving it around for a couple of minutes.

"But I don't have the time right now. From what my mice have told me, Mort has been very busy. If what I suspect is true, you need to get the counter spell to your father as quickly as possible."

"So you were able to make something better than the get-well card?"

Carl nodded. "The pattern on the card was never a cure." He wheeled over to the table and picked up a rock about half the size of a hen's egg.

"Hmm. I'm going to need a full sized table again."

Dot accepted it in both hands. "Is it dangerous to anyone else?"

"It shouldn't be, but be careful of handling it too much. There are scratches on the rock surface that you don't want to erase."

She nodded. "How does it work?"

Carl expected that question from her. "Do you still have clocks that wind up with a key?" She nodded.

"Then you know the spring gets tighter and tighter. The gestalt your father has absorbed generates a stress in his mind that builds up tighter and tighter just like the spring. When something triggers it, a sight, an event, a thought—the stress powers the rage, and once started, the rage feeds on itself.

"The spiral pattern on the card just lets the tension release harmlessly, like a gear with a broken tooth. It's only temporary because the mind can heal that kind of trick—heal the broken gear.

"This rock, as it is fingered, begins to erase the rage-building part of the gestalt itself. As he rubs out the scratches, the damage inside him is smoothed out as well. It will stop building the stress that triggers the rage.

"Once he gets home, I can locate the remnants of the pattern and wipe it out completely. But it is up to you to get this to him and get him back home."

...

"Shul! Shul, pecare?" The voice echoed down the tunnel.

Dot turned, "What's that?"

"It's Ned. Didn't you hear his motorcycle?"

"No. I didn't."

Ned? That doesn't sound like his voice.

He eased into the room from the tunnel entrance and held out the printouts.

"Shul, vo tene com alese. Ec non folne 'jaca."

Carl nodded. "That will be very helpful."

Dot watched the strange guy talking away with Carl.

"That's not Ned! And what's he saying? He's speaking gibberish."

The two men looked at her strangely.

"Jenu? Grenu?" The Ned person asked.

Carl held up his hand. "Dot. You understand me, right?"

"Yes, but who is this, and what is he saying?" Horror was building in her stomach.

Carl turned to the stranger, "How about you?"

"Ec jene." He shrugged.

Carl looked from one to the other. "Okay, hold on a minute." He wheeled out of the room.

Dot watched the unknown person suspiciously.

If it really is Ned, then I'm going crazy.

Carl was back quickly with two little metal pieces. "Here, catch." He tossed one to Dot and the other to ... Ned.

"What's this supposed to do?" asked Ned.

"Ned! It is you!"

He shrugged, "Always has been."

Carl said, "These are resonance enhancers. Stick them in your pockets for now."

Dot put her hand in her pocket, reluctant to release the thing shaped like an extra thick quarter.

"Carl, am I going crazy?"

"No. I'm afraid it's Ned who has shifted."

Ned looked upward and breathed in, a solemn look on his face. "I was afraid of that. I've been angry and upset all day long. I almost punched Larry's teeth out.

"And on the way here, I passed close to a huge crop-circle thing. I could feel it doing things."

Dot nodded. "I've been angry too. I've been biting my tongue to keep from saying ugly things to people."

Carl picked up the photos that Ned had set on the table. He looked at them all, frowning at the images.

"Probably the whole valley is feeling it." He looked at Dot. "We will have to build a counter spell for the whole population. The rage is low key, but it will still have to be inverted.

"Ned, did you get a picture of this 'crop-circle' you mentioned?"

"Yes, but on the way here. I haven't had a chance to print it out yet."

Dot sighed, "Ned, give me the camera."

He handed it over. She pressed a few buttons and the back of the camera lit up with the last pictures taken.

"Here, press this to get a close up view."

Carl hesitantly worked the controls.

"This is bad." He looked up at Dot. "Is this the thing your father was working on before he started exhibiting the rages?"

"Yes. He was working with Aaron Locke."

Ned added, "And Locke is dead. I heard from the policeman. He committed suicide."

Dot put her hand over her mouth.

Carl shook his head. "We're too late for him then. But we still have time to get the counter spell to your father, Dot."

Ned said, "You had better make another one. Greg Cooper has been doing the same work for Mort. He has the blue uniform, and Hallee Cooper, his niece, is now wearing a black eye."

...

"Are you sure you can do it alone?"

Dot wasn't sure, but she nodded. "You've got to get Greg Cooper healed, and find a way to stop Mort. Carl can't go above ground. You're needed here."

Carl nodded, "And Ned can't leave here until we remove this latest change." He looked at Ned. "As far as the rest of the valley is concerned, you would be a stranger talking a foreign language."

"How long will that take?"

"Two or three hours, at best."

Dot took a deep breath. "That settles it. I can't wait, not if Dad's disturbance is turning suicidal."

Ned frowned. "I understand, but Dot, any policeman will know at a glance that you are too young to have a driver's license."

Carl waved that aside. "I can make her look older."

Dot didn't even ask how. "Good, I'll need that."

She shivered. Driving a few miles on a dirt road to school with no other traffic was one thing. Driving hundreds of miles on a highway into a major city was frightening.

"Here," Ned dug into his wallet. "This is my dad's but you might need it for emergencies." He handed her the credit card.

Carl gasped. "What is that?"

Ned said, "A credit card. You can buy gas and other things with them."

Carl wheeled closer, and with trembling hands, reached for it.

He looked it over, felt the embossed plastic lettering, and squinted to read the fine print on the back side.

"It's just a credit card. Everyone has them."

Carl snapped, "Don't tell me what it is!"

Dot asked, "Carl? Is there a problem?"

The light was faint, but she could see the tears in his eyes. Finally, he slumped back in the wheelchair and handed the card back to her.

"Carl? Talk to us."

He shook his head. "Everyone has credit cards? How many is everyone? Be specific."

Ned shrugged, "I don't really know. Most adults have several of them. Dad is poor, and we have three. This one we occasionally use for gas. The other two are in the file cabinet so we don't use them by accident. But regular people use them all the time."

"And how many people are you talking about, Ned?"

"Oh, several hundred million people in the US. Maybe the same number for the rest of the world. I'm really just guessing, but maybe a billion people."

Carl closed his eyes, his head tilted back against the headrest.

"For decades, trapped down here in the darkness, I was comforted to believe that I had saved the world from a great plague."

"Credit cards?"

He nodded. "One of those weapon systems I told you about. The government wanted a way to defeat a nation financially. We invented one."

Dot shook her head, "Credit cards? How?"

Carl asked, "Do you have one? Have you ever used one?"

"No."

Ned nodded, "I have, just the other day."

Carl straightened himself back upright.

"Credit card use is a different gestalt than spending real cash, but in a very subtle way.

"With cash or barter, you give up something of value to you and receive something else in its place. With a card, you take out a card, magic happens, and you receive your goods, and you keep your card unchanged.

"Yes, of course, your conscious mind knows that invisible credits are being exchanged and that a bill in the future will reflect this, but that is all too abstract. It's not in the real world, where you touch things and move things around and build your habit patterns.

"With cash, it *hurts* to hand over the bill or coin, as a counterbalance to the pleasure of the acquisition. With the card, it is painless. Spending is instant gratification. It can become immediately habit-forming."

Ned interrupted. "My dad said about the same thing, but what makes it a weapon? I don't see that."

Carl nodded, "You're right. Credit has been with us for thousands of years. Making it highly portable and available for impulse use just adds one more destructive addiction to a list already too long.

"What our research added was the way to use this addiction to drain off a nation's resources—invisibly, secretly. As we designed it, government agents could set up credit card systems in target nations, and then funnel the money back here over time, keeping dangerous enemies depleted and under control."

Carl hit his fist on the armrest of the wheelchair. "It was Dwight—Mort, who suggested the next step. Infect America along with everyone else. Forget using credit cards for national security. Drain the money off into the private account of a small group of individuals. Maybe even one person.

"It was the last straw. By then we were enemies. Time and time again, my new discoveries were being sidelined, held for 'more research'. Very little was being fed up to the committee in control of the project. I suspected that Mort was planning a more personal use for our weapon designs.

"I went over his head. Surely, I thought, if the general in charge knew, he could get rid of Mort, and we could get back to the project's original goals—finding a way to stop tyrants from coming into power in the first place.

"But I was the one who didn't understand human nature. I thought at the time the general had been bribed, but if Mort already had copies of the research notes, there could have been a dozen ways he could have taken control away from the military.

"Mort took command of the base and ordered it de-commissioned, officially. To the people on my research team, there was a different story. There was a security leak to the communists. We were going 'underground'. Hiding so deep that no one could find us. We would report to him only."

Carl paused. "I ... I decided to take matters into my own hands. I burned our notes. I thought they were the only copy. I constructed an official memorandum and sent it up the chain of command. Everyone who read it forgot about the project, the base, everything. It should have gone all the way to the President.

"The base shutdown was already underway, and I added an exit interview for everyone. Every person re-assigned or fired forgot the place as well. I was down here alone, checking every room for any leftover notes, anything that Mort could use to turn our research to his own ends.

"I can still remember when the lights went out and explosions went off."

Dot gasped. The darkness of the place made the image seem too real.

Carl nodded. "Fear. It hit me so hard I could hardly breathe. In the darkness, I raced to the exit, but by the time I reached it, a second explosion went off, and the arch of the main entrance collapsed. A large beam fell across my legs. I was trapped.

"I waited days, it seems, for rescue. But it never came. My scheme to make everyone forget worked far too well. Maybe I was too bland a personality.

Maybe I was too caught up in the project. My 'forget-me' patterns made everyone forget the project, forget the base, and forget me.

"I should have died." He shook his head. "It is strange how powerful the will to live can be.

"I amputated my own legs to get free. The shock alone should have killed me, but I already knew a gestalt shift to combat that. I stopped the bleeding, eventually.

"Eventually, I learned where the food stockpile was. Eventually, I learned how to turn on the thermocouple lighting system and stop wandering around crawling with my hands and dragging a burning pot of oil for light.

"Eventually, I healed, and accepted my fate."

Dot reached out and clasped Ned's hand. "I would have died."

Ned nodded, "Me too."

Carl's mouth was grim. "I lived. And what kept me alive many long days was that tiny spark of pride—pride that I had sacrificed my life so that a greedy maniac would be kept from turning the whole world into victims."

He waved his arms wide. "But that was all a lie! I did it. I let loose a plague on humanity that must have ruined countless lives by now. How many people have succumbed to the addiction of credit cards and lost their hopes and their future?

"I should never have been born." He slumped in the wheelchair.

"Carl?" Dot's pulse shot up. She reached to touch the old pallid skin of his hand. "Carl, I need you. No matter what you thought. You are still alive now. You have survived! And now you are the only one who can help us stop Mort."

Quietly, she whispered, "You are the only one who can help me heal my father."

Carl took a breath. His eyes were closed, but he nodded. "All right. I'm okay."

Ned took the other hand. "And you'll win this time. This time you have help."

Carl gripped both of their hands. "Thank you. Don't mind this bout of self-pity. I have had far too much practice with it over the years."

Dot asked, "One more question, Mr. Stellman. How does Mort drain off the money?"

"I forgot to explain that, didn't I? It's the credit card number. We discovered a class of numbers that people can't remember. That long credit card number is specially designed. Among all the possible valid credit card numbers, there exists one 'forget-me' pattern of numbers.

"The holder of the card with that number can charge anything, but by the time the charge disappears into the maze of transactions, it is forgotten. No charge ever accrues to the account. No bill ever needs to be paid. If the pool of users is large enough, and one billion users is indeed large enough, millions, billions of dollars worth of charges can be drained out of the system with no one noticing.

"With one credit card, a man like Mort could build a huge financial empire, and no one could stop him."

Losing Ranch Exit

Ned shook his head in amazement. "A magic credit card. Oh, I would love to have that!"

Dot said, "He has it. I've seen it. It's white and old-fashioned looking." She caught Ned's eye. "It has no magnetic strip."

Carl asked. "What is that?"

Ned read her mind. "It means that we now know why Mort is doing this stuff in Ranch Exit."

He held out his hand and Dot handed back his father's card. "See here. This brown stripe is a computer memory. Today, for most credit card transactions, people don't even look at the number. It goes directly into the computer. It is processed with no human intervention. There are no humans in the loop to forget the number.

"When they issued the new style cards to combat theft, it turned off his flow of money."

Dot said, "There are a few instances where you can still use the number alone—phone transactions."

She related the story of Mrs. Baker and Mort's purchase of the camera.

"So he can still raise some cash, but it explains the collapse of his company."

Ned added, "And computers will still wave the red flag on his illegal transactions, but the human investigators must be handicapped, if they keep forgetting stuff."

"So he needs a secure base. A place to hide." She looked around. "And that's why he came to Ranch Exit. He hopes to find another way around the system, buried down here with your bones."

"A magic credit card," Ned mused. "Mort isn't the only person who would kill for that."

...

After feeding Pokey, making sandwiches for the trip, getting cleaned up and changed, it was already past sunset. Dot realized she was just making excuses.

I've got to get on the road.

I'm scared.

She cleaned out a school folder and replaced reports on the Lewis and Clark Expedition with her own 'supplies'.

All but one of the charms went into clasp envelopes and into the folder.

Staring into the bathroom mirror, she took a small lock of hair from the right side of her head, much smaller than she did when braiding her hair. Around it, she tied the colored threads in a knot, so the little bit of color lined up even with her eyes.

Okay, Carl. I don't see anything different.

She turned her head, looked at her profile—still no change.

The clothes made more of a difference.

In a single suitcase her father had stored in the back of his closet were a collection of June Comal's clothes. When Dot had first found them, she had been too small to wear them and Dad had firmly put them away. But now, some of them fit, and she would need every edge she could use to make the doctors at the hospital take her seriously.

The matching beige outfit she now wore was nicer than anything in her own closet. And it made her look older.

No more excuses.

With sandwiches, spells, and thirty-four dollars scavenged from her dad's desk and the bundle of Christmas and Birthday cards she had been keeping since she was six, she started the pickup and headed towards the interstate.

Driving by headlights on the dirt road kept her moving slow.

Not that Mr. Wanekia is going to jump out and scare me off the road. Not any more.

The funny old man was gone. Dead. She blinked her eyes.

No time for tears. He wasn't even my friend.

But that didn't feel right. Maybe it was just Indian philosophy about healing the land, but it had touched her. Could friendship click in an instant, living in shared beliefs?

She looked at her hands on the steering wheel and held up the palm of her right hand. *Am I a Healer?*

Ned's voice seemed to echo in her head, *"Judge people by their actions."*

Have I healed anyone? Her memories were as dark and confused as the landscape outside.

But as the road topped the rise, festive lights drew her attention. The Ranch Exit Roundup was just a one-day affair, but preparations for the fair had kept the community in a multi-day frenzy of activity.

If I am going to sneak out of here, I had better turn off the headlights.

Or no! That would be a dead giveaway.

She put her hand on the folder of spells. Maybe she would need them, but not yet.

She slowed as she neared the lighted booths. *I'm just coming to help with the preparations. I'm just ordinary old Dot. Pay no attention.*

Latoya waved, and trotted over to the road. Dot pulled off to the side with two other old pickups. *I can't run. If people guess I am headed out of town, they would stop me, 'for my own good'.*

"Hi Dot, come to help?"

"Just a spectator, this time." The breeze hinted at smoked beef and sweet berries being cooked down to jam.

"Well come on. I've got to show you Larry's attempt at metal art."

Dot shook her head.

Latoya cocked her head, eyed her change of clothes and then spied the items in the seat beside Dot.

"You aren't going to run out on us, are you?"

Dot sighed. "I'll be back by Saturday. I've got to be here for the Roundup, don't I?"

"I should stop you. Where are you going?"

"I've got to go. This could be the last chance I get to see my father. You know they're taking me away to Seattle after the Roundup don't you?"

She nodded. "I'd heard. Your aunt won't take you to see him?"

Dot shook her head. "I can't risk it—an old family feud. Latoya, please don't tell anyone I've gone!"

The older girl glanced back at the lights. "I'm getting in." Dot re-arranged the things on the seat.

"Okay," said Latoya, "drive slowly past the booths, and smile while I point out things. You are just taking me over to the school building."

Dot did as she was told, and smiled honestly at her neighbors having fun. They parked on the far side of the school.

Latoya stepped out. "I thought about doing this myself a dozen times this year, but I was never brave enough to try. Isn't Ned going with you?"

"He has his own job to do. This is mine. Don't worry about us."

"I'll walk back. What do I say when they finally realize you're gone?"

Dot shrugged. "Tell them the truth, I guess. If I'm gone long enough, they won't try to chase me down. Try to give me a head start, okay?"

"Good luck."

...

"That's enough, Ned. You should be back to normal."

Ned put down the metal thing shaped like a dinner plate and nodded. "Great. I'm tired of banging my head against a manhole cover."

"You weren't really hitting your head with it were you?"

"No, but it felt like it. Every time my forehead touched the metal my head rang like a gong."

Carl wheeled closer and checked his pulse. "It was the quickest way. You weren't likely to get close to Cooper if he saw you as a stranger he couldn't even understand."

"I just hope he doesn't start shooting at me."

"If he does..."

"Yes?"

"Run away."

"Thanks a lot." Ned picked up the ornate pattern Carl had drawn on card cut from a 1930's era file folder.

"How come Greg gets a card but Mr. Comal gets a rock?"

Carl shrugged, "Each case is different. Comal had been working for Mort far longer than Cooper. Plus I know a lot more about Ruben Comal from the reflection he left on Dot than I do about Greg Cooper. The change in gestalt is what's important, not how you get there."

Ned slipped the card into his wallet. "They're different people all right." *Like apples and horse-apples.*

...

Dot gripped the steering wheel, and watched the headlights approaching in her rear-view mirror.

Nobody told me I had to drive fast!

She put more pressure on the gas pedal and tried to edge the speed up closer to seventy. It still wasn't enough.

The huge truck blinked its lights and whipped past her in the other lane.

What do all these light-flashes mean? Am I supposed to do that too?

She sped up even faster, ignoring the speedometer.

If I can get behind him and keep a few hundred yards back, then people won't pass me, right?

She kept it up for ten miles, and then had to slow down. The old pickup could cruise at eighty, but it didn't like it. The engine didn't sound right. The steering felt soft on every curve. Something even smelled wrong, like hot oil.

I can't afford trouble. I can't afford a breakdown, and I can't afford a ticket.

Back down to fifty-five, she could sense the engine was happier. *Carl didn't give me anything to keep the old pickup running, and Ned isn't here to do his magic with the engine, so I'll just let the trucks pass me.*

...

Ned took the long way, down to the store and then out to the Cooper ranch on the regular road.

"Don't get too close to any of Mort's artifacts. You are sensitized to them, and they could affect you stronger than a normal person."

Driving by moonlight and a motorcycle headlight with a weak bulb, Ned had no desire to re-visit the crop-circles. They had been spooky enough in broad daylight.

Knock, knock. At the Cooper house Ned could see shadows behind the drapes, but no one answered the door.

I bet they are afraid to let Greg in the house.

"This is Ned. I am looking for Greg Cooper. Is anyone home?"

There was no answer. Ned walked back to his bike.

Where would he be hiding out, if they have barred the door? There was the other, disturbing, possibility—Greg could be in the house. Hallee and her folks could be hurt or tied up.

What could he do if that was the case? Get help? Who could he go to? Who would believe him? And what if he was wrong, and all the Coopers were one big happy family and Hallee's black eye was just a temporary cosmetics disaster?

No, I have to track down Greg. I should have stopped at the store and checked if anyone there had seen him.

...

The single headlight of the approaching motorcycle was bright enough to push Greg's headache up a notch.

"Stupid idiot!" He spun the steering wheel hard over, and slid into the ditch.

Greg had the door open, choking in the dust, before the bike came rattling up, blaring in his ears.

"Are you okay?"

"Stupid kid! You trying to kill me?"

"No, Mr. Cooper. In fact, I was looking for you. I've got a message for you."

The kid walked into range and Greg knocked him out with one blow, a roundhouse right.

"Now you've done it!" Greg screamed. He kicked the body laying in the dirt. "My stupid brother said he'd call the cops. I didn't mean to hit her. He said he'd call the cops if I hit anyone. Now what'll I do about you?"

...

The roaring startled Dot awake. "What?"

A flat tire! She jerked the steering wheel, and the sound went away.

Her pulse hammered, as she checked the mirrors. No headlights were close.

What was that noise?

A little experimentation located the groves at the edge of the lane.

I was drifting off the road. I should have stayed at that Rest Area.

But that place had been like an alien landscape—the orange lights and the trucks parked for the night with their engines still running.

And people looked at her strangely. Men smiled. Women frowned. It wasn't like Ranch Exit, or even the people in the towns when she went on a shopping trip with Dad. There was something ... protective in the eyes of people she knew. That was gone.

It's just the age charm. She reached up to touch the threads in her hair.

"People who don't already know you," Carl had explained, *"will see you as older—somewhere in your mid-twenties. It will still be you, just an older version."*

She needed it, to get past the traffic police, and to get close to her Dad, but it was disturbing.

Will people look at me like this when I'm really twenty-five?

The way grown men looked at her was disturbing enough that she had fled the place after using the restroom and raiding the vending machines.

I'm not going to be able to drive all night—not if I'm falling asleep at the wheel.

But it wouldn't be terribly safe to park beside the road either. *I'll find some place off the road. Under a bridge or something where people won't see me.*

Across the median, she saw the back side of a sign and smiled. Every mile, all the way back to Ranch Exit, there was one of those signs. She had checked out a few of them.

The sign crew had been busy, advertising the Roundup. If the highway department didn't knock them all down before the weekend, it should draw quite a crowd.

...

The last lights in the booths went out after one AM. Mort started up his Humvee.

He eased past the school and the store and the booths, making sure that no one was still there.

Well, that is the last time I allow a policeman into my valley. Too bad about the fair, but I can't let a windfall like this slip through my fingers.

The advertising signs should be completely installed by now. He rubbed his hands with glee, something he couldn't have done when he walked by the sign painting booth and overheard the debate over who would make the run to install all the completed signs. For the ranchers, it was a huge, thankless job. The signs had to go out no more than a day or so before the fair, since they were going up on highway right-of-way and the state would make them remove them immediately. Putting them up legally, on private land, would be prohibitively expensive. This way, they could say 'oops, sorry' and take them down after the fair.

But Mort already had several hundred resonator rods. How lovely the idea to hire a crew to put up the town's signs on his poles, and then when the wards activated, no one would care about the signs anyway.

I was worried about how to get all those resonators in place without people asking questions.

Things were finally falling into place. After searching for years, he had found the old base. It seemed impossible that Stellman was still alive down there, but putting the place behind wards would hold him until he trained someone with more loyalty than brains to go down in that tunnel for him. It also gave him a chance to try out the new series of ward poles his Florida plant had manufactured. Installation had gone so much easier than the ones he had used back in the Sixties.

He parked the Humvee near the big green Ranch Exit sign and pulled out the post-hole digger. The fat screw, driven off the Humvee's engine, cut a precise hole into the earth. Staking a cable into the ground he pulled a twenty-foot tall ward pole from the rack on the roof and winched it into place. Some wooden stakes and some fast-drying cement had it firmly mounted within twenty minutes.

Four more to go, and then I can activate it.

In a little over an hour, Ranch Exit will vanish from Utah and become my private little kingdom.

...

Trying to measure the crop-circles from the tiny little images on the back of the digital camera was frustrating. The ratios were key. Carl noted down his calculations with a pencil stub on the back of a mess-hall memo so old the paper threatened to crack into pieces.

The data he had collected, the images from the kids, the patterns from the mice, and now an actual ward pole Ned had pulled into the tunnel for him—the pieces were shaping up into a ugly whole.

Mort had been at the process for years. Some of his efforts, the giant apple for example, had been experiments in detaching the valley from the common gestalt. The iconoplaks were a wholesale attack on the residents of Ranch Exit, preparing their minds for a radical shift in perception.

The crop circles, powerful and deadly, were driving a change that couldn't be stopped. Unless they were linked to a major gestalt pattern, the insanity would bleed out all over the valley, affecting minds large and small.

Ned had been affected the strongest, but he could see the effects in Dot as well.

Mort had set in motion a plan of such scope he must have planned it out years ago. What chance did a slug and two children have to stop it?

He wheeled over to the file-cabinet. As he put his hand on the handle, he looked up at the top two drawers.

I haven't even looked at those in so many years. What else have I chopped out of my mind just because I lived on the floor?

A simple thing like a wheelchair, getting his eyeline up off the ground was changing him in many subtle ways.

He straightened his back. *I'm not a slug in the dust. I'm a man.*

...

Mort loaded his tools back into the Humvee. In the moonlight, the primary wards looked like Pacific Northwest Indian totem poles, with wings spread high.

He pulled out a cloth band and tied it around his forehead.

I can hardly wait. He hopped in and drove up the access road until the school building was in sight.

He extended the antenna on his radio remote control unit, turned the dial and pressed the activating switch.

Little motors rotated the patterned wings on the poles, correcting any minor errors from the hasty installation. Then as one, they synchronized their orientation towards the center of Jed Fellerman's ranch, the center of the power circles.

Like a flash, the gestalt of Ranch Exit shuddered like a bucket of rocks being dropped.

...

Carl gasped. He gripped the sides of the chair. *What was that?*

He felt his pulse race, but he stilled it with a thought. *Don't lose focus! King Mort has just launched another spell.*

But the sense of the power of his enemy was overwhelming. What chance did he have of defeating the most powerful person in the whole world?

There was just him, hiding like a worm in the ground, with his only help a single boy who didn't understand the forces they were dealing with.

He put down the pattern he had been etching. *That can wait.* Carl wheeled out of his workroom and down the hallway. His bed called to him. Sleep. He needed sleep.

Mice scattered as he went through the door. They danced in a strange pattern, but he couldn't seem to care. He locked the wheels and slid down to the ground. Crawling like a worm, he prepared to sleep. Sleep a long time. Hadn't he been working too long as it was?

His hand touched a cloth bundle. He closed his eyes.

The texture of the strange cloth under his hand wasn't the only irritant. The unknown nagged at him.

I'll never get to sleep this way. He shifted on his mattress and moved his hand away from the bundle.

It smelled different. *What is that smell? I think I remember it.* He lay in the dark, taking deep slow breaths.

Soap. He remembered! *That's the smell of soap. How long ago had the last of his soap run out? Fifty years ago?*

Carl frowned. If the last of the soap was gone fifty years ago, why did this bundle smell like soap?

Ned. Ned must have left this for me.

He shook off the sleepiness like a drug. He opened the carefully folded bundle.

Clothes. Clean clothes. He fingered the shirt. Everything was there. Shirt, trousers, underwear. The only things missing were shoes and socks. Carl laughed. Not that he would miss those.

The sleep could wait. He would take a bath, and then put on clean clothes! Like a flood of energy, he felt his whole body tingle with anticipation.

The Kingdom of Ronchex

Dorothy Comal woke up on the bench seat of the pickup. Dawn had come. She twisted under the blanket, and rubbed her neck.

No wonder I never sleep in the pickup. My neck is killing me.

She took a short walk around the vehicle to stretch her legs. A truck downshifted on the grade. She could hear it over the hill.

By the time she had given up driving for the night, she was too tired to be particular about her campsite. A gap in a fence line where it dropped into a gully showed old tire tracks, so she followed it. Trespassing on private land seemed more desirable than falling asleep at the wheel or parking on the shoulder where passing vehicles would bother her.

But it was time to move on. Dad needed her.

She checked her face in the rear-view mirror.

Nothing new. You would think working killer hours at the Emergency Room would show more damage to my looks.

She scratched at her teeth. *I need a toothbrush.*

Her clothes were all wrong. *When I walk in there, I'll need to convince them that I'm a competent medical professional. It's a shame I don't have my papers with me.*

She tapped the folder with her finger. It looked like the kind of thing she used when she was a teenager back in high school. But if her theories of the mind were right, this would solve her father's case.

It's strange how the ideas just came into my head, but if I'm right about this telepathic connection, this 'collective unconscious', then I suppose it's not too surprising after all.

It would be nice to think I have a connection with everyone else. I'm such a loner. No husband, no boyfriend.

She shook her head and pulled back on the interstate. A wave of loneliness swept over her.

"Who am I kidding? No boyfriend. I don't have any friends. Just Dad and a few remote relatives. I've got to save him."

...

Ned woke with a mouth full of dirt. He coughed, and tried to gasp— and that was when he realized he couldn't move. He panicked.

But it did no good to panic. His arms wouldn't move, neither would his legs. And pressure around his chest wouldn't let him breathe deeply.

Another clump of dirt dropped into his mouth. Frantically he tried to spit it out, but he was too dry. He pursed his lips and blew.

I'm buried. The memory of last night came rushing back. *Greg buried me alive!*

He struggled, and then stopped, trying to catch his breath. *I am getting air. I can't be buried too deeply.*

Heart beating away, Ned concentrated on the lifegiving air. He feared to open his eyes. The texture of dirt on his face was too immediate a warning to ignore.

Greg's an agent of the King. Did he have warning?

Ned could tell that his body had been dumped in a hurry. His left arm was trapped under his own weight.

But the right arm was above him. He pushed. No luck.

I've got to get free!

He concentrated on his fingers. He poked and wiggled them.

A rock moved.

...

King Mort sat under the awning and nodded benevolently to the people who had come to work on their fair booths.

George Filmore walked by with a frown on his face.

"Hello, George. How are you this morning?"

George bowed. "Your Highness."

"It's a lovely morning, George. Smile for me."

The storekeeper made the attempt.

"My apologies, Sire. It's just that something feels wrong."

The King said, "Explain it to me."

George sighed. "I wish I could. I checked my inventory this morning. The numbers are all wrong. As the storehouse for the Kingdom of Ronchex, I know I should have food and supplies enough for everyone in the world, at least until the harvest comes in.

"But I have far less than that. Food will run out in weeks, days for some items. And the varieties! So many varieties, and I have no idea of how to replace them."

King Mort nodded, "But you know that I will supply the needs of my people. The King can command resources from the sky. I've done so all of your life. Why do you doubt me now?"

George shook his head. "There is just too much strangeness to take in all at once. Look at all these people." He pointed at a nearby booth, with shelves covered with glass jars. "Cactus butter! She has enough there to supply every family in the world with enough cactus butter many times over. All the booths are like that. Cactus butter will keep, but Jake Cartulio has so much beef and goat for his barbeque pits that all of us together won't finish it off.

"It's just crazy. The valley is all there is. We can't will more people into existence just by having more goods to sell. I don't know why this fair has taken everyone's imagination. I don't even know how it started."

King Mort nodded. "Dot. Quite an infectious little mind."

George frowned, "What?"

"The student who proposed the fair."

"A student started this? Who?"

"Dot Comal."

George shook his head, "Sorry, I didn't hear you. What did you say?"

"Nothing. Don't worry about your supplies, George. I'll take care of everything.

"However, I need something from you."

"Yes, Sire."

"Prepare a list of everyone in the world. I want names, which homestead, ages, marital status, gender and a comment on what they do for a living. Have it ready by this evening."

George nodded, "I believe I have all of that information. May I ask what you need it for? I probably know everyone personally."

The King nodded. "Our population is too low. Unless I take action, it will continue to shrink and become unsustainable in a couple of decades. I think we need more weddings, and we don't have time for random meetings and extended courtships.

"I want you," he pointed at George's stomach, "to immediate destroy all contraceptives in your store. You aren't married are you?"

"No, Sire."

"Well give some thought to the prospects."

When Filmore took his leave, it was Mort's time to frown. *He is too close to the truth. I should have known that the shopkeeper would see the leftovers of the other reality.*

And how did the girl go missing? Dot Comal was the one who suggested the fair. She turned the town instantly to her way of thinking. *I don't trust coincidences. Could she have discovered the old base? I can't have pretenders to the throne here. And what about that boy she is always with? The one with the motorcycle?*

He looked in the direction of his ranch. *I'll bring George there and dispose of the body behind wards. If the townspeople can't remember him, they won't grieve. No chance of resentment that way. I'll have to track down the meddling kids as well.*

I'll have to use a compulsion on the wedding list. Maybe a few general loyalty posters as well. I don't want a repeat of what happened in my Manhattan townhouse.

...

Carl rummaged through storerooms he hadn't visited in decades. He worked efficiently; the clean red plaid shirt and the jeans made him feel stronger than he had in a long time.

"Ah, ha!" Several mice dashed to safety.

"Oh, come on! I've spoken out loud before."

The object of his satisfaction was a large floppy hat. He had seen it long ago. It was amazing what trivia collected in long term memory.

Ned had promised to come by at dawn to report what happened with Cooper. He was hours late. Ned was his only human contact with the outside world. There was only so much mice could do. If Ned needed help, he would have to find a way to go outside by himself.

Outside had raw sunshine, but in his new clothes, the unthinkable was suddenly not so impossible. Long-sleeved shirt, gloves, and now a hat to shield his head—if he could just get the wheel-chair out through the tunnel, surely he could make it to the High Road?

The King would recognize Dr. Carl Stellman, but he won't be expecting a cripple.

...

The traffic was intense. Dorothy kept the pickup in the far right lane and passed nobody. That worked until the lane vanished and she was forced to exit the highway.

I've never been good at city traffic. But there was nothing to do but get back on. She sailed through the intersection and headed for the on-ramp.

A short burst of siren and the flashing light behind her changed that plan.

Pull over to the right. She remembered that much. There wasn't much room to park, but she had no intention of ignoring the police.

What'll I do? All my papers are gone, my driver's license included.

She rolled down the window. The policeman was approaching, clipboard in hand.

Dorothy made the first move.

"Officer? Could you help me? I'm lost." She gave him a timid smile.

He smiled back.

...

The booths were nearly deserted, as most people suddenly realized that they were over-prepared for tomorrow's festivities.

Ms. Carson checked her calendar. Today had originally been planned for a student party. With the fair, that seemed redundant. She had a 'fair committee meeting' penciled in. *That will be a fiasco. With no one in charge, we will just sit around and look at each other.*

No students, no activities. *It will be nothing more than a babysitting day when a few parents start to realize I'm sitting here doing nothing.*

My last day of the school year.

And what of the future. *I hadn't planned on teaching these kids next year. But what else can I do?*

She could teach next year, or else try to find something else to do.

Cultivating the four or five unattached men didn't appeal to her. A rancher's wife needed all those homemaker skills she had never been interested in.

Of course there is one unattached male who would be different.

King Mort had no queen. Of course he was old, but not too old to ignore a pretty face. She glanced at the mirror she kept in her desk. *I look better when I smile.*

And the smile was real. *Now I have a summer project.*

...

Dorothy watched the police car dwindle away in the rear view mirror.

He was nice. The driver's license never came up. *A damsel in distress, that's me.* She had a map to the hospital, advice on how best to navigate the city, and his phone number in case she needed rescuing again.

Bill Radcliff was her age, twenty-four, and cute looking in his uniform. *It could work. A cop and a doctor. We would both have horrible schedules, but off-duty we could build a nice h....*

Her mind stuttered. She shook her head. It was like mental indigestion. Heartburn. Her mind drifted off in different channels.

The hospital was only a dozen blocks away. *I'll need to get myself ready.*

...

Carl crawled through the airshaft tunnel, pulling the folded wheelchair after him. *If it looks good, I'll go back for the canteens. I just hate getting this shirt dirty.*

The sunlight was blinding, even with the hat for shade. *I should make an eyeshade, like a headband over my eyes—just look through the holes in the cloth.*

The chair unfolded easily, and he locked it in place.

I've got to follow that trail, and get on top of the High Road.

The trail was steep and very rocky. And probably there was no easier path. The motorcycle tracks and horse hoof prints testified that this was the way Ned came.

Horse? He remembered the horse. But why would Ned ride a horse? He loved that motorcycle, and he couldn't bring both.

Carl frowned at the tracks. The hoof prints were a glaring inconsistency. *They make no sense.*

Carl tapped his fingers on the wheelchair armrest.

When reality doesn't make sense, people tune out the offending data. I can rationalize away these prints, or face the other possibility.

There were two people who have discovered me. Ned and ... someone else. I can't remember ... whoever it is. The latest gestalt shift—King Mort removed someone, someone close to me. What else has he removed?

He looked again at the trail up the side of the High Road. The wheelchair would never make it.

He sagged. *So I'm not an action hero. I've got to get back to my work desk, and my mice. If Ned needs rescue, he'll have to find it elsewhere.*

I've got to figure out what has changed and who the unknown horse-rider was.

...

Latoya Harris wandered over to the school building.

School is over, my last year. Now what? Help Mom doctor the horses?

The main schoolroom was empty, but she heard voices in the teachers' office.

"So you don't remember which student came up with it?" the King asked.

"No. The idea of a fair just happened spontaneously." Ms. Carson had a strange lilting tone in her voice.

"Have you heard of a girl named Dot?"

"There's no one by that name—and by now I know everyone in the world." She chuckled.

"Hmm. How about that boy with the motorcycle?"

"Ned? What about him?"

"Watch for him. Give me a call the moment you see him, okay?"

"For you, Sire, anything!"

"One more thing. Make a list of students, and which have romantic interests. I feel like playing match-maker. In addition, tell me anyone you know who would be good working at my palace. I need house-servants."

"Will you be needing a hostess?"

There was a long silence before the King said, "Perhaps. Perhaps. I'll keep that idea in mind."

Latoya eased back out.

The idea of the King setting her up with a guy sent shivers down her spine. The pool of available men was terribly small. Her mother hadn't found anyone interesting since her father died. In her age group the numbers were as bad.

Forrester is brainless, and Ned or Larry would need to grow up a bit.

She liked Larry, for some reason, but she wasn't going to raid the cradle. *If he just had an older brother, that would be perfect.*

But if the King acted, she would be out of luck. Everyone obeyed the King. It was odd that she even thought about being disloyal.

It's just ... I know my choices are all wrong. It's as if there is someone else out there for me.

She hurried to get out of sight before the King left the school.

What does the King want with Ned? And who is this Dot he was asking about?

...

Dr. McCormick nodded to the young lady. "I've been told you have come to see your father." He looked down at his notes. "I'm afraid that he has taken a turn for the worse since he was admitted."

"Take me to him."

"He is currently asleep. The medications he is on...."

"Regardless." Dorothy stood. The doctor hesitated, but the look in her eyes had no hint of compromise.

He called an attendant to come with them. As they walked the long hallway, the doctor asked, "Your father has had a high priority with us because his symptoms matched another patient's, Aaron Locke. Did you know him?"

Dorothy shook her head, "I've heard the name. He worked with my father, I believe."

"Are you from 'Ranch Exit' as well?"

Dorothy shook her head. "I don't know what you're talking about."

"Well, the admissions paperwork had...."

"Please, just let me see my father. I'm not interested in talking paperwork right now."

The room was down a separate hallway, marked 'Authorized Personnel Only'. A huge man in whites stood at the door.

"Blake, would you come with us? Ms. Comal wishes to see her father."

The growing collection of men in white was a little intimidating, but Dorothy kept her eyes straight ahead. It only confirmed her worst fears.

"Dr. McCormick, when my father arrived, he had a small, hand-written get-well card. If he has gotten worse, I have to assume something has happened to that card."

The door was wide and sturdy with a window re-enforced with a wire grid. When her eyes came level with the view into the room, she felt a jolt.

Her father was strapped to a bed. She had been expecting a hospital room, with spartan but pleasant furnishings. This was something different. There was no furniture, other than the bed. No bedding, just leather straps to hold him secure.

"What have you done to him?" She pushed at the door, but it wouldn't budge. She glared at the doctor.

"Blake?" The big man inserted a card into a slot and the door locks clicked.

"Miss," said Blake, "please be cautious. The rages come on him without warning, and he is very strong." For such a big man, his voice was soft and gentle.

"I know exactly how he is." She entered and approached to within four feet.

"Daddy? It's Dorothy. Can you hear me?"

His eyes snapped open, and she could see the madness in them. But they were hazy as well. The drugs had him in their thrall. Ruben Comal gave no sign that he recognized her.

She asked the doctor, "That get-well card. Where is it?"

McCormick answered, "When he arrived we had reason to suspect an environmental poison. I ordered all personal effects removed for testing."

She was angry, "So you took away the one thing that had been keeping him sane, a get-well card written after the disease had struck him?

"Well, get it! Immediately. He is this way because of you."

The doctor showed a flushed face, but he had years of keeping his own anger bottled up when facing patients and families. "Blake, go get it."

Ruben groaned, reacting to the voices.

They insisted that she wait outside while Blake was gone. Dorothy looked at her notebook while she sat in the waiting room.

I'll have to get him calmed down first. Then I can give him the touchstone. Getting him released will be the hardest.

Blake entered the room with a sealed plastic bag.

"I'm sorry, Miss. He didn't want to let go of it."

Inside the bag, the get-well card was mangled and torn.

...

Latoya saw her mother at the store. "Hey, Mom, I'm going to go back to the house for a bit."

Ruth Harris paused in her talk with George Filmore over how many bags of grain to buy.

"Sure. Nothing doing at school?"

"It's dead there. How long will you be here?"

"Come back for me in a couple of hours."

Latoya checked the cars again, looking for a motorcycle among them. No one had seen Ned this morning.

There are not too many places he can be. The entire world had only a few miles of dirt road, plus the High Road. She could cover that in less than two hours.

I shouldn't do anything disloyal to the King, but Ned needs to know that the King is looking for him.

She headed down the eastern branch, driving slow, and keeping the crest of the High Road in view.

Hallee Cooper drove over the hill, heading in the opposite direction. Latoya waved and slowed to a stop.

Hallee was wearing her hair different, down and across her face on the side. She held her hand up, partially obscuring her face. "Hi. Have you seen Ned?"

"No, I'm looking for him myself. What's up?"

"Oh, nothing. My uncle Greg just found his wallet."

Latoya asked, "What happened to your face?"

Hallee hesitantly lowered her hand, and pulled the hair back. The black eye was easily visible under the make-up. "It was an accident."

"Who did it?"

"Uncle Greg, but it was really just an accident."

Latoya shook her head, "Nobody gets away with hurting my friends. Where is he?"

"He's at home. Really, Latoya, let it be. He was sick, and he's better now. He's the King's worker, you can't bother him. He's asleep—out cold really. My dad will handle it.

"He came home last night all irrational and confused, but he seemed sorry for what he had done. It was this morning before we found Ned's wallet." Hallee looked worried.

"Mom is afraid Greg did something to Ned while he was sick. I'm out checking, so is Dad."

"Well, he's not at school, or at the store. I've already checked."

"Just keep looking."

Dr. Dorothy

Dorothy approached her father gingerly. Ruben Comal was more alert. He howled, without recognition, and struggled against the straps.

Carefully taped together on the back side, she held out the get-well card. His eyes passed over the pattern, but nothing changed. Dr. McCormick watched with an impassive expression.

She could feel her face start to turn red. *It's not working.*

He lurched, his face muscles tense with rage. She jumped back.

The doctor cleared his throat.

Dorothy dropped her arm to her side.

"Perhaps," he said, "there is more here than a get-well card can cure."

She turned to him. With her teeth clenched, she said, "Perhaps, if you hadn't mangled the pattern, I would be done by now!"

He looked at Blake, standing impassively to the side, waiting to jump into action if needed. "I have other patients to attend to. Give the lady what assistance she needs." And then he left.

She looked at the card. There were smudges and tear lines. A pattern with new lines was a different pattern.

Ruben strained at the straps again. Each groan cut right through her heart.

The lines of the pattern started to blur through her tears.

"Miss, don't give up. Can you fix it?" His voice calmed her. "I have seen many patients here. There is something about your father that is different. I don't know what your treatment is supposed to do, but don't let Dr. Mc-Cormick discourage you."

Dorothy nodded, and blinked her eyes clear. With a sniff, she asked, "Do you have a copy machine, and a whiteout marker?"

...

Ned crawled painfully to the top of the High Road.

I'll kill for something to drink. Not only was he dehydrated, but his mouth was still gritty from spitting dirt.

He had taken too long to dig himself out of the shallow grave. *People can last five days without water, but does that count when you've been beat-up and buried alive.* Something about the pains in his side made him realize Greg had kicked him repeatedly after he had been knocked out.

From the appearance of North Mesa he was about a mile past his home. It was past the stretch where the regular road paralleled the High Road.

Nobody is going to find me here. I'll have to walk it.

He moved slowly, each step triggering a pain in his side.

If Greg attacked me because of the uncontrolled rage, that's one thing, but if the King is after me—wants me dead—then I'll need to hide.

And where is my motorcycle?

...

Carl heard the engine noise far in the distance. *Ned! Finally.*

He wheeled his way to the access tunnel and crawled up to the entrance where he could greet the boy.

But it wasn't Ned moving slowly along the High Road.

Who is that? And what kind of a vehicle is that?

The man was obviously searching for something. His vehicle looked like a four-wheeled motorcycle, ridden astride like a motorcycle, with handlebars.

He peered down at the trail Ned and the unknown horseman had left on the side of the High Road.

The engine stopped, and he got off to take a better look.

Carl was in the shadows, obscured by the brush piled over the opening. Still he made no movement. With the King solidly in power, and the air reeking of a loyalty pattern, the chances the man could be an ally was slim.

The man looked around, never focusing on the tunnel entrance.

"Ned! It's Samuel Cooper. Ned?"
Carl waited until he left before he moved.
Cooper. He must be a relative of Greg.
Something must have happened to Ned.

...

Blake returned to the waiting room where Dorothy worked with white-inker and a fine-tipped black ink pen to reconstruct the pattern. She made a dozen photocopies of the original, with the brightness tweaked differently on all of them in an effort to remove the defacing tear lines and smudges.

"Miss, we don't have much time. The doctor is going to ask you to leave and come back tomorrow. It is past the official visiting hours."

She blew on the evaporating ink softly. *It is working, even on me, I haven't felt this calm all day.*

"Surely he won't run me off yet?"

Blake sat down on the chair next to her. "Oh, the doctors can get stubborn about their rules. I know you're pretty special, and I think Dr. Mc-Cormick senses that, but he does have a lot of other patients to deal with."

"What do you mean 'special'?" She set the finished pattern down, and collected all the false starts and swept them into the trashcan.

Blake smiled, "Oh, there is something. I don't know what. Half the time I look at you and you look like a young professional woman, and then I catch a glance of you down the hall and you look like a little teenager, worried about her daddy.

"But if you need to stay longer today," he stood back up, "you had better have your arguments ready."

She heard footsteps. "Thanks, Blake." She opened her file folder and pulled out an envelope. She removed the crude paper badge and clipped it to her collar.

Dr. McCormick entered with a solemn look on his face. "Ms. Comal, it is past visiting hours. Perhaps you should come back another time."

She stood straight, grateful for the calming influence of her reconstructed get-well card. Now was not the time to yell at him.

"Dr. McCormick, I am not quite a simple visitor. I am Dr. Dorothy Comal. I received my M.D. at Harvard Medical and I am currently doing my residency at St. Joseph's in Denver. When I heard of my father's condition, I took an immediate leave and left, unfortunately leaving my papers behind.

"Doctor, his condition is something I have treated before, and time is critical.

"And he is my father.

"I will need a few more hours, and it truly can mean the difference between his total recovery and his death."

The doctor blinked. He shook his head, puzzled that he actually believed everything she said.

"I wish you had told me this earlier. We have seen nothing published on a rage affliction like this."

"There hasn't been any publication. The diagnosis and treatment plan are both very new.

"But may I have your permission to continue?"

He nodded. "Blake, stay with her, and take notes. I don't want to be caught un-prepared the next time one of these patients arrives."

He glanced at his watch and gave her a nod.

Dorothy picked up the get-well card, used it herself for a second, and then waved Blake to follow her.

...

Ned listened to the conversation, just barely loud enough to carry all the way to the pump house where he was hiding.

"Albert, I know Ned hasn't done anything. If anything Greg is the criminal."

"But then why does the King want Ned?" His father was out on the porch. Ned could hear his crutches on the boards.

Sam Cooper sighed, "I don't know. The King wants what the King wants. But I worry about what happened last night. Here's Ned's wallet. Greg came back to the house with it.

"I don't know what to do. I can't believe my brother is a murderer, but if he has done ... something, I don't want him in the house. But he is a King's worker! I couldn't throw him out if I tried."

Ned's father's voice was strained. "You haven't seen any signs of my boy?"

"Not a one. There are five of us searching. We've covered all the roads, the school, and the store. We're going house to house now."

"Well, come in and look around. He's not here. I can hear a mouse moving in this old place, and there hasn't been a sound all day. Yolanda is at the booth. Has she been told?"

There were footsteps, and the voices went out of range.

They'll come looking in the outbuildings next.

The water from the hose, where he had drunk gallons and hosed the dirt off his clothes was still wet on the concrete. Ned turned the hose back on to a trickle and left it coiled on its hanger. The water splattered over the floor.

He still winced from the memory of the tongue-lashing his father had given him a couple of years earlier when he had left the water running in the pumphouse. With the door closed, the water had crept up several inches inside before it had been discovered. The trickle should flood the floor well enough to cover any tracks.

Ned closed the door and tiptoed from rock to rock as quickly as he could to get out of sight without leaving plain tracks.

I'll be in trouble, but there won't be any proof I was here this morning.

Dad wouldn't turn me in to the King, but it's so unthinkable to do anything against the King's will. I can't trust anyone.

...

Ruben Comal focused on the pattern, and Dorothy could see the madness fade from his eyes. He sagged, no longer struggling against the straps.

He blinked, puzzled, and then in a hoarse whisper he said, "Dot?"

She closed the distance between them and hugged him. Blake moved to stop her, but even he could see that something had dramatically changed with his most violent patient.

"My little girl," her dad cried.

Dorothy shook.

Dot felt a wave of confusion vanish from her mind.

I'm Dot. I'm a teenager. Why did I think I was older?

She looked at Blake. He watched contentedly. Whatever change came over her, it hadn't been visible to him.

"Dad," she whispered. "You understand about the pattern on the card?"

"Yes!" He kept his head turned where he could see it.

"Then here, in your hand." She moved the touchstone into his grasp, the action hidden from Blake. He closed his hand tightly on the rock. "It will cure you."

He nodded, his face covered with tears. "I love you, Dot."

She backed away, leaving the card propped up on his chest. His hand was working, as he could feel the etched pattern on the touchstone.

Blake asked, "What did you give him?"

She asked, "You saw it?"

"I don't think there is a patient on this floor who hasn't tried to hide things from me. You get an eye for the signs."

"Well, let him have it." She gave him a superficial description of the touchstone.

He nodded. "I won't mess you up. But you didn't make this pattern discovery did you?"

"What do you mean?" Of course she had.

"I mean I hear all kinds of stories, from medical textbook diagnosis, to delusional fantasies, to ancient Chinese mystical theories. Your descriptions aren't your own. You are paraphrasing someone else."

"Well," she tilted her nose a little higher, "you are wrong."

He tilted his head and dropped the subject. He moved to the other side of the bed.

"How are you doing Mr. Comal?"

Dot reached for her truth badge and stuffed it into her pocket. *He believed me, even though he had no evidence. I would rather he kept his own thoughts for now.*

Ruben tried to focus on the big man. "Do I know you?"

"Not well. How are you feeling?"

"Tired, and jittery. My throat hurts."

"That's just reaction from your fits. I can bring something that will help your throat. Try not to talk much." Blake smiled. "And no more yelling."

Ruben frowned, "You took my card away."

"My mistake. But your daughter came and fixed it. Just get some rest now."

Ruben nodded. His fingers worked the touchstone urgently.

Dot absently touched her hair, and felt the threads tied there. *The age illusion. Now I remember. I look older to people who don't know me.*

But why did I not know myself?

Blake nodded at her and went to get the throat medicine.

Even Blake could see through it sometimes. That made sense. She suspected Blake was a very perceptive man.

A very perceptive older man. As they had worked making the copies, she had felt a more embarrassing admiration for the muscular attendant.

Her daydreams about the traffic cop came back in a flash, and she could feel her face starting to get hot.

This age illusion is dangerous. I should be thinking about boys my age.

An image flickered through her memory, a boy on a motorcycle. But it was gone in a flash.

...

Ned hid in a gully out of sight. *I need food and a canteen. Ranch Exit is huge without wheels.*

As long as I'm in hiding, I'll need resources.

He reached into his pocket. There was little there—a pocketknife and a few coins.

The image of a girl's face flashed through his mind as he fingered the change. Most of the coins were familiar, with anonymous faces and the King's eagle on some of the quarters. The fat coin was strange, but he felt drawn to its touch. Carl had given it to him for some reason, but it eluded him now.

Money won't help, even if I had a lot of it.

As he rubbed the fat coin absently, he remembered the horse.

Pokey! He lives at that deserted ranch down the road. A horse will at least get me from place to place.

...

Ms. Carson circled the chairs and it wasn't long before George Filmore and Jake Cartulio arrived. By the time the fair committee's seven adults were seated, the conversation had already drifted.

"The King has certainly started to take a more personal interest in the community, hasn't he?"

Ms. Carson sniffed, "The King has always had our welfare at heart."

"Still," Jake continued, "I never remember the King telling me what crops to grow, and how many cattle to run. Bill is going to have a lot more chores this summer than he's used to. Probably do him a world of good."

George nodded. "He'd better get used to hard work. Have you heard the latest proclamation? I just hammered it up on the store post board. The King has just lowered marriageable age to fourteen. Get prepared for grandkids a lot sooner than you'd expected."

The conversation stalled, as everyone started reviewing which of their children, or their neighbors' children would be affected.

Carol Samuelson started to object, but that would have meant criticism of the King. She said nothing. She couldn't.

...

"How are you doing Dad?"

"Fine, Dot. Fine. My head is clearer now than it has been in days."

She nodded and turned her head to check the room. Blake had left the door unlocked for her, still under the compulsion to believe that she was a doctor.

I believed that myself when I said it. It just rattled off my tongue. How did I even know about Harvard Medical or St. Joseph's hospital in Denver?

"Dad, how soon do you feel able to travel? We need to get out of here."

"Honey, I'm committed to a mental hospital. It will take a court order, or something like that, to get me out. I committed myself, so unless I broke some laws I don't remember, I'll get out, but it can take days, weeks, before that can happen.

"By the way, who brought you here?"

"Dad, I've got all that covered. Believe me, we need to leave as soon as you feel up to it."

Ruben moved his hand toward her, but was restrained by the strap. It was exasperating, but no longer enraging as it had been just a couple of hours before.

"Honey, some things are just impossible."

She patted his hand, just as he had tried to pat hers.

"Dad, there are fewer impossibles than you know. Just rest now. I'll see if we can't get these straps removed."

...

Dot reached into her pocket for some change. The vending machines were calling to her. Her last meal had been a day-old sandwich for breakfast, and it was catching up with her. Perhaps it was better to wait another day. She could get some rest and a meal, and her dad could rest up and throw off the anti-psychotic medicines the staff had been pumping into him.

The fat coin felt warm to the touch. She paused, standing there in the hallway.

No, I've got to go, immediately. It's important.

She stuffed the money back into her pocket and strode toward Blake's office.

He was sitting at his desk, working with a stack of papers. Her papers— the copies of the get-well card she had discarded.

Blake looked up, embarrassed. "I think this one works. I feel something when I look at it."

Mixed feelings swirled in her chest. "Do you usually raid the trash can?"

He shook his head. "No, but I can see what is happening to your father. I don't throw away good medicines. There are dozens of people in this building alone who could use a way to throw off rages without suffering the side effects of our standard drugs.

"Your discovery is too important to hide away."

Dot felt the same way, but nothing was more important than getting her Dad safely out of there. In just hours, Blake would be off duty. A new staff would arrive, and she would have to convince them all that they didn't need to keep her dad bound and drugged. And she would have to convince them that she was a doctor. *And I don't believe that any more.* They would make her leave.

She pulled the truth badge from her pocket, but kept it concealed in her palm.

"Blake," she said, pulling up a chair. "There are more potent patterns than the get-well card. With your help or without it, I will be taking my father out of here tonight."

He looked alarmed. "I would have to stop you."

She clipped the truth badge to her collar.

"You will not be able to stop me. I have a release document that will let us walk out with no problem. Tomorrow, everyone will believe he was here because of a clerical error. The day after that, they won't even remember we were here at all."

She took the badge off again.

"Blake, I'll make you a deal. Help me get past the front desk and help me load Dad into the pickup and I'll leave you the get-well pattern. The only gotcha is that you must never read the dismissal paper. It will wipe your memory of our visit here."

He believed her. "It's that potent?"

"Yes."

He sighed deeply. "This is the kind of thing that gets people fired."

He took the photocopies and filed them in the drawer.

"Okay. When do we start?"

Fugitive

Pokey the horse smelled Ned on the wind, and covered the distance to the barn at an easy trot.

Ned was moving a lot slower. He had drained the canteen. Two miles in late May was a long hot walk, especially when his ribs still hurt. He bypassed the horse with a wave, and even bypassed the watering trough. It had green scum growing on the top of the water. The ranch house, although deserted, was in good shape and the water was fresh at the faucet. The place felt very familiar.

Have I come here often? I don't remember.

That was strange. Could the beating Greg gave him have left him with amnesia? If so, what was missing?

He put his hand in his pocket, after filling the canteen. He jingled the coins.

It is odd that a horse lives here—water in the trough, obviously fed regularly. The house looks clean.

He walked in the unlocked front door. There were signs of people living here. He looked at the pictures resting on the mantle over the fireplace. A family of three, father, mother and daughter, and there was a separate picture of the mother, in a fancy frame.

The daughter—she caught his eye.

The fat coin in his pocket seemed warmer to the touch.

She looked at him with an amused smile. But the memory vanished as soon as it had appeared. She had been older than in the picture, wearing a motorcycle helmet.

Ned dashed back out of the house and faced towards the northwest.

What am I doing? I don't know the girl. I've never known her, and I've lived here for years.

The whole ranch had acquired a spooky feel, like it was a place he shouldn't be—a place he shouldn't even think about.

The horse was waiting for him at the fence line.

I've got too many questions, and Carl is the only person who can answer them.

...

The nurse at the front desk took the paper from her and started to read it.

Dot had no idea what it said. She dared not read it herself. All she knew was the effect it would have on people.

Carl had based it on the forget-me document he had used to hide the base. It started out like a legal document, but the legalese, the fine print, took the reader's mind off on a side trip. Any person who read it would daydream about something unrelated for a few seconds, and when they were done, certain facts were loaded into the mind past the point where they could be examined.

The nurse's eyes seemed to glaze over, and then after a moment, she took a deep breath as if waking up.

"Okay, looks good to me. I apologize for the mix-up. Can I help you with your father?"

"Blake is helping me, thank you."

They wheeled Ruben to the door. "Stay here. I'll bring the pickup around."

Blake picked her father up with ease, as if he weighed no more than a child, and set him in the pickup.

"Fasten your seatbelt, sir." He then put the wheelchair in the back of the pickup.

Dot was surprised at the gift, but she wasn't about to turn it down. Blake came around to the driver's side.

"How can I contact you? If the pattern works, or if it doesn't, I'll want to talk to you some more."

Dot struggled inwardly. She had no objection to giving him contact information, but it was like trying to find just the right word. She strained to remember her address, but it just wouldn't come.

"I'll have to contact you. Give me your phone number."

He whipped out a pen and wrote it out on a business card. "Have a safe trip home."

She nodded, but her mind stuttered. On automatic, she started the engine, and with a wave, she headed for the highway.

Ruben Comal muttered, "I am going to sleep. I can't hold it off."

"It's okay Dad. That's how it's supposed to work."

His head dropped and he was out.

"Okay. Time to head h...." Her brain stuttered again over the h-word. *Where am I headed?* She shook her head. *The best bet is to retrace my steps.* It was a long drive, and she would need gas again, but she knew, deep in her bones, that it would be a mistake to spend the night in the city.

She touched the fat coin in her pocket—for some reason she had to head southeast. It was important.

...

Ned was sure he had ridden horses before, but Pokey wasn't happy. He kept turning his head back towards the barn, looking for someone else.

"Come on! We've got distance to travel." Ned pulled the reins and urged him on.

Pokey was familiar with the route, heading for the High Road with little correction.

How does he know where Carl is? I seem to remember him there at the tunnel, but why?

Ned pulled the fat coin from his pocket and rubbed it between his thumb and index finger. *Something is wrong, seriously wrong. The King ... what about the king? Why don't I feel right about him?*

Engine noises. Ned urged the protesting horse off the side of the High Road.

"Down. Get down. I don't want them to see us."

Pokey shook his head, but carefully chose his path down the steep embankment.

Anyone can be working for the King. King Mort. Mort?

He's not a king!

The revelation felt like truth, and yet it directly contradicted what he knew.

For several minutes, he guided Pokey down a gully. When there was no sign of anyone following on the High Road, he headed towards the tunnel cross-country.

He strained to remember. *What memories do I have of the King?*

Ned remembered him in the classroom in his business suit. He remembered Mort driving past in his Humvee. He remembered seeing the large house in the distance.

But the very first time he remembered thinking of him as a King was today, digging himself out of the dirt.

The knowledge of Mort as King was timeless, ancient. His memories were different.

Mort was just a neighbor, a rich one, with no power over the people of the valley other than money.

No, that wasn't right either.

Mort is a wizard, with mind-bending powers, putting up signs to trick peoples' minds. Building crop-circles for power, putting up ward poles to....

Ned gasped. *He's warded off the entire valley! That's why this feels familiar. I was caught behind a ward before, when he tried to hide Carl's underground base.*

If Mort has warded off the valley, then there had to be a bigger world outside! And someone he knew—someone who lived at the deserted ranch—was trapped outside the wards.

...

Back on the highway, after stopping in Provo to get gas and hamburgers, Dot was energized. Dad was still sleeping, but she knew that was part of the healing process. He still clutched the touchstone, even while sleeping. Unless he dropped it, she was content to let him stay put no matter how uncomfortable he looked.

It was several miles down the road before she saw the first of the signs. They made no sense to her, but they did catch the eye. "Free—Ranch Exit— Your Off-Ramp to Fun!"

...

Ned was a half-mile from the tunnel entrance when the eagle swept overhead. The plane banked sharply and shrieked as it gained altitude.

He saw me.

Pokey reared and stopped dead in his tracks.

Mort knows about the tunnel entrance, but does he know that we took down the wards? Carl would be no match for anyone Mort decided to send down into the tunnels.

They're after me.

"Come on, slowpoke. Get a move on!" He urged Pokey towards the High Road. If he could get up there, he could get better speed out of the horse and maybe make it to the gullies west of his house. That land was so rugged only a horse, or maybe his motorcycle, could make any time through it.

Pokey complained as Ned urged him up the steep slope. Ned clung to the saddle, hoping he had secured it tightly enough. Horses weren't his thing, and he feared Pokey would lose his footing and drop the both of them down on the rocks.

Finally, they reached the crest of the High Road. To the west, Mort's eagle was wagging its wings at the Samuelson's vehicle. To the east, Sam Cooper was kicking up a cloud of dust as he raced across country.

"No help for it boy. Let's go. He shook the reins and pointed the horse eastward on the narrow top of the High Road. Any doubt that this was a hunt for him faded as Sam Cooper's four-wheeler changed course to cut him off.

If Ned had trusted the horse to navigate the narrow roadway at a full gallop, he might have made it. But he didn't trust the animal.

The four-wheeler topped the High Road within minutes, just ahead of him.

"Ned!" called out Sam Cooper. "Don't run!"

Pokey pulled up and he turned towards the open land to the north. But the machine took the downgrade faster than the timid horse.

"Wait! Ned! The King just wants to talk to you!"

But he wasn't taking any chances. Ned urged Pokey around the machine and towards the nearest mesa.

Only seconds later, Ned felt a blast of hot air above him, and the eagle swooped into view.

Only this wasn't the airplane painted to look like an eagle, this was a real flying beast, an eagle with a thirty foot wingspan, eyes that looked at him as prey, and talons that glistened sharply in the fading sun. Banking sharply, it turned for a closer pass.

Ned knew it would have no trouble yanking him and the horse into the sky with those claws.

He pulled Pokey to a stop. He raised his hands.

The eagle pulled up and passed overhead.

Sam Cooper roared up and snagged Pokey's halter.

"Hang on, Ned. You're not going anywhere."

...

Carl heard the chase, and from mice-sized eyes, filtered through mice-sized brains, he observed Ned's capture.

At least the boy is alive, for now.

King Mort is flexing his muscles. That eagle manifestation isn't something the others can ignore. He isn't afraid to push for god-king status, and that means he intends to keep the population as serfs permanently, or kill them.

Without Ned, Carl was trapped, just as surely as if the tunnel had never been opened.

But I can't just leave him to die either.

What resources do I have?

Carl wheeled over to his worktable, and spread out the photos Ned had left him. Two mice scurried up onto the table to join him.

He crooked a finger to stroke the closest under its snout.

"Are you up to this?"

...

Ned rode behind Sam Cooper.

"I wouldn't worry about it, Ned. The King just wants to talk to you. We were worried about you. After what Greg said last night, and finding your wallet, we feared the worst."

Ned shouted back, "Greg tried to kill me. He thought he had. He buried me."

Sam hunched his shoulders and lowered his head and concentrated on his driving.

Luke Samuelson met them on the road. "I'll take him on to the King's place."

Ned dismounted. He was tempted to make a break for it, but both of the men had rifles. Neither of them pointed them his way, but neither of them met his eye.

They wouldn't have the guns out if the King hadn't ordered their use. "I'll go quietly."

They were plainly relieved. Ned sat up front with Mr. Samuelson. Mr. Cooper headed off towards his place.

"Why did you run, Ned? Was it the wedding notice?"

"What wedding notice?"

"The King lowered the marriage age. He will be assigning couples from you and your friends."

Ned laughed. If that was all he had to be worried about!

"No, I hadn't heard. What's he going to do next? Name all the babies after himself?"

"Don't disrespect the King."

Ned could feel that Mr. Samuelson was upset. He was a good guy. What must be going through his mind?

"Don't worry about me. I won't be marrying anyone. Neither will Larry."

"You won't have a choice."

...

Dot blinked and checked the traffic again.

I should really try to drive during the daylight. When it gets dark, I get sleepy.

Even if her father wasn't sleeping off the effects of the healing touchstone pattern, with a broken leg he wouldn't be any help with the driving.

Another sign appeared in the headlights, "Free Ranch Exit...." She glazed over, tuning it out.

I've got to stay awake.

A different sign appeared. White letters on blue, it proclaimed: "Rest Area 2 Miles."

She looked at her father. Glaring orange lights or not, it was a safe place to stop, and they wouldn't likely wake him up.

Just a catnap, an hour or so. It would make a world of difference.

She remembered how bad it had gotten the night before, and she was running short of sleep. It was even worse tonight.

As the entrance ramp approached, Dot pulled in and parked near a picnic bench. *A bathroom stop and sleep.* Weariness settled down over her.

She glanced at the rear-view mirror and pulled the colored string from her hair.

Everything is back to normal. I won't need this.

When the engine died, she could hear the truck noises, but sleep was calling too strong.

It's okay. There is no need to hurry. What difference would it make if it took an extra day to get h....

Dot couldn't complete the thought. She leaned against her dad and fell asleep.

...

King Mort's palace was lit up, and there were several cars parked in front of it. Luke Samuelson pulled to a stop.

"Come on Ned. Let's get this over with."

Ned had seen the ward poles at the entrance to the Mort property, and had felt a slight twist in his guts as they crossed the property line. Mort's ranch was obviously not warded into non-existence as he had done with the underground base, but something was in place here.

Ned got out and walked with Mr. Samuelson through the open door.

"Ah, Ned! I'm glad to see you." Mort ... King Mort was jovial, and clearly the center of attraction in the room. Instead of his business suit, he was wearing an yellow oriental robe. George Filmore, Ms. Carson, Mr. Gibson, the Lee's and Mr. Brown stood around, facing him.

Mort beckoned him closer, and Ned found himself walking. The patterns on the robe kept catching his attention.

"The missing child has returned." Mort turned to the others, "I suppose all of you need to go home and rest up for the festivities tomorrow?"

They all nodded and muttered their apologies. Within a couple of minutes they had all left. Ned was alone with the King.

"Ned, the motorcycle kid. You led us quite a chase this evening." His voice lost a touch of his cheer.

"It's a good thing you surrendered when you did. The Eagle was getting hungry."

Ned opened his mouth, ready to tell him off for what he had done to Greg Cooper, and indirectly to him. Nothing came out.

Mort held up his palm. "No, don't even try to talk. You'll strain yourself. When I want information from you, I'll ask."

Mort moved closer, and Ned realized he couldn't even step back. Something had locked his will to move.

The King put his hand on Ned's head, and with a thumb, lifted an eyelid. "Hmm." He peered closely into his eye.

"You've been tampered with. Carl's at his old tricks."

Mort released his grip and turned back to his chair. It was a huge, high-backed affair, with carved wood and plush cushions. Ned suddenly realized it was a throne.

In his royal robes, the old man looked regal, and evil, as he rubbed his hands together.

"With the right tools, I should be able to read you like a book. You are the key to unlocking Carl's defenses."

He nodded to himself. "But I'm not wasting my beauty sleep on the likes of you. Yes. We'll start peeling the information off you in the morning, while the peasants have their fair.

"Unfortunately, some of the 'peeling' will be unpleasant. I'll have to throw away the core. I'm sure you understand. It is unfortunate. You would have made a good page, with that motorcycle of yours."

Ned struggled to fight the compulsion to silence.

"You have a question?" Mort's face lit up in a smile. "Certainly. One question." He held up one finger.

Ned almost stumbled as part of the compulsion was released. *I have a hundred questions.* But there was just that single finger.

"How old are you?"

Mort dropped his hand, and laughed. Ned could feel the silence descend on him again.

"How old am I?" He looked distracted. "Hmm. I guess that would be one hundred and thirty-four. Yes, Carl's little parlor tricks have some nice side effects!

"But just in case you are hoping I'll drop dead of old-age, forget it! I will certainly outlive you. I will outlive everyone in this dusty little valley!"

He took a deep breath, and then waved toward the staircase. "Now go to the first bedroom on the left at the top of the stairs. Don't even attempt to leave once you are inside."

Ned turned as if his legs were remote controlled.

Mort called after him. "You might as well enjoy the night. It will be your last."

Mouse Tactics

Dot stopped in Green River just as dawn was starting to show on the horizon. They needed gas, and for the past hour she'd sensed they were going the wrong direction.

She felt the fat coin in her pocket, and turned to look off towards the west. A few stars remained in the brightening sky.

The gas pump was lit up, but the store appeared closed. "Pay at the pump."

She reached for the credit card and followed the instructions on the pump, and soon enough the gas was flowing.

The card felt strange in her hand. Holding it up to the light, she read the name.

"Albert Kelso? Who is Albert Kelso?" Where did she get this card in the first place? It seemed natural that she had it, but something was seriously wrong.

Kelso. She put the card away, and reached for the fat coin. *I'm supposed to go back west. It's important.*

"Good morning, Dot." Ruben Comal had straightened up in his seat, and was twisting his head around to ease the muscle cramp.

"Hi Dad. I'm glad to see you back."

He looked at the skyline. "Where are we?"

"Green River."

He nodded.

"Dad? Where are we going?"

"Ah." He frowned, and then shook his head. "I'm not sure. My brain's still a little scrambled I guess." He glanced at the touchstone still in his hand.

Dot sighed. "It's not just you. I have no idea where I am headed. Something tells me to go back west, to turn around."

Her father put his hand on his forehead.

"There's a word," he struggled. "It's the place where you live. H-home. That's it. Shouldn't we go h-home?"

Dot shook her head, suddenly confused. The word meant nothing to her. "I think we should head west."

He nodded. "You're driving. Whatever you think."

...

Carl Stellman noticed the lights brightening. He put aside the pencil and paper.

The sun is up. It's about time.

He rapped the edge of the table with his ruler. Five mice scurried close.

I hope they are up to it. I've never had them try anything like this before.

...

Ned had been awake since first light. He hadn't thought he would sleep a wink, but being beat up and buried for most of the day, followed by several miles of walking had drained him.

He might have slept longer, except his motorcycle woke him up. The sound was muffled by the fancy windows, but he was out of bed as soon as he recognized the noise.

Greg Cooper drove it up, trailing road dust and his brother's pickup. Greg parked it next to Mort's Humvee, and then joined his brother and left. No message.

They don't want to disturb the King.

Ned took it as a good sign. Carl's healing pattern had been in his wallet. Greg stole the wallet and from the looks of things, he was healed by accident. Once his mind cleared up, he returned the motorcycle.

People know I'm here. Not that he could get too hopeful about it. The information inside people's heads existed only at the whim of King Mort.

How many people get buried the day before they die?

Mort's plans for him didn't sound too pleasant, and there was no chance for rescue. Maybe Carl knew what was going on—but there was no certainty of that. His parents, his friends, all of them were under Mort's spell, and had no real concept of the danger he was in. Carl couldn't help, even if he tried. No one else even knew that they should try.

Ned reached for the window, but no matter how hard he strained, he couldn't touch it. *It's only in my head!* He struggled, but even closing his eyes and throwing himself at the glass didn't work. His leg collapsed under him at just the wrong time.

He turned to the door, but it was the same.

What had Mort said? "Don't attempt to leave." I'm attempting, but my own body is stopping me. I couldn't leave even if the door were wide open.

The door opened. Mort looked in, an amused smile on his face. His morning robe was red, and perhaps even more elaborately decorated than the one he wore last night.

"I thought I heard you banging around up here. Anxious to get started on the day, are you?"

Ned lunged at him, arms reaching, ready to tear the man apart. He collapsed to his knees.

Mort watched, immensely pleased.

"No need to bow." He glanced at his wristwatch. "But I'm not ready for you yet."

Ned struggled to his feet, edging back, careful to keep his distance from the man.

Mort moved aside and waved toward the door. "Do you want to leave? Try it."

Cautiously, Ned walked to the door. Nothing happened. He took another step out into the hall. Mort just watched.

He ran. The stairway was just a few feet away.

"Stop!"

Ned skidded to a stop.

"Turn around."

He did.

"Come back to your room."

Woodenly, he walked slowly back. The compulsion was complete. He couldn't even think of doing anything other than what Mort said.

"I still have breakfast to take care of. I would ask you to join me, but it would be a waste, don't you think?"

Ned's head jerked in a nod.

"Good. Now stop trying stupid escape attempts. The door and window are out of your reach."

He snapped his finger. Ned felt the mental numbness leave.

"I'll be back shortly. Consider what you can tell me. Make me happy, and I'll find a way to keep you. If not...." he cocked his head and walked away, not even bothering to close the door.

Ned yelled, "You'll never succeed! I'll...."

"Shut up." Mort didn't even raise his voice, but Ned's words locked up in his mouth.

...

Dot felt her body jerk. She slowed down. *Free Ranch Exit.* The sign flickered past.

She reached for the fat coin. It was pulling her north. She frowned. There was no road heading that direction.

In daylight, there seemed to be much more traffic than when she went through before. There were several cars traveling along with her, as well as a few trucks.

Her father was dozing again. He had been chatting about how well she was driving, and telling embarrassing tales of when he had been a teenager and started driving.

Wait, the signs have moved over to the other side of the road. From somewhere near here to just this side of Provo, the signs were on the south side of the road. From here to Green River, they were on the north side.

That means something. But what it meant was elusive. Thinking about the signs was liking trying to grab a greased baseball.

She clutched the coin in her left hand, and drove with the other. *You've been pulling me in this direction since Salt Lake City. But what are you pulling me towards?*

...

206

The booths were opening up. Here it was, the day of the fair, and the people who had shown up early waved to the latecomers.

Whole families had come this time, with the kids wandering around the booths while the adults sat by their tables and pretended to sell their wares.

George Filmore turned his store over to Quad Brewster, and while the hefty boy kept a wide eye on the place, George walked the booths.

The King wants to know if I've trained someone to handle the store, and then he hires Ned away from me! I'll need to find someone who can handle the job. Quad can run the cash register, but I need someone older to handle the stock.

"Hey, George!" Mr. Brown waved.

George turned to their booth. Kelly held little Sue in her lap while Mel Brown and Luke Samuelson were shuffling dominoes.

"Come join the game."

"I'd love to, but I can't stay too long. I just wanted to stretch my legs. How are things going here?"

Kelly Brown laughed, "I don't know where I got the idea that I could sell all these jars! Every one of the ladies here in town can cook as well as I can, and certainly you men aren't going to buy anything."

Sue whimpered, and Kelly turned to make faces at her.

Luke waved around. "It's the same with all of us. It's like a mass illusion grabbed us and had us believing we could sell crates and crates of this stuff."

George nodded and griped about his own mis-stocking.

"I have a feeling this is going to be a long day."

Kelly pointed off to the northwest. "What's that?"

They all looked.

A thin column of smoke trailed off with the gentle breeze from somewhere up the valley.

Mel said, "It looks like somebody burning a brush-pile."

"Who would that be?" asked Luke. "Everyone is here today." He pushed back his chair. "I think I'll go take a look-see."

...

Ned sat on the bed, holding the fat coin in his hand.

He opened his mouth, but nothing he tried to say would come out.

At least my mind is my own, I think.

He tried to be strong, to shake off the fear, but it was hard. *I don't want to die. I don't want to be Mort's zombie, either.*

Neither of his possible futures bore thinking about. *Escape. I can still think about escape.*

The motorcycle was still down there in front of the house. His bike was freedom. If he could just reach his bike, Carl's tunnel was just minutes away. Carl could break these mental chains. Without the chains on his action, he could escape and reach his bike.

Fruitless worry was interrupted by the sound of footsteps on the stairway. Ned moved the coin and his hand into his pocket.

Mort was dressed for the day, holding a clipboard and an old bound ledger. He went to the desk in the bedroom, ignoring Ned. He opened the book and removed a diagram freshly drawn on a sheet of paper.

Ned tried to avert his eyes, but was too late.

The pain in his head was intense, his eyesight blurred.

...

"I'll curse that hawk out of the sky! I didn't come all this way for my health."

"A hawk, Mr. Wanekia?" he asked.

The wrinkled face looked them over. "Kelso. Did you know you're stretching the valley with that thing? Back and forth, back and forth. Hmmp."

....

"Hello," came a dry whispery voice.

He froze. He strained his eyes to see by the faint light reflecting in from the outside.

"Who's that?"

"Surely Dot has mentioned me?"

"What did you do to her? She won't wake up!"

....

He wondered what Carl was doing. He had vanished, gone to 'do research', whatever that meant.

The old bridge near Dot's house came into view. Some day, he thought, I'll fix that ramp.

He eased the throttle, and turned towards the well-worn rut that took him around the bridge.

The crack of a rifle and the puff-flower of dirt just a foot from his front tire took him by surprise. He jerked the handlebars and went flying.

...

Ned woke, lying flat on the floor. Mort was yelling out the window. "Where is the fire?"

A faint voice came up from outside. "A grass fire over on Jed Fellerman's land."

"Go on," shouted Mort, "Don't wait for me. I'll get some shovels and follow."

Mort glared at him, seeing his eyes open. "I'm not done with you yet!" He grabbed his papers and book, and ran out of the room. By the time Ned gained enough strength to get to the window. Mort's Humvee was on the road.

The crop-circles. Ned chuckled. *That got Mort's attention!*

Ned's mind was dull. Mort had indeed been stripping his memories, and that part of his mind felt bruised.

I've still got to escape. He put his hand toward the window, but the strength went out of his arm before it got there.

...

A team of six mice struggled hard, rolling the bottle, half-full of spring water, towards its destined position, all without spilling anything from the open mouth. With a tiny *clink*, it stopped, propped against two rocks and over a pile of dark, dry leaves.

The bright morning sun bent through the glass and water, concentrating its blazing heat to an irregular patch on the leaves. Shortly, a whisper of smoke curled up from the heat.

The mice scattered, half to find another discarded clear bottle near the creek, and half to prepare another dark pile of leaves.

The roar of men's machines penetrated the tiny minds, panic washing away the calm deliberate work spell. They dashed for safety—away from the men, and away from the growing grass fire.

The men yelled at each other, beating the flames with brooms and blankets, stamping at the grass with their feet.

Ten acres were ablaze, crawling up the hill toward the crop-circles. Somehow the fire had started from three different places near the creek.

A pickup plowed through the fire line and three men hopped out with shovels, hoping to cut a fire lane by chopping through the tall grass. If they could start a controlled backfire, they could keep the blaze from spreading.

The Humvee drove another crew to the upper edge, where fire was eating into the lowest of the crop-circles. The fire spread slower there, where the grass was beaten down, but the driver of the Humvee yelled orders, and everyone within the sound of his voice obeyed.

...

Ned watched the smoke from his window, wishing he could talk, so that he could cheer the flames on.

A flicker of motion caught his eye.

Beside him on the floor, a little brown mouse was watching him. A second one joined him, and then a third. They danced around each other.

Follow us.

Ned blinked. It was just like Dot … Dot?

Dot! He struggled to remember what she looked like. His thumb rubbed the coin furiously in his pocket.

Follow us. The mice insisted, talking through their dance.

He turned away from the window and took a step. The mice moved, but not towards the door.

They headed for the closet. Ned followed.

Opening the door wider, he disturbed two dozen or more mice, chewing away at the wallboard inside the closet.

There was a mouse-sized hole with light streaming in from the other side.

I've got you. Ned looked around the bedroom. The chair at the desk was finely carved wood, and looked very expensive. Ned broke off the leg without a qualm. Mort had been the last person to sit there.

With the chair-leg as a pick and a pry-bar, he went to work helping the mice. Soon enough the opening was wide enough for him to squeeze through.

Ned eyed the destruction with satisfaction. *Mort should have let me use the door.*

The opening in the back of the closet led to another closet in an adjoining bedroom. He walked to the door, and it opened with a quiet click. And he was out.

The troop of mice headed down the stairs, not waiting for him. Their job was done.

Ned raced down the stairs himself. The front door had even been left open. Who would dare enter Mort's palace uninvited?

I would. He stopped. *I can hear Mort's Humvee coming a mile away if he returns. But he will be busy. He can't let that fire burn away the power circles. I'll give it a minute.*

At a run, he began circling through the rooms on the first floor. That's all he would risk.

The library room stopped him in his tracks. Mort had dropped his clipboard and ledger book on the table on his way out to fight the fire.

He was using that to scrape my mind away.

Carefully, avoiding looking at any of the papers, he stuffed the clipboard and all loose sheets between the covers of the ledger and closed it tight. *I'm taking these.* He looked around for some bag to carry them in.

On one shelf of the library, a whole row of ancient bound ledger books stared back at him. The book he held in his hand was one of that set. *Carl's research notes.*

...

Dot pulled off onto the shoulder of the interstate. *The coin is pulling me back here every time. I'm just burning gas looping back and forth.*

She coasted to a wider section of the shoulder and stopped. Her dad had dozed off again.

There is something about this place. Dad goes to sleep, the coin wants to go north from here, the Free Ranch Exit signs switch sides here.

Quietly, to avoid disturbing her father, she got out and walked around.

That's odd. On the pavement ahead, there were two thin stripes of yellow. A joke road sign said "LIZARD CROSSING". She shook her head and went back to the car.

Her head felt like it was stuffed with cotton.

I might as well take a nap.

Fifteen minutes later, a Postal van pulled up on the shoulder near her. The driver, his mind confused and running in circles, rubbed his eyes and fell asleep.

...

Ned put some air under his bike as he roared past the Mort Ranch entrance gate.

Hiding the notebooks won't slow him down much, but anything to throw him off balance.

Ned grinned, and it felt really good. At the rate Mort had been tearing at his brain, there should have been nothing but tapioca in his skull by now.

The High Road was just ahead, and he powered up to the crest.

Off in the distance, he could see the collection of tents, and farther off, the patch of smoke.

They look like they've got the fire under control.

Mort would be heading back soon. *I've got to find Carl.*

Ned waited patiently for the memory to come back. It didn't.

Where is Carl? It was something he should know, but it eluded him. *Mort has messed up my memory.*

He stared into the distance, along the High Road.

'High Road' isn't its name. It's the old railroad grade.

Railroad. Images of locomotives linked together for power and hundreds of boxcars heading cross-country came back to his mind.

That's not a memory from the valley. Whatever Mort did to him had weakened the effects of the wards. Some memories were back, new ones were missing.

I can't just sit here and wait for Mort to chase me down again.

He rubbed the coin in his pocket. *That way.*

He headed south. The bike picked up speed, but quickly he eased off and without conscious thought, slowed and turned north again.

The ward poles at the entrance to Mort's property brought him out of the doze. *It still has me.* Whatever was cutting the valley off from the rest of the world still had him under its control.

But maybe Carl is north. He sped up and raced as fast as he could towards North Mesa. The bridge near Dot's ranch forced him to slow and take the way around.

I jumped it once, but that was when I was under the clarity spell.

Ned navigated the gap and then regained speed.

Out of a heat haze, the shape of a bear appeared, standing in the center of his path.

Wanekia! But he's dead!

Ned braked hard. By the time he skidded to a halt, the image disappeared. *What does that mean?*

He pulled out the coin, still insisting he go south. Carl was probably still in the tunnels north of here, and now the ghost of an Indian shaman was weighing in. What was he supposed to do?

As he rubbed the coin, the memory of Carl handing it to him returned. He gave another to Dot at the same time. *Resonance enhancers.*

To the south, the railroad grade stretched into the unknown. Dot had to be there, outside the valley. He had tried to go that way, but the wards had turned him back.

Wanekia's voice echoed in his head—*"Kelso. Did you know you're stretching the valley with that thing? Back and forth, back and forth."*

He would love to have Dot here to tell him what to do. She wasn't always right, but even when she wasn't, talking to her made things clearer for him.

To get to her, he would have to pass the wards. Was that even possible?

Surely so, otherwise Mort would just be locking himself into a prison and throwing away the key. That's not likely.

Besides, we knocked down the ward poles around the tunnel, maybe we can do the same for the valley.

I just need to be clear on what I can do.

Clarity.

He reached into the saddlebag where he had stuffed Mort's clipboard and the single notebook that had been used against him. In the depths of the bag, he felt a folded piece of paper.

The seeing charm—he closed his eyes and took a deep breath. *An hour or so of clarity, and then I crash.*

He nodded. *It will be worth it.*

Ned unfolded the paper and opened his eyes.

There was something like a click in his head.

Ned took a long look, peering in all directions. The valley was bent, folded in on itself. Nothing human could pass beyond its limits.

Except for one quirk. The valley had stretched slightly along the railroad grade. It wasn't something one could measure. It was something more fundamental than distance. Something not really visible, unless you could *see*.

In the same way wards bent the boundaries beyond human perception, running the 'Kelso Express' as Dot called it, had pushed the edge of the valley past its natural limit.

Ned revved up the engine. Turning south towards the call of the coin, he leaned into the wind. The speedometer edged up into unfamiliar numbers.

He jumped the old bridge as effortlessly as he had before, and kept gaining speed. Ned reached down and adjusted the fuel-mix by touch, pushing the velocity even higher.

Focused straight ahead, he could feel the valley stretch. At the edge of his sight, he saw the store and the school whip by, and then Mort's ranch. The railroad grade didn't go any farther, sliced off by the interstate's construction decades ago. He knew that.

Still he rode. The boundary of the valley approached, visible to his *seeing* eyes like a featureless cloud. In an instant, he tensed and the world around him vanished.

Free Ranch Exit

The roar of a motorcycle startled Dot awake, just in time for her to see Ned sail through the air.

The apparition materialized about ten feet up, and sailed across her lane of the interstate to land gracefully on the far shoulder of the opposite lane. When he dropped out of sight in the ditch, she felt paralyzed.

Ned. Did I just see Ned?

A wash of confusion passed over her, as her brain adjusted to his existence. Years of memories re-emerged, most of them taking place in impossible locations, with other people she was certain did not exist.

The motorcycle put-putted next to the pickup and she jerked when the window beside her went *tap-tap-tap.*

She turned to see Ned's grinning face.

"Ned!" She rolled down the window. "What's going on?" Beside her Ruben was waking up.

Ned opened his mouth, but didn't speak. He frowned.

Dot asked, "What's wrong?"

He twisted her side mirror around and peered into his own face. He shook his head.

Dot watched him touch his throat.

"Can't you talk?" She took the fat-coin from her pocket absently, as she had been doing since they left Salt Lake, and rubbed it.

He smiled and reached for his own fat-coin.

No. Mort told me to shut-up.

Dot gasped. She asked her Dad, "Did you hear that?"

"No. Hi, Ned." He straightened up in his seat, and asked, "What are we doing here?"

Dot clutched her coin tightly. "Ned, I heard you in my head, like when the mice talked to me!"

Ruben Comal asked, "Mice?"

Ned nodded. *I had my own experience with them. Ranch Exit has been hidden behind wards. I broke through to find you.*

Dot concentrated on the coin. Reading Ned felt like she had been doing it all her life. They could always exchange meaning in smiles, gestures, and the subtleties of body language. This was the same, only elevated to a new level.

"Wards! I know what that is, but I don't know why?"

You are outside the valley. Memories from inside are being suppressed.

Ruben asked, "What are you saying, Dot? Hospital wards?"

She looked at her father. "Dad, strange things are happening. It's all a part with the insanity that took you, and just as quickly healed. I don't have time to explain right now, but I will! Can you just roll with it for now?"

He looked at the intense expression on his daughter's face. How like her mother she had become.

"Sure, Honey. Just remember I'm still here."

Dot gave his hand a squeeze.

"Ned, what can we do? And who is Mort?"

Mort is the bad guy, the wizard who stole our valley. Carl is the good guy, the wizard who can help us put it back to right. Once we get the wards down, you will remember all of this.

"Where are the wards?"

Ned moved his bike up a few feet and got off. Dot opened her door, and was startled to see how many vehicles had pulled off the road. There were eight she could see, and all appeared to have drivers taking naps. One was a police cruiser.

Ned pointed. *There they are, next to the Ranch Exit sign.*

Dot tried to focus on where he pointed, but with no luck. If there was a sign, she couldn't see it.

Ned started walking in that direction, and she followed. After a few paces, she stumbled and fell. She picked herself back up and walked back to her pickup.

"How's it going, Dot?" asked her dad.

"Ah." What was she doing here? And why were all these cars and trucks stopped here as well?

A wave of lethargy swept over her. *Maybe I need to take a nap.*

She opened the door and started to get back in.

A hand on her shoulder startled her.

Ned smiled. He pressed a coin into her hand. *It took you over again, didn't it? Keep your resonance enhancer in your hand. You dropped it.*

Dot felt the confusion drop away.

"You're right. That was scary. Did you find the wards?"

Yes. There are several, right next to the sign. But they are too big to bring down by hand.

"Can we help you, Ned?" asked Ruben.

Dot, get in. Let me drive.

"Dad, Ned's going to drive." She scooted inside to make room.

Ned started the pickup and drove it off the shoulder. Before he had gone a few feet, Dot started feeling sleepy, in spite of the coin in her hands. Ruben's chin dropped to his chest.

She could read the tension in Ned's arms. *It's hard to focus on the wards.*

The pickup bounced through a ditch and up an incline. Dot couldn't force her eyes to lock on anything. It was like a fog.

The crash threw her forward to the dash. Her dad groaned as the seatbelt kept him seated.

I only shook it. I'll have to try again.

The pickup backed up and Ned put it in gear. They slammed the pole again.

Dot saw something long and tall. "I can see it."

Good, we must be making some progress.

Ruben protested, "Ned, what are you doing to my pickup?"

Ned put it into reverse for another run.

"Hang on, Dad. We're going to hit it again."

"But..."

Crash. This time the pole was visibly bent, twisted at least thirty degrees off of vertical.

Ruben looked at his surroundings, and peered up at the large green "RANCH EXIT" sign.

"Dot, something has changed. I can feel it."

Dot's eyes welled with tears, as a surge of memories, most of her life, came rushing back. *Home.*

"Ned! We've broken the ward."

Let's take it all the way down. And there are four more. This was just the primary.

"Dad," she said, "we need to knock it all the way down."

Ruben reached across to catch Ned's sleeve. "Son, you'll crack the radiator this way. If we've got to knock them down, then turn around and hit it with the rear bumper. We don't want to lose the engine."

Ned nodded, and wheeled the pickup around. Two more strikes and they had the primary ward bent down to the ground.

They shifted over to the next ward pole and hit it once when the siren started.

Three heads turned. The cars and trucks, which had parked by the interstate, had all started up. The Postal van was in the lead, but the police car was edging around him.

All of them were taking the exit ramp into the valley.

Ranch Exit is open.

...

The fire fighters were walking the black patch, stamping out any individual embers, when the gestalt shifted. They all stopped in their tracks.

Luke Samuelson called to his son, "Larry! Take over here and make sure you get everything dead out. I've got to get back to the booth."

There was a general murmur of agreement. They had stopped the fire, and it was time to get back to the fair.

"No!" called out a lone voice. "Keep walking the burned patch."

"Sorry, Mr. Mort. Visitors should have started showing up at the fair by now. I've got to go help my wife."

Mort's face paled. *"Mr. Mort"? The wards must be down!*

Off in the distance, a siren could be heard. Mort wasted no time. The impossible had happened, but he had eluded the police for decades by being quick on his feet and asking questions later. The Humvee headed off cross the blackened field, and he passed the others.

As he drove past the booths, a dozen or more cars and trucks had pulled in from outside the valley. He saw the police car and never slowed down. Traffic was still coming in, but he took the side road to his ranch.

Cresting the rise at his property line, he reached for the radio remote control and pressed a key. The ward poles at the entrance shifted their vanes. With a shudder, his ranch vanished off the map.

In Ranch Exit, Mort had gone from god-king, to mister, to non-existent in the span of five minutes.

...

Ned hit the brakes.

"What is it?"

Something has just happened in Ranch Exit. I could see the shift.

"You used the seeing charm?"

Yes, otherwise I would never have been able to break through the wards.

"How long do you have?"

Not long. The headaches are pretty strong.

Dot nodded, familiar with the effect. "Okay. Let's get the other poles later and head on in. If there's something only you can see, we'd better take advantage of your sight while we can."

Ruben caught only the basics of what was going on, missing everything that Ned could communicate to Dot. Still he agreed.

"Fine. I'm getting pretty shaken up from this demolition derby. Let's go home while the pickup can still drive."

Ned steered back onto the exit ramp and headed into town. The school was in sight almost immediately.

Hang on. Ned pulled to a stop, got out and climbed up on top of the pickup.

"What's going on?" Dot scooted out where she could see him.

I can see the valley, and we aren't clear. There is this huge section warded off. Can you remember anything about it?

"No, but maybe you do! You told me something, when I was outside." She struggled to recall what he had told her, but without even the memory of spoken words to work with, it was hard.

"There's a good wizard, and a bad wizard." *Right. Carl and somebody else. We broke the ward on the valley, and he retreated to another place.*

Ned hopped down. *Take your dad someplace safe. I'll walk back and get my bike. If I stay awake long enough, meet me right over there, by that road that seems to lead nowhere.*

...

The two gestalt shifts in less than five minutes took Carl by surprise, but he was grateful. Mort's paradise had already been set up. Any change had to be for the better.

He fingered the necklace. It was the original one he had created so long ago. As long as he wore it, his memories were intact. He might not believe what his memories told him, but a gestalt shift would no longer hide the inconsistent facts. He had dug it out of the storeroom, hoping to break through the King Mort's fog of illusion.

Carl viewed the two-page summary of facts he had gleaned from his unleashed memories. It had spilled over into the second sheet when the kingdom collapsed, and many things came rushing back.

Mort, you may have vanished again, but I've caught you here on paper.

...

Ned was glad to be back on his motorcycle, in spite of what the engine noise did to his headache.

Wow. With the valley ward down, he could see where the railroad grade ended and how far he had jumped. *A world record, but I'll never be able to prove it. Besides, I'd stretched the valley, no telling how far it really was.*

The road that headed into the mysterious warded section was difficult to drive, but right where he expected them, ward poles drifted in and out of his charm-enhanced vision.

The bad wizard is behind there. Should we leave him there, "out of sight, out of mind" or try to take down his defenses. He just might be very dangerous if cornered.

Ned kicked the stand and killed the engine. *I'd better mark this place. I won't be able to see it once the clarity charm fades away.*

He stepped back a few paces and drew an arrow in the dirt. "30 FEET", he added.

The effort was almost too much. Even without the motorcycle noise, his head was banging. He sat down in the dirt, beside his bike.

Then, a new noise started, a metallic buzzing. Ned looked around. The ward poles flickered into view, their vanes turning.

Mort! What is he up to?

The Humvee roared up the road, and skidded to a stop right in front of him, choking him with dust.

Mort opened the door in his face.

The old man grabbed his collar. The pasty face was twisted with rage. "What did you do to my notebooks?"

...

Dot unloaded the wheelchair and by the time she got her father out of the pickup, friends were greeting Ruben Comal on all sides.

The Ranch Exit Roundup was hitting full stride. The makeshift parking lot that George had created by mowing off an unused field beside the road now had about three dozen cars parked in it, and more were coming down the road.

But the return of a neighbor was more of an attraction for the locals.

"Ruben! Good to see you. How's the leg doing?"

"Ruben, wheel that thing over to our booth. I'll bring you a plate of Jake's cabrito."

"How were you treated at the hospital? Were the nurses pretty?"

Dot smiled, and then smiled again as she realized how her own memories were being altered. If she hadn't been there, and hadn't retained those oh-so-vivid memories of her father in a rage, she would accept the new gestalt that Carl's touchstone and that magic release paper had worked.

In the new reality, her father had never gone crazy. He had been at the hospital to get his broken leg treated, and that was it.

How would Blake handle the layered memories? He would be having problems remembering events too—if he hadn't read the release papers!

She would need to have a serious talk with her dad about all this. If you can't trust your memories, you could go insane, but if you knew why, you could live with it.

But for now, Dad was in the hands of friends.

The fair looked to be more successful than she had imagined. There were visitors, dozens and dozens of them, and they were buying.

Dot walked the booths. Nora Baker was rolling up one of her art-prints and chatting with a customer. Jake Cartulio was on a platform in front of his smoking cookers, dressed in his chef's outfit and waving his tongs like a conductor directing an orchestra. Off in the distance, the singers were warming up with a John Denver song about home.

That's the memory that scares me the most—off in Salt Lake City, unable to remember what 'home' meant.

Someone had spread a banner between two of the tents. "Ranch Exit, Utah—It ain't much, but I won't trade it."

...

Duncan Bly raced through the crowd, chasing Ross Brown. Mrs. Brewster was selling fudge bars in all kinds of flavors and colors, and Ross had a sack full. He had taunted Duncan with his stash, and then raced off through the cars.

Duncan lost him, somewhere between the silver car and the panel truck. Huffing from his exertion, Duncan walked slowly, hunched over to avoid being seen. Ross was sure to have a rock in his hand, but if he could sneak up on him....

Three little brown critters were waiting for him between the Ford and a pair of big Harley-Davidson motorcycles.

Duncan, they danced, *help us find Dot. It's important!*

...

Dot had been overwhelmed by the smell of Jake's cooking, and bought a flour tortilla wrapped around sweet juicy beef. The only problem was the drips, but she fixed that by licking her fingers.

A policeman was walking the crowd, but he didn't seem to be on duty. There were a few exchanged whispers from the sign-painters, but if he were here about the illegal road signs, he wasn't telling anyone. From Dot's view, he looked like any other tourist, with an ice-cream cone in one hand and fending off questions about his gun from a contingent of underage males.

Ms. Carson had whished by, stopping long enough to get Dot's promise to say a few words when they held the awards ceremony later in the day. George Filmore's face had the biggest worry lines in the place. The turnout was larger than he had expected.

"Dot, if everyone here needs gas they'll drain those two tank cars dry."

Dot could give moral support only. Dad was her prime concern. As she wandered through the crowd, she made a point to keep him in sight.

Latoya raced over. "Dot! Dot, he's coming!"

"Who? What?"

"Roger! I just checked the letter box. Three whole bags of letters had been lost in the mails. He had written me, several times, but they just hadn't been delivered!" She showed the envelopes, ripped open and held carefully in her hand.

"That's great! You say he is coming?"

"Yes! He said he wouldn't miss it, but he might be later in the day."

Latoya couldn't restrain herself, giving Dot a big hug, and then rushing off to share the news with the rest of Ranch Exit.

Dot glanced over to the table where her dad and a rotating collection of friends chatted.

There was a woman sitting beside him. Dot took in a deep breath.

She looks just like Momma.

They were talking. They looked friendly.

A feeling of dread crept up from her toes.

Aunt Elizabeth has come to take me away.

...

A delivery truck pulled up to the store and George went out to meet it. The driver was apologetic. They had attempted delivery the day before, but the other driver hadn't been able locate Ranch Exit.

George waved off the apologies. "I can use every bit of this today. Let me round up a couple of hands to help unload."

Dot watched. It was just like the postal delivery. Starting several days before the evil wizard had stolen the valley, something was already in play that made it hard for people to find Ranch Exit.

And now it was reversed. Every delayed delivery, every late letter was now showing up.

Even random strangers were dropping in for the Roundup, and no one was having any trouble finding Ranch Exit.

...

Elizabeth Jordon shook her head, "No, I had no problem finding the place. I saw the signs and came right here. Dorothy said there would be a fair, and there it was."

Ruben held up a finger. "Go ahead and call her Dot. She hasn't gone by Dorothy since she was seven. We watched the Wizard of Oz on TV and I think she took a dislike to it."

Elizabeth said, "Thanks. It's going to be hard enough without tripping over her pet peeves." She shook her head, "I know she doesn't like me."

"That's my fault. I shouldn't have let old hurts go unhealed. She picked up on my pain when June died. I should have done more to keep talking with both sides of the family."

He pointed, "Oh, look. There she is."

Over by the Brewster tent, where little metal windmills were twirling in the breeze, Dot was talking to a family—no one Ruben knew.

He waved, but she didn't appear to see him.

Little Duncan Bly raced up and tugged on her sleeve. She leaned down and he whispered in her ear.

She looked up, saw her father, but before he could catch her attention, she headed off with Duncan.

Ruben sighed, "Dot is very busy today. Did you know this fair was her idea?"

...

I knew there was something I was forgetting. Dot raced into the parking lot, following Duncan. *I just couldn't remember what.*

The mice were still there, unwilling to come any closer to the human crowd. When they saw Dot arrive, they danced.

Dot, come get me. It's an emergency.

That was all there was. Once the mice transferred their message, they vanished under the cars.

"Thanks Duncan. I've got to go now."

"To help the dwarf?"

"Yes, but you've got to keep it a secret."

He zipped his mouth and nodded.

Dot headed for the pickup. Carl had said, "Come get me." There was more to the message than just those three words. It wasn't just "Come talk to me."

He needs me to take him somewhere. How do I do that?

If it were just her, she would get Pokey and ride over to the tunnel, but she would never get Carl out that way.

A splash of green and yellow caught her eye.

Off to the side of the freshly mowed parking area was a tractor with a large mowing deck. One side was dented.

That's the tractor Dad was using when he broke his leg. Memory fragments came together.

The evil wizard's tractor.

She had an idea.

At Bay

Carl was ready. The mice had warned him as soon as the tractor came to within a mile of the tunnel.

"Dot! Is that you?" he called.

She waved from the top of the railroad grade. He wheeled the chair out into the open. With gloves and hat and dressed in the thick clothes, the only skin visible was his face, and he was determined not to let that ever see the sun.

The tractor noise shifted, and the front wheels started edging down the steep rocky slope.

His heart pounded, and he wheeled back as quickly as he could. The heavy machine was kicking loose rocks as it crept down hill in the lowest of low gears.

There was a scrape of metal, and she stopped. Something adjusted, and then she continued.

She'll never make it.

"Be careful!" he shouted, and then moved back inside the tunnel opening. If the tractor overturned, it wouldn't do either of them any good if he was caught under the rubble.

Old memories—trauma from his first days trapped underground—came back to awaken fears long forgotten.

The engine stopped.

"Carl?"

"I'm here." He wheeled into sight. Dot looked comfortable behind the wheel.

"I was afraid you would overturn."

She laughed, "I've been driving tractors even before my feet could reach the pedals. Now stay back. I've got to turn this thing around, and there isn't much room."

It took a dozen seesaw swings, but she did it.

"Whew. I'm ready to take you out of here."

"Come inside a minute. We need to talk."

She climbed off the tractor, and was nearly blind in the darkness of the tunnel. Carl turned on extra lights for her.

"We have an enemy."

"I figured that out," she said. "There's an evil wizard. He made Ranch Exit vanish, and then when I knocked down the ward poles, it came back."

Carl held out his summary. "Read this."

Dot held it up to the light. His handwriting was crisp and legible. But the content made her frown.

"I don't remember this Ned."

"You wouldn't. From all the evidence, shortly after you and Ned knocked down the ward poles, Mort opened up his secure area and took Ned back inside with him. When the wards closed, you forgot Ned."

"But Ned is on our side?"

"Ned is your boyfriend. He is definitely on our side. Look in your pocket. Do you have a funny coin?"

She found it. She closed her eyes and stroked the surface. "I can feel him. Back that way." She pointed.

"Good. That means he is still alive. But under Mort's control, alive or dead, he is doomed. We have to rescue him. I can't tell you how. You will have to take me outside, where I can see what's going on."

...

Mort paced back and forth in his library. Ned lay unconscious on the floor. A huge empty section gaped where the notebooks had been.

What is it with him?

Mort could remember three different ways to wake someone up—in addition to yelling and shaking. But none of those worked. He even tried releasing the boy's will, fearing the compulsions he used under questioning might have produced this side effect.

There's a whole section in the third notebook on more extreme measures—if I just knew where it was!

The instant he could get the boy's eyes open, the patterns woven into his robe would be powerful enough to get his tongue wagging.

It is a fruitless hope to hide anything from me. No one can stand against my will.

But without his notebooks, he was reduced to waiting for the boy to wake up on his own.

I should never have burned the microfilm copies. The instant I get them back, I'll scan them to digital, encrypt them and then hide a dozen copies in servers all over the world. I was crazy to keep just the paper notebooks.

But the idea of someone else having access to the patterns was equally crazy. And even encrypted, there was that risk. There was only room for one at the top.

The boy had been tampered with. Carl Stellman had to be at large. With the girl, that made at least three who would have to be removed from the world before he could feel safe again.

But not until I get my notebooks back.

...

An old blue Volkswagen bug came over the hill in a cloud of dust, and Latoya dropped her candied apple and sprinted toward the parking area.

Roger Samuelson hadn't even stopped when she stuck her head through the open window and gave him a kiss.

"You're here!" she squealed.

"Almost." He stopped and set the brake.

"You're early." They hugged.

"Yeah," he said, "I must have been gone too long. I was sure I still had another hundred miles to go, and there it was, the old Ranch Exit turnoff."

"Come on, your family is all here. Everyone is here."

...

Carl gripped the arms of the wheelchair, even knowing that if it came loose, holding onto the chair would do no good.

Dot was confident. Her elastic cords with the hooks on them were laced through the wheels and framework of the chair, with another across his chest as a 'seat-belt'. But having the wheelchair perched on the top of the mower deck was a harrowing experience.

As the tractor labored up the incline, knocking more rocks free, Carl was dangled like an afterthought on the contraption. Tension built up in him like on the first climb of an impossibly steep roller coaster.

When, after an age, they leveled off on the top of the railroad grade, Carl let out an involuntary "Ha!"

"You okay back there?" The engine noise made talking difficult.

"Fine!"

"Okay, we'll be speeding up now."

The tractor had two sets of gears, and after she made the shifts and pushed the throttle lever higher, they were speeding along on the narrow pathway at nearly thirty miles per hour.

Carl had to close his eyes. He hadn't traveled this fast since he was a young man.

Ned must have been under the influence of the seeing charm. After my mice broke him out of Mort's house, it wasn't too long after that that he vanished from my memories. Only someone with an enhanced mental state could have broken through the wards.

And in spite of what Dot thinks, it was probably Ned who broke down the ward poles around the valley. It would be impossible to think about the poles, even if you could see them, from the outside.

No, Ned must have used the charm, and so he is probably unconscious now.

Carl cautiously opened one eye. It was very bright outside. He tilted his head back, trying to keep the rapidly passing roadway out of his line of sight.

The open sky, and miles of scenery in the daylight—it was wonderful. How he had missed it! Even if he didn't survive the coming conflict, this was worth it. Living like a slug underground was not living at all.

...

Ned kept his breathing slow and regular. Mort was pacing, and muttering to himself, and just agitated enough to miss the clues that Ned had finally woken up.

He'll force me to tell where the notebooks are and then kill me. He won't make the same mistake again.

Memories were fading in and out. He knew who Mort was, and remembered vividly the power that the man could call up with just a word.

Those patterns on his robe were compelling. If I look at them again, I'm doomed. Maybe Mort had spells that worked with spoken words alone, but he had no way of guessing.

Close my eyes. Earplugs?

Luckily Mort was making enough noise so that Ned could keep track of where he was in the room without looking. As Mort passed by, Ned slipped his hand into his pocket, feeling for paper or anything he could stuff into his ears.

The touch of the fat coin sent a shiver of recognition through him.

There is someone else in the universe. It's not just Mort and me.

Someone important to him was out there, and coming his way. Someone outside the world.

Leftover clarity from the spell, and the simple fact of someone *outside*, let a few more memories into his personal gestalt.

I'm inside a warded area. A vivid memory of Mort throwing him into the Humvee and hitting a radio remote control switch flashed by.

...

Dot slowed to a stop.

"What is it?" Carl could only see to the rear.

"We're at the end of the railroad grade, and I can see a motorcycle on a dirt road just ahead."

"It must be Ned's. Get us down there."

Dot took the tractor down a mild incline and pulled to a stop. Unhooking the cords, she lowered the mower deck. Carl pushed on his wheels, moving around the tractor. His arms were strong and he made light work of moving over the uneven ground.

Dot was rubbing her coin. "I feel like I should have come here. I was supposed to meet him, but I forgot."

Carl examined the tracks in the dirt. "So he was likely here when Mort captured him. The wards must be close."

Dot found the marked arrow in the dirt. "Thirty feet in this direction. This has to be it."

She climbed back on the tractor and put it in gear. Carefully, she lined up on the arrow and plowed straight ahead.

Seconds later, she was startled to find Carl wheeling hard to get out of her way. She slammed hard on the right brake pedal and pivoted the tractor in a circle.

"What's going on?"

Carl moved closer. "It's the wards. You can't drive through the barrier."

"I was able to take down the ward pole near the tunnel!"

"You were under the influence of the seeing charm, just as Ned was, when you two were outside the valley.

"But now, when you approach them, your mind rejects their existence and you turn around."

"So I'm doing it myself? In some kind of a trance?"

"Close enough."

"Can you get to the poles? I could let you steer while I hold on and deal with the brakes and throttle."

"No. The seeing charm won't work on me. I might be able to construct something else, though. Do you have paper, and a pen?"

Dot shook her head, "No, but maybe in the motorcycle's saddle bag!"

She looked and pulled out an old notebook.

"Dot! Stop! Don't open that!"

Carl wheeled over and took it from her hand. He examined the book without opening it, and cautiously verified that it contained loose papers inside.

"Dot, in my day women carried little mirrors for applying powder to their faces. Do you have something like that?"

She shook her head. "No. I don't use cosmetics—not yet. What do you want it for?"

"I need a mirror. Remember the tale of Persius and Medusa? The sight of her would turn a warrior to stone, but he used the mirror surface of a shield to see while he attacked her.

"It's the same with many of these gestalt patterns. The mirror image can be safe to view, even if the normal version is potent. This is one of my notebooks, we included template patterns drawn in mirror image. It looks like Mort has made active patterns on these sheets. I need to see what he was doing without being affected by them."

"There's the rear-view mirror on the motorcycle."

She moved the handlebars where he could get close, and then at his instruction, moved to the other side of the tractor where she couldn't get even an accidental glimpse of the papers.

Carl peered into the mirror while extracting the sheet of paper.

Dot could hear him gasp. "What's the matter?"

Carl began tearing the paper into shreds.

"There are days when I wish I had never been born."

"Carl?"

"You can come out now."

He was tossing the confetti to the breeze.

"What was it?"

He looked to the ground, looking sad and beaten.

"We were under military direction. We were looking for weapons, tools to be used in case the European unrest became a war.

"We were requested to come up with a way to interrogate the enemy. I found a way, and before I had thought it out, I reported it and put it in the notebooks.

"But Dot, it tears information out of a subject's memory. If the interrogation continues too long, very deep memories get affected. Some parts of the mind are never supposed to be accessible to the parts that can speak them."

He pointed at the scraps of paper on the dirt. "That one was constructed to rip out everything. The notes Mort took show he had started on Ned. Depending on how long he was at it, the boy may have brain damage."

Dot held her coin tightly. "I think he is awake now."

"Then we may not have time. I can't make a pattern to help me see the ward poles, not with what I have here."

She nodded. Through the warmth of the coin, she had feelings for this Ned, even though her brain refused let her remember his face.

"Can we send just the tractor? If I'm not there to turn it around, will it continue to go straight?"

Carl shrugged. "It's worth a shot."

Dot did the hard work, lining up the tractor with the arrow, securing the steering wheel with elastic cords, setting the gears and throttle, and then jumping off once it started. In low, low gear for power, it crept away.

Dot blinked. "What are we doing here?"

Carl felt the necklace around his throat. "We sent a tractor through to knock down the ward pole. I don't think it worked."

"What tractor?" Dot was confused.

"Come on, we need to get to the town. I can't do anything without writing tools."

Dot grabbed the wheelchair. "Let me push. It's not far."

...

Ned heard the motor noise in the distance. So did Mort, coloring the air with curses and heading for the front door.

Ned took his chance. He eased up on hands and knees. Steeling himself not to look back, he took the side door out of the library as fast as he could without making a sound.

The hallway led to the kitchen. He ripped a paper towel from the dispenser and wadded earplugs while he crept out the back entrance.

Blind and deaf. Or not quite. He could still hear the muffled motor noises and as he edged towards the corner of the building, he was alert to any sign of shadows.

He moved away from the noise, heading around the back of the east wing. Mort would surely head towards the noise. He hoped.

A garden sprinkler resting next to a hedge caught his eye. The Y-shaped foot was chrome and reflective. He unhooked it from the hose. At the edge of the building he poked it around the corner at ground level.

Distorted and reduced to a smudge, the colorful reflection of Mort was visible, stalking back towards the house. The Humvee was parked by the door.

He'll see that I'm gone!

The instant Mort vanished from sight, Ned dashed towards the vehicle.

Go for the remote control first. If there are keys, use them.

Crouched low, he circled behind and opened the driver's door. *Keys!*

Almost immediately, he could hear Mort's howl. He fumbled with the ignition. A figure appeared in the front door. The Humvee was nosed in towards the house. Ned clamped his eyes shut, started the engine and plowed back in reverse as hard as he could press the accelerator.

Twice, the Humvee bucked as it surged over something like a bush or a small tree.

234

By feel, he shifted into a forward gear and twisted the steering wheel. He let a crack of light in through his eyelids. Mort wasn't in front of him, so he opened them enough to steer.

A riderless tractor was heading straight for him. He swerved, and kept on going. *Go to the road. Head for the entrance.*

The remote. Where's the remote?

It wasn't in plain sight. He checked everything that might be a storage compartment. In the third one, he found it.

I remember this. He pressed a button, and a light came on.

Up ahead, he suddenly noticed his motorcycle on the road near the entrance gate. *The wards are open.*

He drove through the gate and past the motorcycle before pressing the button again. *Now they're....*

Up ahead he saw Dot and Carl. He waved and pulled to a stop.

"Hi. Out for a walk?"

"Ned!" Dot squealed. "You're free from Mort!"

Ned looked at her puzzled. He pulled the paper out of his ears. "I didn't hear what you said exactly. Who is Mort?"

...

Carl tried to explain, as Ned drove back to get his motorcycle. Dot made him read the summary. He giggled, "So now you're my girlfriend. I don't remember that."

She hit him. "Just read." He stopped the vehicle next to the bike and kept reading. She rubbed her coin. A smile crept across her face when she saw him absently reaching into his pocket for his.

"Okay," Ned put down the papers. "I believe everything in there." He caught her eye. "Almost everything there. So what do we do now?"

Dot shrugged. "Mort is trapped inside his own wards, with the key in our control. Why don't we just leave him there?"

Carl was strapped into the front seat with them. He had been looking at the radio remote control. "These are Mort's wards, and I don't believe for an instant that this is the first time he has used them. This gadget is just too convenient. He has had a lot of practice.

"There are a dozen or so ways I know of to break through wards. Probably three of them are in the notebooks. Even without pushbutton convenience, he could get out again. Wards are most potent against people who don't know that wards exist."

Ned raised a finger, "Ah, I think my memories are a little scrambled, but it seems to me that I hid those notebooks."

"What?" said Carl.

"Where?" asked Dot.

Ned wrinkled his forehead with the effort, but then shook his head. "No. I don't know where."

Carl said, "That's okay. We know enough. If you can't remember where, then it was somewhere inside the ward. With enough time and motivation, which he has, Mort will find them. Are you sure you didn't destroy them?"

Ned shook his head, "No, I'm not sure. It just seems that I hid them."

"Well, we should have some time before he finds them, in any case."

Dot looked solemn. "Yes, you and Ned should be able to keep him locked up. I won't be here." She didn't have that much time.

Ned frowned. "She's here?"

Dot nodded.

"Who is...?" Carl was interrupted by the shriek of a giant eagle. A loud bang shook the Humvee.

...

Carl looked outside, where the rapidly moving shadow was already turning back towards them. Against the sky, he could see something moving faster than any airplane he had ever seen.

"It's Mort's eagle!" Ned put the Humvee in motion and began turning around.

Dot put her hand on his arm. "No! We can't go anywhere near the town. He would kill dozens, just to get to us."

"We can't stay here! Do you want to be inside if he can get a claw on us? What if he rips open the roof?"

"Children! Tell me everything you know about this bird?"

Dot started talking. Ned watched the approaching eagle. Encased in a heavy metal cab made him feel safer than the last time, but not by much.

He turned the wheel and gunned it at the last minute. The talons missed.

The railroad grade was just a few hundred yards away. He cut across the open terrain, bouncing against the shoulder harness. *If I can get close enough to that pile of rock, it'll protect us some.*

Carl was saying, "So, it is a painted airplane?"

Ned yelled, "Sometimes. When it chased me before, I could have sworn it was a real bird—an eagle the size of a fighter plane."

The Humvee titled sideways as Ned put the right two tires on the high embankment. The eagle screeched in anger and slowed to avoid hitting the ground.

Carl watched, "No airplane can maneuver like that."

There was another metal scraping thud. The eagle couldn't hit them as fast, but they were by no means out of its reach.

Ned looked forward and back, checking to see if there were any lower spots. There was nothing.

"He uses it as a search plane." Dot was spilling out anything she knew or imagined about it.

The Humvee sagged as the bird landed on the roof. Talons scraped the metal like chalk on a blackboard. They shook from side to side under the weight of the monster.

"How did Mort get free?" Carl shook his head. "He was behind the wards, and I would have known if he dropped them to get out."

Dot said, "His landing strip! Dad said they had mowed a pattern around the edge of the field."

Carl nodded, "Ah! A bypass! He planned to keep his 'Kingdom' intact, the peasants ignorant, but leave the ability for himself to fly out into the wider reality.

"That gives me an idea. Are there any writing tools in here?"

Dot crawled into the back seat. With every shriek of tortured metal, she glanced up to see if the bird had clawed through.

"Here." Not surprisingly, Mort had drawing supplies in his vehicle. She passed a drawing tablet and set of fine-tipped inking pens up into his hands. The tablet looked well used. Half the sheets were already gone.

Carl's eyes lit up. He glared up at the roof, and Dot felt a shiver of fear. Not fear of Mort, but fear of Carl.

Ned steered the motorized rear view mirrors up so he could catch a glimpse of the giant wings, flapping to balance the bird on the roof while it tried to claw through.

"I think I can shake him loose."

"Not yet! Let me finish."

The scrapes were getting faster, more regular, as the bird made progress.

Dot could see the roof flex. "He's getting close." She looked around for something, anything to use against him. There were shovels, and some kind of power tools, but nothing she could imagine as a weapon.

Carl spoke in a calm voice, "Ned. Get ready to drive. Can you get up on the railroad grade?"

"He would overturn us. We would be vulnerable."

"But can you do it?"

Ned looked out the windshield. "Yes. No problem."

"Okay, here's what you do. Drive to the top. Mort will have to fly in wide loops like he did at first to build up speed. I'll get out."

"No!" Dot put her hand on his arm. "He'll kill you. He'll swoop down on you like a mouse!"

"Dot! Trust me on this!

"Now the instant I get out, head back to the wards. Use the remote and go through. Close the wards behind you.

"This is very important, kids. Destroy the pattern around the airstrip as quickly as you can. You may only have minutes. Can you do this?"

Ned nodded. "We'll do our best. Will we forget anything, closing the wards after us?"

"Keep your resonance enhancers in your hands. It will help. Just don't forget to destroy that pattern!"

Dot squeezed his arm. *Carl is going to sacrifice himself.*

Ned shifted to a lower gear and stamped on the gas. The eagle toppled to the ground and shook itself. A cry of anger chilled his blood.

But he had to concentrate to get the Humvee up the steep, unprepared slope. Off in the distance, he could see the bird already in the air, circling around to gain speed.

With a lurch, they reached the top.

Carl called, "I'm out." He opened the door and fell outside.

Ned steered frantically to avoid running him over.

"Dot, get that door closed."

In the rear-view mirrors, he could see Carl. "I don't believe it."

Dot slammed the door shut. "What?"

"Look back."

Already a couple of hundred feet behind them, Carl stood up. He was a man in his thirties, dressed in a lab coat, with two ordinary legs. With the drawing tablet in his hands, he stood fearlessly, facing the monster eagle, approaching at a hundred miles per hour.

Bird in a Cage

"Hang on." Ned concentrated on his driving and went over the edge. Dot wasn't strapped in, and the roller coaster ride threw her against the ceiling and across the seat. She latched onto Ned, then released him. It wasn't a good idea to interrupt his driving.

They reached the valley floor and Ned raced straight toward the place where he knew the ward poles had to be.

"The coins!" Dot dug for her's. Ned tried to steer with one hand and it was hard.

His bike still lay in the dirt, doing a noble job marking the edge of reality.

"Can you see anything?"

Dot cried, "No! The eagle is still in the air. I can't see Carl."

"Get the remote. It's beside your leg."

The warm familiarity of the coin against his finger steeled him. He clutched it in his hand.

"I've got it."

"The red button in the center. Push it. Push it now!"

The ward poles blinked into existence, their vanes turning. Ned felt returning memories hit with an almost physical impact. They drove onto the ranch.

"Press the button again."

He gripped his coin tightly. Ignorance slammed down on them.

Dot shook her head. "Ah. What are we doing here?"

Ned looked at her. She looked shaken up, but she was clutching her coin in one hand, and the remote control in the other.

"We are fighting Mort, by whatever way we can."

"Look," she said. The tractor was caught straddling a big rock, its rear wheels still turning. "Let's get that free."

"Why?"

"Mort has mowed some kind of pattern around the landing strip. Let's mess that up."

Ned nodded. "Good enough."

The Humvee's winch pulled the tractor free, and Dot hopped on. "I'll mow it. You drive through it."

He headed out first, fishtailing around the decorative edge of the field. By the time he had made one loop, Dot had the mower deck down and was cutting a wide swath through the lace-like pattern.

She's destroying it.

There was something at the house that he could do. He headed over. Inside, he raced to the library.

There was a ladder. He climbed to the shelf two levels higher than where he had found the notebooks. Reaching behind a set of finely bound classics of world literature, which he could tell had never been opened, he could feel the notebooks where he had left them.

Hiding them in the library had been a desperation move. There hadn't been time to hide them well, so all he could hope for was distraction. Moving the books up two shelves had taken little time, and had done the job.

Carrying them in stacks of five, he carted the books out to the Humvee and stacked them on the floor in the rear.

Dot was making good speed around the field.

One last pass through the house.

...

Dot glanced behind her. With this second sweep, there was hardly any sign that there had ever been a pattern around the landing strip.

Ned drove up in the Humvee and they exchanged gestures. They were both on target. Ned paced her until she reached the end of the final sweep.

"Get in. I don't like you being out in the open if you don't have to."

"Good idea."

She closed the door behind her and locked it.

"The field is wiped. How did you do?"

Ned looked very pleased with himself. "Mort will find himself disarmed if he comes back here. I've got the notebooks, the special clothes, even ... " he whipped a wallet out of his pocket and extracted a worn, white credit card.

"Oh." She looked at her friend. "You know you can't use it, don't you."

Ned's face twisted in a crisis of conscience. "Yes. I know. Still, it wouldn't hurt to hang on to it for emergencies."

Dot resolved to get it away from him some time when he was feeling more reasonable.

"Okay, what do we do now?"

Ned put away the card. "Open the wards back up?"

"That's dangerous. What if Mort attacks?" She glanced up automatically, and was puzzled to see the roof torn, as if by giant claws.

"Then we run." Ned frowned. "We can't hide forever. And if the worst happens, I've got a can of gasoline in the back with all his toys. If he takes us out, we'll go out in a blaze of glory."

Dot shivered. She didn't like that phrase.

"Okay. But be ready to run."

She pressed the remote control.

Off in the distance, the ward poles appeared.

"Carl!" they shouted in unison as memory came back.

Ned hit the gas.

...

Officer Lakey put down the little model car that the rancher had made out of sheet metal.

What am I doing? I've got a hot warrant in my car and I've been wasting most of the day at the fair.

Hurriedly, he wound his way through the crowd towards the parking area.

Jake Cartulio noticed the look on the policeman's face, but he had his own worries.

"George!" He waved the shopkeeper over.

"What is it?"

"I am totally out of meat, and people are still coming."

"I've got hamburger and a few chickens."

"Send 'em over, everything you've got."

George nodded. *I wish I could find Ned.* Jake wasn't the only one running out of supplies. He was spending half the time wheeling his pushcart through the crowds. He could have used a delivery boy.

He nodded to the lady in the city hat and gloves, admiring Nora's photo prints. *Dot Comal's aunt.* The grapevine was working overtime and all the Ranch Exit locals had given her a close inspection. *By now everyone has heard the story. If Ruben weren't being so friendly to her, she would be run out of town by now.*

No one wants to lose Dot.

He looked around. *Where is the girl?*

...

Officer Lakey followed the directions a local had given him, easily finding the road that led to Ellis Mort's ranch.

What is that?

On an old elevated railroad grade, two people were waving shovels in the air, fighting off....

That's a bald eagle. He put on the sirens and lights and drove as close as he could. He climbed the rest of the way, ready to arrest them.

When he reached the top. *Oh my, what's that?*

Lying on the ground, protecting himself with only a writing tablet, lay a man with no legs.

"Hey! What's going on?"

"Help us!" The girl waved her shovel, trying to keep the eagle from getting too close to the man on the ground. "He's trying to kill Carl!"

Lakey hesitatated. The eagle was an endangered species and the rules were strict, but the bird was plainly intent on attacking the helpless man.

He's huge. The bird's wingspan was at least six feet. He'd never been this close to one.

Lakey pulled his gun and fired randomly into the air. The eagle shrieked, and flew off. The two teenagers dropped their shovels.

"Are you okay, Sir?" Officer Lakey knelt down next to the old man, who still held the writing tablet over his head.

"Fine. Fine." There was a trickle of blood down his face. "I just need my hat. The sun, you see."

The man was indeed remarkably pale.

"I see it," said the boy. He brought it over.

"You are Ned Kelso. You found that body."

Ned nodded. Dot came back from the Humvee with a cloth to clean the blood.

"Well, it seems we have a new suspect for that death, don't we." Lakey shook his head, looking at the bird, now more than a mile away. "I've never heard of an eagle attacking humans like this. You weren't bothering a nest were you? You do know that bald eagles are an endangered species and there are severe penalties for interfering with them?"

Carl looked at Dot, and then said "Yes, of course. Everyone knows that. No, I saw no evidence of a nest."

"What were you doing up here?"

Carl showed him the ripped and shredded drawing. "Just making maps."

Dot clipped a nametag to her collar.

"Carl Stellman is a naturalist. That's his car. He hired Ned to drive him, and I came along for the ride. See, it's just an environmental map. It's all perfectly innocent."

The policeman believed every word she said. There was nothing illegal going on here, and he had his own job to get back to.

"If you have things under control here, I'll be going. Have any of you seen Ellis Mort?"

Dot nodded. "I saw him fly away in one of his planes!"

Lakey drove on into the ranch and checked out the house with its door wide open. There was clear evidence that he had bolted with books scattered and dresser drawers left open.

I was an idiot for spending so much time at the fair. He was tipped off and made his escape.

The arrest warrant for embezzlement was three years old and he had wondered why it had been ignored by everyone in the office. Mort was something of a legend in this part of the state. Everyone should have seen the connection. *I'm glad I didn't tell anyone where I was going today. They would have a good laugh on me.*

He looked in the barns and hangars, but there was no sign of the man, but one of the hangars was empty, just like the girl said.

When he drove out, a flicker of motion caught his eye.

That eagle. What is it up to?

The bird was landing in the middle of the grassy landing strip, looking puzzled, and then taking off for another try. It looked like one frustrated bird.

...

"So he's a real bird now? How is that possible?"

Carl was soaking up the air-conditioning, his hat pulled down to keep even reflected sunlight away from his sensitive face.

"Ned, Mort had done the hard work. The animal spirit gestalt shift is just one of many that has occurred naturally through the ages. We documented the process in the notebooks, but I'll have to give him credit for pushing beyond what I had imagined. Using the plane with an eagle's eyes to spy from the sky is one thing, but he had almost completely crossed over. Once I realized that, all I had to do was tempt him close enough to complete the shift."

Carl fingered the gash on his scalp. "I forgot how dangerous an enraged eagle could be."

"Can he shift back?"

"The landing strip pattern is gone?"

Dot nodded. "Completely mowed over."

"Then he may be trapped. He's reduced to the eagle's brain, with an eagle's instincts. Even in time, I suspect the human rage would be submerged. If he stops attacking people, he may be able to live out a the rest of a normal eagle's lifespan.

"If so, then it's the end of a long mistake."

Ned asked, "What mistake?"

"My mistake of ever letting my discoveries get out of my hands. We need to burn the notebooks."

Ned shook his head. "No. I want to learn this stuff. When I used the seeing charm, I saw a more magnificent world that I could ever have imagined. The difference was knowledge. How could I live in this world, knowing that what I see is just a simplified shell hiding a bigger reality?"

Dot added, "I agree. I want to be a healer. I have healed pain with the touch of my finger. Off in that hospital where my dad was kept, people need something like that get-well card, to let them heal from their personal demons without having to live in a drug-induced haze. How much of the evil and pain in this world is due to a bad gestalt? There's the possibility for healing. We can't burn it to ashes!"

Carl hesitated. He saw the dangers all too clearly. Dot had pulled the truth badge out quickly to protect them from the policeman. Ned was a teenage boy—the definition of act first and think later!

"We should burn them now, in case they get into the wrong hands again. You saw what Mort was able to do with them. I can teach you myself."

Ned said, "Don't get me wrong, but you are an old man. How long would it take to teach me what I need to know? I would rather learn from you than from some old worn-out notebooks, but if you have a heart attack and Mort stumbles across another way to disrupt his eagle-gestalt, what do I do then? How do I protect my family? How do I protect my home? The notebooks are insurance."

...

Dot put in her opinions, and then left Ned and Carl to argue about the notebooks while she collected the shovels.

A hundred yards down the path, a swirling dust-devil formed itself into the shape of a bear.

"Wanekia!"

The bear didn't respond. It peered over the valley, pacing back and forth, looking upset and uneasy.

In a strange way, it was like the dance of the mice.

She paled, and raced back to the Humvee. She opened the door.

"Guys. We've got a problem."

...

Ned drove. Dot talked. Carl listened. "We didn't think about it. Once the ward around the valley lifted. The cars started driving in and Ned could tell Mort was doing more gestalt changes. We had the primary pole down, but the others are still up.

"I heard the guests talking at the fair, but I didn't put the pieces together. Roger Samuelson was able to get here a hundred miles sooner than he had planned. Delivery trucks that hadn't been able to find Ranch Exit yesterday now found the entrance much sooner than they should have. All of the outsiders mentioned how easy it was to find Ranch Exit."

Carl frowned. "It could be that instead of collapsing the ward, it was distorted instead. There could be dozens of Ranch Exit signs all along the highway. How many resonator poles are there?"

"Every mile for a hundred miles in either direction. I saw them when I went to get Dad. I just didn't notice that the poles were resonators."

Ned slowed down as they approached the fair. The parking area had overflowed and people were parking on both sides of the road. Ordinary cars could get through, but not a Humvee.

"I'll have to go around."

Sam Cooper and his brother Greg were trying to direct traffic. Sam waved them down.

"Dot. Your father needs to see you immediately."

She looked at Ned and Carl.

Ned stopped. "Go on. This thing has a winch. Carl will be able to tell me what to do. Go take care of business. We'll shut the ward poles down."

Carl added, "We'll have to mow down the power circles too. See if you can scare up help to do that."

She nodded. Ned took the Humvee off-road.

Greg asked, "What is Ned doing driving Mort's car?"

Dot sighed and pulled out the truth badge.

...

An hour later, she was sitting on the stage that had been built for the singers and for the awards ceremony. For a town with so few people, there were an outstanding number of prizes awarded.

Ms. Carson was front and center. This was her time to shine, and she loved it. She announced and handed out the ribbons. Maybe Dot noticed that she scanned the crowds every few minutes, hoping to see Mr. Mort, but no one else did.

Dot had barely time to be introduced to her Aunt Elizabeth and exchange a few minutes of small talk before Ms. Carson had pulled her away by the arm and ordered her to sit on the stage with several of the committee members.

I'll have to say something. Ms. Carson made that plain. *It was my idea.*

Looking over the crowd make her feel good. Today was a day that a town of hermits had the chance to feel like one big family. It was a day for total strangers to complement them on their art, their cooking, their singing—and to pay them cash money for their efforts.

Latoya and Roger sat next to each other in the audience, paying no attention to anything but each other.

Hallee Cooper was chatting happily with her friends. After leaving Sam Cooper with the conviction that he had promised Mort to get the crop circles mowed down after they had stopped the fire, Dot had seen her hiding in her car.

Dot was still wearing the truth badge. "No one will notice your black eye." The suggestion had done wonders. No longer self-conscious about it, others hadn't made much of it either. The memories of Greg Coopers insanity were fading rapidly out of people's memories. The black eye was nothing more than an accident.

This is what healing means. We can't let Carl's discoveries die, not while a word truly believed can make such a difference.

Aunt Elizabeth seemed to be enjoying all the activity. Dad had invited her to stay an extra day.

The truth badge was in Dot's pocket now, and just a few careful sentences would put a stop to this summer trip. There was so much that had to be done, right here in Ranch Exit.

Ms. Carson tapped her pointer on the makeshift podium.

"Friends and guests. The Ranch Exit Roundup was the brainchild of one of my very best students, Dot Comal."

There were cheers and applause. "Come on up, Dot."

Panic and stage-fright threatened to freeze her to the spot.

Oh for one more shot of the seeing charm!

Hesitantly, she got out of her seat and stood before the faces. Ruben Comal was practically bouncing out of his wheelchair with the fury of his clapping.

She didn't know what to say. Could she remember what she had said that day she proposed the fair?

Aunt Elizabeth was clapping too.

Dot took a deep breath.

"I see my family out there." She looked over the crowd. "I see all of my family. I see all the kids I play with. I see all the mothers that took me into their hearts when my own mother died. I see all the fathers that watched over me and made me feel, to this day, that of all the places in the world, no place is more secure than Ranch Exit, my home."

There was more applause.

"'Home is where the heart is.' We have come together today to celebrate our shared hearts and our shared home. We have come to honor the best of us, and to keep on sharing with those of us who will be leaving."

She nodded her head in Latoya's direction. "You know and love our graduate this year, and I think we all know where her heart is."

The laughter was loud. Latoya and Roger squirmed under the well-meaning scrutiny.

"Some of you know that I will be gone this summer as well." She was surprised to see the mixed reaction in the crowd. "This is my own choice. I love Ranch Exit. This is my home, where my heart is. But I don't intend to hide my heart away from the world.

"I will be gone, but nothing will keep me from coming back."

She waved to the applause.

Ned and Carl were at the edge of the crowd. Ned whispered something to Carl and dashed off—a strange expression on his face.

Ms. Carson was up immediately, as Dot stepped back to her seat.

"And now, the final award! As you know, profits from the booth sales, as well as contributions from local businessmen and our guests as well have been earmarked to provide a scholarship for our outgoing seniors. This year, our spectacular turnout has enabled the community of Ranch Exit to provide our daughter with an educational fund of ... over thirty-thousand dollars!"

Latoya was on her feet shouting. The crowd broke into a thunderous applause. Ms. Carson had to step down and bring her up to the podium. While Latoya spoke, almost incoherent in her joy, Dot scanned the crowd.

Where did Ned go! Dot only partially heard Latoya's thank-you's to everyone, and the special thank-you she gave to Dot.

He knew I would have to go. I've got to find him. I've got to explain.

...

Albert Kelso moved through the crowd carefully on his crutches. Many of the men knew him, but he was one of the most reclusive people in a town of hermits. For years he had been content to let Yolanda be the public face for the Kelso family. The noise and chaos were nearly more than he could handle.

As the awards ceremony wrapped up, he located Ruben in the seats. He made his slow progress in that direction.

Innumerable people paused to congratulate Ruben for Dot, and Albert waited his turn. Finally the crowd began to thin. It was getting late, and most of the guests had a long way to drive home.

"Ruben?"

"Albert! It's good to see you."

"Ruben, could we have a few words, in private."

Ruben nodded, whispered to his sister-in-law and rolled over to the Samuelson's tent, sold out and closed up.

"Have a seat, Albert."

He settled. "Ruben, I've come to talk to you about my son.

"I know you've been protective about Dot. We all know how wonderful she is and how proud of her you must be.

"Well, I'm proud of my son too. I know he's been a little wild, but this past year he has matured faster than I did at his age. He has taken on responsibilities. He has demonstrated, at least to me, that he has a great heart. And he hurts—hurts! This grudge you've held against him the past couple of weeks has torn him up inside. He's trapped between respect, for you and me, and his deep affection for Dot.

"I know you think Dot deserves better than a dirt-poor rancher's kid with no prospects, but his heart is good. I think you're wrong to keep them apart."

Ruben took in the rebuke. After a bit he said, "Thanks Albert. Ned and I have worked out our differences, but you just helped me to see what an idiot I have been.

"Substitute me for Ned, and my June's family for me, and you have the hellish mess that kept me bitter over her family for years. I'd do anything to spare Dot having to live through something like that.

"You're a good man Albert. From now on you won't find me in Ned's way. Dot is old enough to choose her own friends."

...

Outside the tent, Ned hovered, listening to what his father had to say. When he had seem him moving toward the tent, Ned was amazed that his father had left the house. What could have been so important?

He stepped quietly away. Every word was etched into his soul.

...

"Hey, Dot!"

She turned, feeling a wash of relief as Ned walked up, a huge grin on his face.

She gripped his hand. "I saw you in the crowd. I wanted to explain why I decided to go with Aunt Elizabeth."

He gripped back. "I know. What your dad wants is important. You will be back."

Dot struggled to find the words. "It's more than that. I've still got the truth badge. I could make Dad and Aunt Elizabeth change their minds, and not even know why.

"I decided for myself that I needed to go.

"When I went to Salt Lake City, the age charm backfired when Ranch Exit vanished. I thought I was 24. And you know what I thought about myself?

"I thought I was a doctor. I thought that I had struggled through medical school and was on my way to being a real doctor. This is what popped out of the back of my mind, and I've come to realize that maybe it's always what I've wanted to be. Old Man Wanekia called me a healer. He could see it in me before I could.

"But you know what becoming a doctor means? You can't get a medical degree in Ranch Exit. It takes big schools in big cities, and it takes years." Her face showed the agony.

"I love Ranch Exit. This is my home. But I need to know now, before I have to choose a college, whether I have what it takes to survive in a big city. Do I have the guts to live away from Ranch Exit? Away from my home? Away from my friends?"

"Away from you?"

Ned reached into his pocket. "As much as I need you here, I knew this was coming. So here's a present."

He held out a plastic card.

She realized after a second that it wasn't a credit card, not the magic credit card. She read the text.

"It's a pre-paid long distance phone card."

"Yes. And I bought it with my own money, so don't give me that look. I have a phone, and now you have no excuse not to call me all summer long. I'll be busy cleaning up Mort's mess, and I'll need your advice.

"The resonators are still out there on the highway, and until the crop circles are totally destroyed, there will be echoes. I'm not looking forward to pulling up two hundred resonator poles, but I'm the logical one to do the job.

"And there's more, once that's done.

"Carl and I talked while we brought the main poles down. His underground base fell off the map years ago. It's now almost all underneath the Kelso property. We're going to start up a salvage operation. Old office furniture, old collectibles. When we make enough money, we'll get Carl an aboveground home, maybe some teeth.

"And all the while, he'll be teaching me the wizard stuff.

"Dot, this is going to take years, and I'll be stuck right here in Ranch Exit. So you'll have to get used to calling me on the phone."

She blinked away tears. She reached into her pocket and pulled out the fat coin. "I'm keeping this."

"You'd better." He showed his coin and put it safely back into his pocket. "Now dry your eyes before someone see it and thinks we're boyfriend/girlfriend or something, okay?"

"Okay." She smiled.

He bent over and gave her a quick kiss, then dashed off.

Dot held her hand to her face, her brain awash in confused emotions. "I've got a charm for that."

Carl wheeled up out of the shadows. She was surprised to see him wearing trendy mirrored sunglasses—which booth had sold them, she had no clue.

She straightened and cleaned up her face with her sleeve. "I'm okay. It's just been a busy day."

"I know you're okay. Stress takes a lot out of all of us. You've just chosen to embrace more stress than most people. Remember, you still have a few years before you have to make the most serious decisions."

She nodded. "I know that. I'm just afraid of losing Ned."

Carl fished out a picture postcard he had purchased from Nora Baker showing a glorious Utah sunrise. "'Home is where the heart is.' I think someone said that recently." He turned it to the back side. It was covered with an intricate pattern. He put it into its mailing envelope and handed it to her.

"You know that standard-reality's concept of distance isn't the only one?"

She nodded. Otherwise how could dozens of different Ranch Exit off-ramps all arrive at the same place?

"Home is a very basic concept. Very central. Very powerful. More powerful than most people understand.

"Some evening in Seattle, or Boston, or Paris for that matter, go for a walk and take out this card. After a few minutes, you'll arrive home. In the morning, it will take you back where you came from. It doesn't wear out, but if your heart has moved on...."

"I understand." She lifted the brow of his large floppy had and kissed his wrinkled old forehead.

With a cheer in her heart, she asked, "Is Ned going to get you back home? Dad and Aunt Elizabeth are looking for me, and I still haven't packed!"

He nodded. "Ned's got it all covered. I'll see you in the fall."

She smiled, "In the fall."

Carl watched her head off with renewed confidence.

THE END

Small Towns, Big Ideas

Many titles, and more are coming. This series that appeals to age 12 and up by Henry Melton is available now. Starting in the here and now, these tales follow the trials of high school aged heros that take that extra step into the fantastic when something unexpected drops into their lives. Many of the classic science fiction ideas like teleportation, alien contact and time travel are explored in a way totally accessible to many readers who "don't read that kind of stuff" as well as being an exciting adventure for those who do. Available as paper and e-books on-line everywhere.

Henry Melton is often on the road with his wife Mary Ann, a nature photographer. From the Redwood forests to Death Valley to the Great Lakes to Delaware swamps to the African bush, scenes out the windshield become locales for his fiction work. He is frequently captivated by the places he visits, and that has inspired his latest series of novels; Small Towns, Big Ideas. Check his website, HenryMelton.com for current location, his stories, a blog of his activities, and scheduled appearances. Henry's short fiction has been published in many magazines and anthologies, most frequently in Analog. Catacomb, published in Dragon magazine, is considered a classic

Falling Bakward

by Henry Melton

ISBN 978-0-9802253-6-5

Jerry Ingram wanted to be special, more than just a sixth-generation farmer in South Dakota and spent hours after school digging at the mystery spot in the back fields, searching for Indian artifacts. With Sheriff Musgrave always picking on his family and Dad always worried about money, an important discovery would be a great lift. But those bones he found weren't Indian, and when a cave-in drove him into the metal craft buried since the last ice age he found a portal to the world of the Bak, and discovered that the gentle, zebra-striped giants had been waiting for his family for thousands of years!

❧

"...just about everyone in Jerry's family has secrets...the story flows well and is easy to follow. The Bak are an engaging race, and the Kree are suitably terrifying. I can almost see this as a '50s monster movie, but with much better characterization. Lots of thrills, plenty of suspense, and widescreen action... If you're looking for YA science fiction in the sense-of-wonder vein, check out Falling Bakward." Bill Crider, author of the Sheriff Dan Rhodes series, among many other things. 3/15/09

"His writing style is much like that of Robert A. Heinlein and Isaac Asimov when they were writing what was known at the time as Juvenile Fiction...a satisfying read for adults as well... It was quite awhile before I put it down again and then only reluctantly." Elizabeth J. Baldwin, author of Horses 3/10/09

Lighter Than Air

by Henry Melton

ISBN 978-0-9802253-1-0

Winner of the 2009 Eleanor Cameron / Golden Duck Award

It could be the best prank in the history of Munising High School's unofficial Prank Day. Working for a next door neighbor inventor had left Jon Kish with unlimited quantities of lighter-than-air foam, perfect for building...say, a full-sized flying saucer! High school honor demanded it. Plus with the family stress of his mother's surgery, he needed something to keep his mind occupied. But little sister Cherry had her own schemes in play, and events more serious than high school pranks or Mother's cancer were about to focus the world's attention on this little northern town.

❦

"Lighter Than Air is a good read for the whole family that teenagers will love from start to finish! Ample scientific facts are scattered throughout the story, thus enriching the plot and feeding the mind. It is entertaining and exciting to read" Liana Metal, Midwest Book Review 12/2008

"Melton weaves a tale of secrets and suspense, science and pranks, emotion and intrigue...the tedium of the scientific jargon is minimalized by Melton's exquisite ability to tell a story...the scene where Jon and his friend and co-conspirator, Larry, unleash their UFO on an unsuspecting Halloween Festival crowd is priceless. The scary part of the story, though, is not how the characters deal with the issue of death, but that of Internet predators...I found the possibility all too real, and you might as well." Benjamin Potter, October 13, 2008

Extreme Makeover

by Henry Melton

ISBN 978-0-9802253-2-7

Lightning brought a towering redwood crashing down around her, and something dripped on her skin. After that, high school senior Deena Brooke struggled to make sense of the impossible changes to her body. She was grateful for the interest Luther Jennings had in her puzzling insights and quirky urges, until she discovered that he was hiding a deadly secret of his own. Alien nanobots had invaded her body, an unseen influence that was changing her into something else! And was Luther helping her or dragging her into some criminal scam of his own?

❧

"I've recently read the #1 best-selling YA novel, and Henry's is much better written. It's also better paced and has a better story and better-realized characters. Trust me." Bill Crider, Author of the Sheriff Dan Rhodes series and others. 10/08/08

"The plot is quite tight and believable, and so are the characters. They are 'real' kids with their own family problems who try to solve the riddle of Deena's sudden change. It is a very exciting story from the very first page to the last one." Liana Metal, Midwest Book Review September 2008

"Once in awhile you read something that is really fun. If you pick up a Henry Melton book that's what you'll find...this is a superb example of young adult science fiction." Benjamin Potter, August 11, 2008

Roswell or Bust

by Henry Melton

ISBN 978-0-9802253-0-3

Teenager Joe Ferris was raised to help guests -- he was third generation in his family's motel business -- but once he connected with mute Judith, they were off on an epic thousand mile road trip through the Southwest, all to help the most unique guests of all -- the Roswell aliens stranded far from home since 1947. With the Men in Black hot on their trail, and discovering that the aliens had more tricks up their sleeves than their captors had ever discovered, Joe and Judith have to wonder just who is taking whom on the ride of their lives!

❧

"Reading Roswell or Bust will give let you enjoy Science Fiction, even if you haven't been a big fan in the past, and will clue you into why Melton was chosen for an award from the SF community in his first outing as a novelist. It's a great escape (and not only for the aliens who've been kept captive for many decades) Benjamin Potter, April 7, 2008

"The plot is tight... A strange talkie, a mysterious courier and a couple of spies are all involved in this exciting story that will entertain kids of that age... It caters to all the family." Liana Metal, Midwest Book Review July 2008

"...whimsically amusing. The story inside is a wonderful read...His characters are real, complete with the small concerns and everyday trials... adventures are zany and compelling, keeping the reader enthralled to the end when the book can be closed with satisfaction." Ethan Rose, coauthor of Rowan of the Wood

Emperor Dad

by Henry Melton

ISBN 978-0-9802253-4-1

Winner of the 2008 Darrell Award for Best Novel.

His dad was up to something, but it wasn't until James Hill saw the theft of the British Crown Jewels live on CNN and the bizarre claims of this new Emperor of the Earth, did he realize Dad might have invented teleportation in the shed in the back yard. Bob Hill had a plan to protect the world from his disruptive invention, but when the police forces of the world move in on him, no one knew James had hacked the family computer and had taken the power of teleportation himself. Now only he could save his family, and the world.

❧

"It follows in the best tradition of other juvenile SF/action adventure novels in that it follows a young man trying to solve the usual problems that confront any young man (the search for self-identity, relationships with girls, family, and society) at the same time as he must solve the larger problems that surround him (such as whether his father is a mysterious shadowy figure branded as a global terrorist, and what to do when FBI agents show up at the door)... great job of balancing suspense and humor...no real belly laughs, but there were quite a lot of chuckles." Chris Meadows, Teleread January 7th, 2009

"It's a fast-moving SF adventure that's a lot of fun ... Cool cover." Bill Crider -- August 1, 2007

"I had a blast reading this book! With every page turned, you don't want it to end." J. Stock August 16, 2007

Golden Girl

by Henry Melton

ISBN 978-0-9802253-5-8

Debra Barr was barely out of bed when she found herself thrust into a pivotal role in the future of the human race. Plucked out of her bedroom in small town Oquawka, Illinois to a future Earth destroyed and poisoned by a major asteroid impact, the future scientists explained how she could walk a few steps differently, and with YouTube, save the planet. But everything they told her was wrong. Instead of returning to her bedroom, she appeared two hundred years in the past, in the wilderness on the banks of the Mississippi River and it was up to her to discover the rules of time travel without killing herself or anyone else in the process. Bouncing through time, only one thing was certain, anything she decided to do could mean life or death for her family and friends and the route she chose would likely cost her everything. Unfortunately, the more she discovered, the more she suspected that everyone was lying to her.

❧

Not Your Usual Time Travel Story

"Stories that give serious consideration to the issues of paradox and causality in time travel are few and far between. But Henry Melton's latest young-adult book, Golden Girl, is one that treats time travel the right way. It starts from an interesting premise, adds a unique time travel mechanic, and puts a teen-aged girl at the center of an interesting dilemma—with nothing less than the survival of the entire human race at stake!

One of the things I have always enjoyed about Henry Melton's books is that they feature intelligent, self-reliant teens who are by and large able to solve their own problems. There is nothing juvenile in how these young-adult novels are put together. Henry Melton is a master storyteller, and I will be anxiously awaiting his next work."

Chris Meadows TeleRead

Home Planet Adventures

Pixie Dust
by Henry Melton
ISBN 978-0-9802253-8-9

Jenny Quinn's life was on course for her advanced physics degree until a lab experiment in vacuum decay turned her life upside down. With career hopes destroyed and her professor dead in an unexplained fall, she is forced to cope with a strange change in her own body. With nothing but her own resources, a childhood infatuation with old comic books may be her only guide to help solve the twin mysteries of cutting edge physics and the murder of her professor, before one or the other puzzle gets her killed.

Henry Melton, award winning author of the YA adventures Emperor Dad and Lighter Than Air, takes us on an adventure with a slightly older heroine, even if she is just four foot ten and everyone calls her Tinkerbell.